D0948519

THE MATCH

BY THE SAME AUTHOR

Reef

Monkfish Moon

The Sandglass

Heaven's Edge

THE MATCH

ROMESH GUNESEKERA

BLOOMSBURY

First published in Great Britain in 2006

Bloomsbury Publishing Plc,
36 Soho Square,
London W1D 3QY

A CIP catalogue record for this book
is available from the British Library

Hardback ISBN 0 7475 7858 3
Hardback ISBN-13 9780747578581
10 9 8 7 6 5 4 3 2

Trade paperback ISBN 0 7475 8024 3
Trade paperback ISBN-13 9780747580249
10 9 8 7 6 5 4 3 2 1

Typeset by Palimpsest Book Production Ltd, Polmont, Stirlingshire
Printed in Great Britain by Clays Ltd, St Ives plc

Bloomsbury Publishing, London, New York and Berlin

The paper this book is printed on is certified by the © Forest Stewardship Council 1996 A.C. (FSC). It is ancient-forest friendly. The printer holds FSC chain of custody SGS-COC-2061

Helen

CONTENTS

Shooting a picture is holding your breath . . .

Henri Cartier-Bresson

VIEWFINDER

2002

T*IMING IS the thing*, the ageing Hector wrote from his home on the outskirts of Colombo. *Our troubles may soon be over. I only hope it is not too late.* He enclosed a cheque for Mikey's sixteenth birthday. *Get him a good bat as a present, Sunny. You remember how you suddenly got the cricket bug?*

The day the letter arrived, Sunny's morning paper in London reported that a ceasefire, brokered by Norwegian mediators, had been signed by the Liberation Tigers of Tamil Eelam, the LTTE, and the Government of Sri Lanka. A Memorandum of Understanding to erase the maiming and killing of nineteen years. It seemed to Sunny that the impossible was beginning to happen. Roadblocks in Colombo had been swiftly dismantled, the army backed into barracks and politicians on all sides were said to be making gleeful holiday plans. As the rest of the world was gearing up for bush warfare and a state of permanent terror, it finally seemed as though in Sri Lanka violence might be repudiated in favour of weekend shindigs at five-star beach hotels with gunslingers and majorettes prancing in bikinis. Colombo columnists had already begun to write about fjords and smorgasbord as though these things were native to Trincomalee. The Tigers, they claimed, were learning to souse fish. It looked as though this was a lull that would last. In his letter, Hector had added: *The cricket team is due to tour your part of the world. They've had a run of nine Test victories. England could be the tenth – 2002 might be a year to remember.*

The prospect cheered Sunny. The old man Hector – nearing eighty – was still able to do that: raise his spirits, even with his wavering handwriting, with the tiny dented words he crammed between the faint lines of his notepaper. If things were looking up, Sunny thought, if the war in Sri Lanka was really over and the cricket promising once again, then perhaps it was time to go back, to focus on the fast ball as he had done when he was his son Mikey's age. To go back at least to his halfway house, between the Colombo he had been born in and the London he now lived in, the forgotten city of his unexpected upbringing, and find the hidden heart of his life.

WRISTWORK

1970

FOR THE first years that he lived in Manila, young Sunny Fernando knew no other Ceylonese in the city apart from his father's friend Hector. Then in the long, dry heat of 1970 the Navaratnams turned up. Sunny was nearly fifteen and had recently acquired a pair of tinted glasses. Tina Navaratnam was unlike any girl he had ever seen.

He first heard of her from Robby, his best friend.

'Sunny, you lucky prick,' Robby whined down the telephone.

'Hey, you are back?'

'Thank God.' It was nearly the end of the summer holidays and Robby had been away with his parents. His mother had been a Filipina beauty queen, but his father, a burly, balding, Algerian businessman, was deemed by even Robby to be an alien. 'Have you seen that astounding piece that has come? A girl from Ceylon right next door, man. Sunny, you know her?'

Sunny sighed at his friend's crass ignorance. 'Impossible.' In Ceylon, as it was called then, he had never been near a girl – that is to say within fifteen feet – who was not one of his mother's prissy piano protégées, or a passing vagrant, or possibly a dubious relative pinched into a gloomy printed frock. 'Ours was a very divided society.' He trotted out one of his father's phrases.

'You should, dickhead.'

'Yeah?' Sunny thought how far he'd come into this bright Americanized world where girls wore hardly any clothes and pouted with alarming ease.

He headed over to Robby's house. The other two in their gang – Herbie greenfingers and speedy Junior – were coming round too. While waiting for them up on the balcony, Sunny saw her. Tina Navaratnam dashed out of the house next door straight into her father's silver Mercedes. The car eased out like a royal horse and carriage.

'Nice?' Robby leered.

'Neat wheels,' Sunny replied.

'Oh, *cojones*.'

Sometimes Robby could be an absolute lout. Sunny did like the car. The sharp European styling, the tight hum of precise engineering, the barely suppressed b.h.p. From an early age he had been fascinated by horses – their flaring nostrils and breezy tails, the potent idea of bucking broncos. Tina, with her abundant mane and long, smooth, graceful racing nose was almost too much.

For the rest of the holidays Sunny found solace in centre-fold fantasies and cold showers. He dreamt of lassoes, love knots and star-spangled spurs and dreaded going back to school because she'd be there and he would not know what to do or say. But it turned out that she had been sent to a boarding school up in the hills, beyond the reach of the hot fingers of any young *Manileño*, home-grown like Robby or like Sunny, temporarily resident.

Sunny didn't see Tina again until the Christmas break. He was in the menswear section of Rustan's, the Makati department store voted best in Asia, if not the world. He had just selected his gear for the new season – Jockey's naturally – when he saw her from behind, shying away from a grey plastic torso sporting the latest 100 per cent all-man nylon Skants.

Tina's languorous fingers strayed over an imported string vest.

After three months, here was the chance to get close to the girl that plagued his dreams. An agonizing minute passed, he removed his specs and stepped forward. 'Er . . . Hi.'

It was enough to keep him going for several days. He couldn't remember what she had said in reply, whether she had spoken at all. He had revealed the tip of his tongue to her, and that was electrifying. He thought soon they might have a good thing going. With time-lags, of course, and hesitations. That was only to be expected. A conversation was a complex thing. He was old enough to know that.

On the day of the jeepney strike – the 7th of January – when the principal mode of public transport in Manila, the folksy converted US army jeeps, came to a halt, Robby declared that revolution was in the air. Marcos, six months into his second term as president, was already being called a tyrant. The student protests of the year before – the so-called First Quarter Storm – had created widespread dissent, but nothing obviously

Maoist or Marcosist was going on in his part of town – Makati. The car park of the Commercial Centre was full. Sunny headed for Dulcie's to dig into a crisp, puffy *merienda* pastry.

Sally, a breezy American girl from his class, was sitting at the nearby soda fountain with Tina. She called him over. 'Hi, Sunny. You know Tina? She's from wherever too. India?'

'Ceylon.' Tina adjusted her teeny orange sun dress.

'Yeah, an island,' Sunny added. It was something his geography teacher liked to bang on about, comparing the continent Sally knew – North America – to the seven thousand, one hundred and seven islands of the archipelago on which she was now marooned, tipsy on Del Monte juice and wanton capitalism.

Tina looked at Sunny and smiled knowingly. He blushed, heady with the sense that they already shared more than one secret – an island in the Indian Ocean, Rustan's Menswear. Possibly a sublime attraction to erotic dressage.

'Do you . . .' Sunny started.

'So, you are Sunny.'

'Yeah.' Sunny beamed. 'You live in San Lorenzo.'

It seemed easier to speak for each other.

Tina hid her smile with a sip from a huge bowl of *Halo-halo* – the ever-present Filipino mélange of shaved ice, diced pineapple, papaya, tinned milk, green jelly, ice cream and a spoonful of red kidney beans. The concoction wobbled in front of her nose. 'I saw you in Rustan's.'

'You like *Halo-halo* . . .' Sunny groped for something to keep the conversation going.

'You don't?'

Sunny lunged for the safety of the everyday. 'Coke?'

Sally, who had been fiddling with her pigtails, picking at split ends, had had enough. 'Tina, hurry up. We have to be there in ten minutes.'

Sunny didn't want her to hurry up. *Halo-halo* should not be forced down any throat, however inviting it may be.

'I'll see you,' he said in hope to one – Tina – and resignation to the other. But he was happy. He had managed an almost intimate conversation – spanning weeks – of about twenty-five, maybe thirty, words including Americanisms like *hi*, *OK* and *yeah* which he had learnt to say without flinching. He turned the corner with studied nonchalance and once out of sight, did a quick wobbly skip of delight.

Robby turned up the next day in new red flares and a fancy foreign shirt. His tight curls had been teased out into a bush and a modest moustache was beginning to show itself. He had one of his smuggled Gitanes dangling from his mouth. 'Sunny, you know this game cricket? Can you play it?' He broke into an impressive cough. French smoke was so very cool.

Sunny hadn't heard the word cricket mentioned since he'd come to the Philippines. Amazed, he stared at the sexy packet of blue and white swirls in Robby's hand. Eventually he nodded. 'Yup.'

'I wanna know how to play.'

'Why?' Robby was not the sporty type.

'I read about it.'

He was not the bookish type either. Reading was an unnatural act for him, except perhaps for a page or two of his father's Henry Miller and some indecipherable Parisian porn he'd picked up on holiday. Even those he'd tried to barter for the local 'bedtime stories' of rampant fornication illustrated with fuzzy photos of fat dongs and bare bottoms.

He took another puff and spluttered. 'Papa was talkin' about it . . . I wanna impress him, *sige*. We are due for serious talk about bread.'

Robby always had an ulterior motive, although he often pretended whatever happened was pure luck. *'Bahala na,'* he'd simper.

'We need a bat, a ball and a wicket – stumps and bails.'

Robby's right eye narrowed in a vain effort to look like James Dean. '*Bails*? What is it? Bails is what? Come on, Sunny, *putanginamo*. Tell.'

'It's not so easy, Robby. Let me find the stuff, then you'll see.'

Back in Ceylon, Sunny had had all the paraphernalia of a minor enthusiast, but he'd never played in a proper team. He'd consoled himself with the smell of linseed oil and crotch boxes like the other outcasts at his Colombo school. Now he saw the possibility of a captain's cap.

Sunny's father, Lester, had come to Manila in order to work as a journalist in 1967, as so many others did – from Ceylon, India, Malaysia, Hong Kong – because President Marcos, the new Ilokano clean broom, had pledged that the Philippines would have the *freest* press in Asia. The then heroic champion of social justice and civil liberties had promised Utopia. Lester Fernando, desperate to leave the constraints of Colombo, had become delirious at the dream of a land that might combine El Dorado with Fleet Street.

'Guaranteed total freedom we have here,' Lester used to

say in those early days, opening a fresh tub of Magnolia flavour-of-the-month ice cream. 'You know how important independence is? Nothing can ever be hidden, any more.' He'd check his plastic scoop like a professional sleuth and use a stubby little finger to get the last bits out.

Manila, he had believed, was destined to become the centre of a new journalism that would make the American heroes of the day blanch. The city would provide a refuge for any correspondent under threat; a free Filipino press would enable all of Asia to open its eyes, shake off the yoke of imperial bureaucracy and join the twentieth century with reporting that was pure and true. No censoring, no toadying, and a circulation that would rise to the hundreds of millions.

His dreams were short-lived. Living in a society of conspicuous consumption on what was still a hack's salary proved too much for Lester. He soon saw how money controlled the media. And so he gave up journalism and went into the more lucrative business of marketing and PR. Within two years he had moved with his son into a swanky Makati enclave of executive households, charmingly called the village of Urdaneta, outside the limits of the old town.

When Sunny first heard the name he thought it came from the moon, or some place in outer space. He knew nothing yet of Fraya Andres de Urdaneta, the crotchety flag-waving monk and his fellow Basque, Miguel López de Legazpi – their 1564 journey of appropriation from Mexico to Cebu, and on to Manila, for the glory of King Philip II of Spain. He knew nothing of the history of the Philippines, the Namayan Kingdom, the *datus*, rajahs and sultans who had ruled before the conquistadors blundered in; nothing of America's smutty imperial adventure, the commonwealth of *baryos* and *barang-gays*, the Tondo, the river Pasig; nothing of the Catholic Church or cardinal sin, never mind the *Ave Maria*. But he liked the word – Urdaneta – even though the place was, as he quickly learned to say, kind of *weird*.

Sunny's mother Irene, a woman with the striking features of a thirties screen idol, had been a pianist in Colombo. She had never been one to show a great deal of affection, but Sunny had accepted her remoteness as a feature of her prized artistic temperament. The delegation of childcare to servants was not peculiar to her – it was common among many mothers of her class and generation in a mid-twentieth-century backwater – and her need to concentrate on her music seemed perfectly natural to him. What he found difficult to understand was her bizarre decision to draw into their house dozens of freakish children in an effort to develop their musical abilities, while at the same time assuming that he, like his father, had none. She'd wear gorgeous dot dresses, bright lip-stick, Chanel by the gallon and play minuets, polkas and duets with anyone but him. He was not even allowed in the piano room and had to suffer outside, in the front yard, until the last note had faded and only her perfume still lingered. Sometimes he was sent further, to scout meetings or on school trips he hated. One day, when he was eight years old, he came home from a special rice-planting camp and was told that something had happened to his mother. Something had gone wrong inside her and she'd died. Her complete disappearance was hard for him to comprehend, but slowly he came to believe that in death she was much closer to him and safe from distractions. He had a portrait of her – a photograph by the outrageous Kandyan photographer Alphonso – that showed her sharp elongated face in the three-quarter pose of a Madonna, her graceful fingers poised above the keys of a polished piano. Finally it seemed she was ready to play for him. Nobody could come between them.

Lester's unmarried sister Aunty Lillie was drafted in to look after Sunny after his mother's death. She was a small, hardy woman of great misguided determination who had never been pleased with her brother's choice of a highly strung, preening artist for a mate. While Irene had been alive, she rarely came near the house, but immediately afterwards she had rushed in and turned the place upside down. She had the walls distempered, the cupboards fumigated and the linen steeped in bleach for days. She banished the piano to a convent school in the hope that the devil in it might be tamed. Her profound aversion to secular music and the modern world meant that toys, films, records, ice cream – anything plastic, artificial or sweet – was also forbidden. She put her chubby young charge on a special diet of lentils and raw spinach. Astrological forecasts of impending Armageddon were her lullabies of choice.

In Aunty Lillie's considered opinion Sunny was a born idler and his father – her brother – a thoroughly useless loafer. The long years wasted at a corroded typewriter in the semi-darkness of a suburban house polluted with ungodly sounds and distilled spirits had, she reckoned, dulled her brother's senses. She declared his plan to abscond to the Philippines an even bigger mistake than his marriage. 'You can't see for toffee, Lester. You've been sitting on your backside for too darn long, just listening to that . . . rubbish and dreaming of dirty money.'

Now, in Manila, Lester had achieved a balance of affluence and sloth that would have turned Aunty Lillie's stomach. Luckily she never got the chance to see him thrive in his consumerist paradise. Lester never brought her over. Family life, Sunny had heard him confide to his friend Hector, was a much overrated business. He was glad of the chance of a new life in a new land with none of the impediments of the past. Despite being free of Aunty Lillie, Sunny didn't entirely agree. Although he didn't much grieve for his mad aunt, her rickety Morris Minor or the faggoty boys' school she'd unwittingly sent him to, he recognized that there was a piece missing from his sense of himself. Because of his mother's antics – genius perhaps – he'd felt a little out of the ordinary, but now as a teenager in Makati's shallow wonderland he found the void created by that abandoned world almost too scary to think about.

Robby's mention of cricket launched Sunny into a reverie. By five-thirty, when Lester was due back from his uptown office, Sunny was ready. He had a plan that was simple and rather beautiful. It was going to transform their uprooted lives. There had been a time when Sunny and his father had played garden cricket on a strip of lawn barely wide enough to swing a bat. Lester favoured the leg-spin; Sunny wanted to be a fast bowler. He'd aim for the body, while Lester tried his best to get his little boy to learn to go for the wicket instead. But golf was Lester's sport in their new world. Big broad fairways and luscious, well-watered greens were where the word was for a lapsed journalist of his inclinations, the real news: Manila moolah. Sunny wanted to get it back, that closeness they'd once contained on a makeshift pitch.

He heard his father's Buick roll in, the car door open and shut. Lester was an incredibly slow mover. Even in his journalist days he'd never rushed, whatever the story, walking as though he had to weigh every step. 'To catch the little ones, you have to run, but to catch the big ones you have to be patient,' he liked to say. Sunny thought he was more suited to fishing than chasing stories of any kind.

By the time Lester reached the front door, Sunny had banished the cartoons from the TV and was on his feet. 'Dad, did we bring my bat?'

Lester pulled off his brown knitted tie and looked at his son suspiciously. The Sunday supplements had recently declared the discovery of a 'generation gap' and his son, he reckoned, was very unlikely to be the one who would bridge it.

'Or *your* bat?'

'Bat?'

'I wanna – *want to* I mean – play cricket . . .' Sunny remembered the time he'd bowled a hard ball, dead on, and hit his father right between the eyes.

Lester opened his mouth and the metal flints in his teeth sparkled. 'Ah . . . ha.' Something moved across his face. There was almost the hiss of gas in the guarded Makati air. 'Cricket?'

'I thought we might have brought some gear with us.'

Lester narrowed his eyes. 'There are a couple of boxes in the back. We might have a bat and a ball in there.'

'Stumps? For the wicket?'

'You can use sticks, you know.'

Sunny wasn't sure about that. A few bits of bamboo were

unlikely to impress a trendsetter like his pal Robby. 'Isn't there a weird shop in Ermita, or someplace, selling the stuff? Like on the black market?' Manila was famous for every kind of vice.

'Cricket gear is not contraband.' Lester rubbed the edge of his grey sideburn. 'Why don't you ask your Australian friend – that Thompson boy? He is sure to have the lot.'

Sunny was horrified. 'He's not a friend.'

'Why not? Any fellow can be a friend. If you are in need.'

As it turned out there was no need for Steve Thompson. Not yet. The box in the storeroom did contain a neglected bat and a barely used red leather ball. With the two essentials in his hand, Sunny agreed that he could improvise a wicket.

'Hey Robby, I have the bat and the ball.'

There was a pause at the other end of the line. Sunny could hear Robby aerate his brain with a smoky intake of breath as he searched for the right word. Eventually it appeared, a little mangled. 'Baileys?'

Sunny laughed. 'Bails?'

'Yeah. What about them?'

'No problem.' Sunny told him to come to the park. Urdaneta Park.

'I can't. Not today.'

'This is *not* good news, man. You must come.'

'I've got to go to Cavite with my Dad. Export presentations, *na*.' Robby's father was said to be in the garment industry, although Sunny suspected it was something much shadier.

'Tomorrow then?'

⋆

Sunny put the cricket ball in one of his white gym socks and tied the end of a rope to it. Then he hung the rope off one of the metal poles supporting the tin roof of the porch outside the kitchen. The ball swung eighteen inches off the ground, perfect for rehearsing the basic block, forward punch and offside cut. Within seconds Sunny had launched himself into what was once his favourite fantasy. Out on the playing fields of Kingston and Port of Spain, clocking in the runs to cheers of adulation. His first heroes – West Indian cricketers all, especially Kanhai, who looked almost like Sunny – appeared, wowed by his every stroke. They were toasting him on the beach. The daydream grew and soon all Urdaneta, Makati, the whole of the Philippines basked in the glow of his Caribbean innings.

As he made his second imaginary century, his father's car turned in at the gate and stopped. Lester hauled himself out with a pipe in his fist. He lit the pipe, puffing with great determination, shifting his concentration from his lumbago to his lungs. He had bought the pipe after reading about the Royal College of Physicians' report on the dangers of smoking cheap cigarettes. He didn't look at Sunny, but kept sucking and puffing until the smoke enveloped his whole head. 'So, how is it? Hit the ball?'

Sunny didn't answer. He showed his father a neat flick of seasoned willow. A boundary on tap.

'Good. Use those wrists. You have good wrists.'

Sunny was chuffed. It had been a long time since his father had said anything like that. Lester's natural tendency was towards the sardonic – Hector called it the Fernando house style of total annihilation.

Lester ambled over and held out his hand for the bat. 'Let's see.'

Sunny handed it to him. Lester adjusted his pipe, clamping hard on the stem. He pulled up his sleeves and grasping the bat firmly, went into a block position with his right leg trailing behind like a superhero's cape, his back straighter than it had been for ages. He nudged the ball with the face of the bat. It swung out. On the return arc he almost missed it, but managed a slight glance off the side, somehow giving the impression that this was deliberate. He made a clicking sound out of the side of his mouth and handed the bat back. Unplugging his pipe, he grunted before going inside.

When Lester reappeared after a nap he found Sunny with the newspaper open at the TV page. 'You have no homework?'

'Saturday night, Dad.'

'Not even geography homework?'

'No.'

'You are doing what, then?'

'I have to see Herbie.'

'See him for what purpose?'

'We might go over to Bel-Air together. He's got my geography book anyways.'

Lester hesitated as though he had something important to say, but then he shut his eyes and rubbed his back. His lumbago reminded him of more pressing problems. 'Desai has a party tonight, but it'll be impossible to get a decent drink out of that stingy fellow. I can't stand in that damn house for very long sipping bloody calamansi juice. Shall I pick you up on the way back?'

Sunny shook his head. 'We might go bowling, or something, later.'

'Are you sure you can take all this sport?' Lester tried to catch his son's eye and share a joke at his expense, but Sunny ignored the gibe and went to phone Herbie.

'Bowling? No way. Listen, I'm going to Quiapo with Ricardo. You wanna come?' Herbie's voice creaked.

'What about the Black Naz thing? Isn't the big Jesus procession over there this weekend? It'll be chaos.'

'Yeah, yeah. Perfect timing.'

'OK. I'll come over to your place.'

Herbie lived on Cerrada Avenue, a ten-minute walk away. Sunny slipped out of the house while his father was still yodelling in the shower.

The streetlights hummed fat and bright. The night was hot. Nobody was around. Cerrada Avenue had a curve to it unlike most of the others slotted into the Urdaneta grid and Herbie's house was one of the last on the street. Sunny's canvas shoes barely made a sound on the white concrete. The hum in his ears could have been pure electricity, or fireflies beating their wings.

Sunny rang the bell and waited to see who would come to the door. He'd never met Herbie's parents, or any siblings. The only people who ever appeared were Herbie's peculiar friends and a stream of hapless maids, none of whom lasted longer than a month or two before going berserk. He didn't recognize the one who opened the door, but she smiled sweetly and showed him in.

Herbie's room was dark. 'Herbie?' Sunny called out above

the familiar refrain of The Doors playing in Herbie's home-made speakers. 'What's happening?'

Someone scrabbled in the dark.

'Cool, man.'

'Is Ricardo here?'

'Not yet. He's coming. Relax.'

The tape came to an end and the hiss of the air-conditioner filled the space. 'Any new sounds, Herbie?'

'Ricardo. He's bringing the new album.'

'Which new album?'

'Their new album, man. You know?' The music started again.

Sunny tried another tack. 'So, what's in Quiapo besides the fiesta?'

Herbie giggled. 'It's a big deal. Ricardo . . .' He didn't bother to finish the sentence.

Two hours later Sunny was still waiting to hear about the big deal. Ricardo had not turned up. Or if he had, he was lost somewhere in Herbie's room. Sunny had listened to The Doors bang again and again until *his* fire at least was quite blown out.

'Hey, I'm going home, Herbie.'

'Wait,' Herbie started. 'Ricardo.' The mantra. *Ricardo.* He switched on a red lamp as though that might conjure up his fiendish friend. Herbie's moonlike face was flat and thin and sloped to one side like a severe mudslide.

In the glow Sunny made out a cricket ball snared inside an empty pickle jar. 'Hey, Herbie, you have a ball.'

'Fuck you, too.' Herbie snorted.

'A cricket ball, yeah? You know how to play, right?'

Herbie groaned as the tape wound itself around the tiny metal capstan inside the cassette machine.

'Do you?'

'What are you talkin' about?' Herbie forced the cassette out and pulled the tape until his hands were full with the brown plastic ribbon of Jim Morrison's unspooled words.

'Robby and I are looking for people to play cricket.'

'Robby?'

'Yeah. He wants to learn.'

'Learn?'

After a while Herbie admitted that he had played cricket in junior school when he lived in Hong Kong and that he was pretty good with the googly.

Sunny yelped, thrilled, when he heard the word: *googly*. 'Fantastic.' It was the kind of bowling he wished he could perfect, alongside the bouncers and bodyliners he'd spent so long practising.

Back in the Fernando house, Rosa the maid and Beatriz the cook had gone to sleep. Rex the driver, who had been given the night off, was out on the town undaunted by the continuing jeepney strike – down to Grace Park where, he said (usually for Rosa's benefit), he liked to have his buttocks massaged.

Sunny was still up, fantasizing, when Lester got back from his party with Hector in tow, both men uncomfortably hamstrung by starched pineapple-fibre shirts – *barongs* – the Filipino national dress. The two men had been friends since their school days, but it was chance that had brought them together again in Manila. Hector was an administrator at the new Asian Development Bank, the ADB. He was a great listener and a great nodder. His large, sharp head would regularly bob, up and down, like a pecking bird. His eyes tended to be wide open, as though he was in a continuous state of surprise. For an ex-hack like Lester, he was the ideal companion. Everything Lester said he took as breaking news. He lived down the same road as Lester and Sunny and often walked over. He had no family – no wife, no children – and took an avuncular interest in Sunny. 'Look at the world every way you can, Sunny,' he would croon. 'There's a lot of world out there to see.'

Lester brought out a bottle of whisky and an ice bucket. 'Soda?'

'Soda.' Hector nodded.

Sunny came and stood at the doorway.

'Ah, Sunny, *Mabuhay* eh?' Hector raised a hand in greeting. 'How's the young fellow?'

'OK.' Sunny shrugged.

'So, you went bowling with Herbie?' His father measured out three fingers of Scotch.

Sunny didn't reply.

Lester poured a pretty stream of bubbly soda. The glass ended up too full. Hector's tongue peeped out of his lips while he considered his options. Lester filled his own glass with half an inch to spare. 'Cheers!' He took a loud sip. 'That's better. How those fellows can throw a party without any whisky is beyond me. No liquor at all. Are they paid to make enemies, these diplomats? And that Mrs Desai, poking her nose into everyone's affairs. Always on about the need of a woman's touch in my house . . . *Tcha.* Cheeky ass.'

Hector started to reach for his glass but then, hand in mid-air, hesitated. 'I say, Lester.'

'Yes, Hector?' He chuckled at the pat little rhyme that echoed each time they addressed one another.

'This is a little full, no?'

'What? Your hand not steady any more?' Lester hooted merrily. 'Drink up, drink up. Very good for the old sciatica.'

Sunny decided to intervene. 'We didn't go bowling, but you know what, Dad? Herbie is a bowler. Googlies.'

Hector looked up. 'Googlies? What's this about googlies?'

'Cricket, Uncle. Cricket.'

Hector nodded solemnly.

'I found my bat and ball and some friends who want to learn the game.'

Hector managed a sip, spilling just a few drops from his glass. He smacked his lips and settled back. 'I see. A cricket team. But is there another team to play against? The Quezon XI perhaps?'

'You,' Sunny declared. 'You and Dad. You must have a team you can get together? The Old Boys' Brigade.'

Lester slapped his thigh, a habit he had developed to aid his thinking, particularly after a whisky or two. 'Desai. Those fellows must have a cricketer or two among them. Bloody soberers, no?' He took a big mouthful. Slap, bang, his hand went again hard against his thigh.

'Navaratnam can play,' Hector added.

'Who?'

'Our Harvard economist. The Colombo chap.'

Sunny pricked up his ears at the mention of Tina's father.

'Of course, you are quite right. He even played for Royal, no?' Lester kept files in his head of all sorts of random information, including the schooling of Ceylon's growing band of international vagabonds.

Hector nodded again. 'He was always in the cricket crowd,

you remember. Major league. Out here he has a bit of a craving . . .'

So Rudolf Navaratnam was not just a rolling stone, he was a colossus of cricket – someone in the order of Grace, Bradman or Walcott – in whose presence Sunny would wilt and expire. Sunny imagined Tina's father stepping out of his silver Mercedes and striding up to the crease in Urdaneta Park with a bat that would smash the hell out of a wimp like him.

In Makati, Manila, at nine-thirty on the morning of Sunday, 10 January 1971, Sunny was the only one among his gang of spaced-out zonks who was awake. The prospect of cricket, and Tina, had upset the equilibrium he normally achieved through his reclusive passions of sleep, TV and minor self-abuse.

He walked into the kitchen and found his father giving instructions to Rosa and Beatriz.

'I have asked some people around for lunch,' Lester said. 'You will be here?'

'Oh?' Sunny was careful to reserve his rights, one syllable at a time.

'Your cricket idea, last night, got me thinking.'

Sunny cringed, aware that they were on dangerous ground.

'I thought it would be a good idea to get the Navaratnams over. Hector will come, and the Thompsons. The Navaratnams have a girl, I think. And the Thompson boy may tag along.'

'Why?'

'Why, what?' Lester looked puzzled.

'Why everything? Why Steve Thompson, for God's sake.'

'I thought we might get the team going, you know. The Thompsons will provide two – father and son. One for you, one for me. By the way, you shouldn't swear. It achieves nothing, unless you are particularly religious.'

'I was going to meet Robby and Herbie for a bit of batting.'

'Ask them over here. Navaratnam was a first-class player in his day, you know. He can give us all a lesson.'

'Anyways, I wasn't swearing. Jeez, Dad.' Sunny slunk back to his room to recuperate in front of his collection of Zen photos. It was all too much, too fast and too out of control. He couldn't understand what had got into his father. This gathering was not of his usual type. No hangers-on. These were the Navaratnams and the Thompsons. Heck, he had even offered to have Herbie around.

Sunny called and left messages for the gang. He said that there would be curry for lunch and that they could go out cricketing later. Herbie and Robby both liked the food in the Fernando house and would happily sneak in to munch leftovers at any time of the day. With their support Sunny believed he had a chance of coping with the arrival of both Steve and Tina at the same time.

The immediate problem that Sunny faced was his room. Personally he didn't mind the limey walls, the pukey bedspread, the dressing table with its wing-tip mirrors and cut-outs from perfume ads; but in daylight with the sun streaming in, the place did look a little girlish. It didn't show anything of the real him, except for the collage of snaps stuck on the wardrobe door and the portrait of his dead mother. Sunny kept her on top of the chest of drawers facing the door. In the furthest corner from the photograph, there was a guitar which he couldn't really play but which could for this occasion be brought a little more centre stage. Placed casually on the bed perhaps. He thought he would keep the curtains drawn, the lights turned down low and snug like at Herbie's. With the murky rug on the floor, Tina might even think there was a kind of purple haze in there somewhere. Sunny turned the air-con high and put a bowl underneath to catch the drips of icy condensation.

Rosa was outside, in the hall, singing along with Engelbert Humperdinck and cleaning the fretwork using a potato peeler wrapped in cotton wool. Sunny asked her for a duster. She giggled. 'Is in the larder, *na*.' He fetched the cloth and set to work on everything horizontal – bed, shelves, louvres – and hid his father's latest Harold Robbins under a poncho. Then, after a shower and tons of deodorant in crucial places, slipped into a bright flowery shirt and his faded blue jeans with the zip that didn't quite go all the way. He wanted to be ready for anything.

Lester arrived back from Guadalupe Market with four kilos of belly pork and called for his son. 'Sunny, you want to fry the pork?'

'We need Coke,' Sunny countered quickly. He didn't want pork fat greasing his hair and the smell of his father's curry clinging to his fresh clothes. It was not the aroma for Tina, regardless of their common culinary heritage. 'You didn't get any Coke, did you?'

'I got a case of 7-Up.'

'I'll go get a couple of Cokes. Herbie likes Coke. And the Navaratnam girl also prefers it. I can walk over to the Supermart.'

'You know the Navaratnam girl?'

'I've talked to her.'

'Good.' Lester handed over a wad of pesos. 'In that case, get some Ajinomoto also. And a lemon. Her father, the champ, is bound to be a G&T bugger.'

Makati Supermart, right in the middle of the Commercial Centre, past the Tempura restaurant, the barber shop and the tenpin bowling alley, was Sunny's first and favourite supermarket. Retail self-service hadn't existed in the Colombo of his childhood. The first time he entered it he realized that this was truly an erogenous zone. Even in Manila it was special: the largest supermarket in the Far East. Customers were requested to 'Please Leave All Firearms at the Desk', an order Sunny wished he could obey with a personal arsenal as big as the best. And so polite – *please*. Everyone in the new Makati aimed to please, from pisspot to gunshot.

Sunny walked down the confectionery aisle, feasting his eyes through a cool light tint, and then loitered for a while by the ice-cream freezers. Further on he picked a lemon and hung a left, thinking of Coke, girls and fretless chords.

He found Hector stranded on a corner by the mini-pretzels. He was leaning on a shopping trolley, stroking his chin.

'Sunny, look at this,' Hector squawked the moment he saw him. 'Look at the way they have done this. Are they trying to build a pyramid? How can you get a packet out of this heap? The whole thing will collapse.'

Sunny led Hector down the aisle. 'Those are for show. The ones to buy are here, Uncle.'

Hector exhaled loudly, relieved. 'You like these pretzel things? I thought I'd bring some along for lunch.'

'Dad's making pork curry.'

Hector nodded vigorously, pleased. 'Yes. Definitely. He's not one for these nibbles, I know, but what about you?'

Sunny nodded back, unconsciously keeping time to Hector's bobbing head. 'I came to get some Coke.'

'So, I'll take you back?'

Sunny was grateful for the offer of a lift. Crossing Ayala Avenue in the heat on the way over he had realized it might have been better to be flavoured with pork fat after all, and found it quite a turn-on to imagine a kiss that turned into a wild tongue bath.

Hector's car was also a Mercedes, a mud-coloured diesel version of the one Rudolf Navaratnam had. 'Does everyone in your office have a Merc?'

Hector looked baffled.

'The Navaratnams?'

'Oh, oh.' He nodded. 'Ceylon, no? We old boys stick together. Team spirit.'

'What about us then? Dad has a Buick.'

'Ah, but he is the captain, no? He leads. Next year we will all have American cars.'

Sunny wasn't sure whether Hector was making fun of his father. His father was not a leader – not even a leader writer any more.

Hector reversed slowly into the kerb. There was the crunch of a can, or a trolley, or some poor Supermart attendant. Hector looked at Sunny and shook his head helplessly. 'Germans make hard cars.'

It was true, Sunny thought. The seats were hard. 'Will you guys really get a team together with Mr Navaratnam?'

'Oh, yes. That's what the pork curry is about.'

'Yeah?' Sunny was lost.

'You see, I happen to know, Mrs Navaratnam – sweet Anjuli – can't ff . . . fry a sausage. He gets only leftover *adobo* from the cook. Rudolf, poor bugger, has been dying for a hot curry for months.'

'How do you know that?' Sunny could imagine his father picking up such a juicy domestic titbit – he had once been an investigative reporter, after all. But Hector?

'It's all he ever talks about when we meet.'

'Really?' Sunny tried to conjure up a conversation at the bank. 'A pork curry, I say, *men*. GDP would double, no, with a pukka red-hot pork curry.' Then he cut to Rudolf at home – a moody, menacing figure flinging Ceylonese recipe books at his clueless wife while Tina cowered in her room, traumatized. 'But if he wants it so much, why doesn't he learn to cook like Dad? Why should his wife have to do all the frying?'

'Well, perhaps your father will teach him, in return for a trick or two with the old bat and ball. Anjuli, you see, is not very . . . compliant.' Hector made a laborious wide turn into Urdaneta.

'No power steering?' Sunny asked.

'It is very precise, this car. European engineering.'

Having parked at the house without further mishap, Hector sniffed the air and chuckled. 'Navaratnam will go absolutely mad.'

Sunny wondered if the smell of pork frying could possibly reach all the way over across the Commercial Centre and seep through the *sampalok* leaves of San Lorenzo village, the next compound, to permeate the arid interior of the Navaratnam household. Would Rudolf Navaratnam already be salivating, bundling his wife into the back of his silver Merc and urging Tina to hurry up?

Hector headed for the kitchen door. He had the brown paper bag stuffed with pretzels close to his chest.

'I say, Lester, I brought you some party snacks.'

Lester looked up from the sizzling pan, one hand bandaged with a small pink towel and the other wielding a ladle made out of a coconut shell. 'Snacks?'

'Pretzels.'

'What the hell for?'

Hector shrugged. 'For Sunny and his friends. The young generation.'

Lester's scowl disappeared and his face relaxed. He put the ladle on the saucepan lid and turned the gas down. Then he saw his son. 'You got the lemon?'

Sunny pulled one out of his bag with a little flourish and tossed it over. 'Catch.'

'Oi.' Lester managed to cup his free hand in time.

'I say, what happened to your other hand, Lester?' Hector asked.

Lester looked down at his bandaged hand as though it had just appeared in front of him. 'Oh that. Just a bit of hot oil.'

'You are not preparing a little excuse to get out of the cricket, Lester, are you?' Hector gave Sunny a wry smile. 'Your father, you know, is a very shrewd fellow.'

'I can play you lot for a six with one hand tied behind my back.'

'Both hands.' Hector laughed. 'Why not both hands, Houdini?'

Sunny left them to their banter and went to his room.

The point was not to try too hard. *Let it be, let it be.* The Beatles' Lao-tzu creed that made a virtue out of reducing effort was very dear to Sunny. *Bahala na* was to his mind a fair Filipino interpretation.

'Zen,' Lester liked to mock, 'is the art of seeing everything but noticing nothing. A gift emulated by politicians, high priests and professional pundits. Divine, but useless.' He was not a great fan of anything remotely mystical. Unlike Aunty Lillie, he preferred the physical world in spite of its difficulties and disappointments.

Sunny picked up his mother's portrait. In this picture he could see everything and notice everything. He could follow the very grain of it. He understood how it had been produced: the play of light and chemicals, the fragility of the paper-thin image. And yet there was more for him in that one photograph than in anything else he possessed. When *Amma* died he had just learnt the heady words, *she loves you yeah, yeah, yeah . . .* from Radio Ceylon's re-broadcast BBC hit parade. *Love?* He had been desperate to grow up and find out about this thing.

At twelve-thirty sharp the Thompsons arrived. Rosa knocked on Sunny's door. He opened it and she gestured frantically. '*Come*, come. Your Daddy calling. Thompson family here already, *na*.' She clutched her head and ran back to the kitchen.

Sunny sauntered out.

The three Thompsons – Martin, a lanky sunburnt man in a yellow shirt, Mary, his freckled bemused wife, and their tall, spotty son Steve – stood trapped in the front garden.

'Hi, there.' Martin Thompson waved a big hand. Sunny nodded, taking his cue from Hector who faced them, dumbfounded.

'Hello,' Mary added with the special consideration some mothers can't help but offer the motherless. Her dress had patterns that belonged in a zoo.

Sunny flinched.

A small brown bird glided into the pine tree by the gate. Lester came and herded the guests through the house to the back patio where an assorted collection of chairs – wood, wicker, rattan – were set out.

'Sunny, you'll do the soft drinks for . . .' He had forgotten the boy's name. He was hopeless with names unless he wrote them down. He turned to Mary. 'What can I get you, Marie?'

'A Cinzano and lemonade would be nice, Lester.'

Sunny decided then that if he was going to get his team together, he would have to rise above the petty prejudices of teenage angst. Steve Thompson had usefully long arms even if his carroty hair was cut square and his pimples a little off-putting. '7-Up?' Sunny asked him.

'Cool.'

Sunny retreated to the kitchen and got a bottle out of the fridge. A curvy Coke rolled temptingly on the top shelf. He thought he'd wait a little longer. He'd read about the pleasures of delayed gratification.

'You know Herbie?' He handed Steve the 7-Up.

'Nope.'

'Robby?'

'Nope.'

'They'll be here. You'll meet them.'

'Good.' He didn't look too excited. Sunny didn't mention Tina.

In the blazing heat of the patio, Lester asked Steve's parents what they made of life in Manila.

Mr Thompson mopped his face with a big hanky and grinned. 'Fantastic.' The class struggle, the strikes downtown and the student battles could have been on another planet.

'He loves the nightclubs,' his wife elaborated. She took a large swig of her drink and her voice sharpened. 'Friday nights and Saturday nights are impossible with Martin. He's so raring to go for those dolly hostesses on Roxas Boulevard. Even last night, he was in such a state . . .'

Her husband interrupted. 'We were in Borneo for two years, you see. Orang-utans are not party people, I can tell you. It makes a change. Never mind Roxas, you seen those all-out floor shows in Cubao? Hey, aren't they something? They just do *everything*.'

Sunny looked at Steve. 'You lived in Borneo?'

'Where?'

'Borneo. Your Dad just said you guys were in Borneo for two years.'

'Not me. I was in Melbourne.'

'Oh, yeah. Not Borneo?'

He shrugged. 'I visited.'

Sunny reckoned even his brief exposure had had devastating effects.

'You play cricket?' he asked eventually. There was an echo

as his father asked Martin Thompson the same question almost at the same time. Thompson father and son looked at each other, bewildered.

'Cricket.' Hector added his own echo for emphasis.

Martin Thompson replied first. 'Why, sure. Crikey, I used to play all the time. More my game than poncy golf.'

His son shrugged again.

'I wanted to stay on in Melbourne for that third Test, you know. I don't know where the rain came from. Pommies must have brought it with them like some bloody good luck charm. It never rains like that in Melbourne. Bradman and dear Sir Cyril had to dream up this one-day match for the fans. You follow that?'

'One-day?' Lester's head lifted.

The doorbell rang and Rosa squealed, 'Sir, sir.'

'Excuse me, that'll be Navaratnam. First-class batsman. He was our number one centurion in Colombo.'

'Right.' Martin Thompson's jaw tightened.

The arrival of the Navaratnams, like that of the Spanish, Sunny knew, could spell the end of simple innocence – his easy life of auto-eroticism. He looked down to see if his blood had seeped out of a hole in his heel, staining his Jesus sandals and ruining the patio. Involuntary fluid loss, he'd learnt from experience, was part of growing up.

Rudolf Navaratnam, the great bull patriarch of the family, had landed what Lester called a comfort job at the ADB. Apparently Dr Navaratnam was an expert on economic development. His wife Anjuli was a plump woman with a smart nose for hot gossip, bouncy and frisky and always on the verge of laughter. Tina had inherited her mother's features but fortunately neither her figure, nor the tittering that was her usual greeting. Tina was altogether more serious, focused and desirable.

Mrs Navaratnam came first, a bundle of kingfisher blue preceded by the jingle-jangle of her gold bangles and a flight of skittering giggles. She jostled her way out between her husband, who was stuck in the shadows of the doorway, and a pot of lusty anthuriums. 'Ooh,' she cooed at Martin Thompson, who couldn't take his eyes off her. 'I am Anjuli.' Then spotting Mary collapsed in the shade, she giggled. 'How do *you* do?'

'Mary.' Mary replied with a weak smile.

Tina nosed ahead of her father and winked at Sunny. Even if he had summoned sufficient motor control to do so, he couldn't have responded. Her father was staring right at him. Rudolf Navaratnam smoothed the side of his Brylcreemed head with the palm of his hand and stepped out into the sunshine in a red shirt and dazzling white slacks. He could have been Lloyd, Walcott, Sobers, all rolled into one. A giant among batsmen.

Lester did the introductions. 'Anjuli, Marie. Sorry, sorry – *Mary*. How could I get it wrong? Mary. Forgive me. Mary, Anjuli, Rudolf, Mary, Mary, Rudolf, Martin, Anjuli, Anjuli, Martin, Martin, Rudolf, Rudolf, Martin and . . . Hector. You all know Hector, of course.' Then he turned to his son in relief. 'The kids, I think, know each other already. For this younger generation the whole world is already such a small place, isn't it? But this, anyway, is Sunny.'

'Ooh, I know him.' Mrs Navaratnam snickered incriminatingly.

'Your son?' Rudolf Navaratnam's tone seemed to suggest that Lester's pronunciation needed some work.

'Sanath,' Sunny managed to sputter. 'Here in Manila they prefer Sunny.' He looked to see if Tina thought he was babbling. How did her mother know him?

'Ah, yes. They like the *ih* sound here.'

Tina butted in. 'But Daddy, you are the one who says "bunny" and "fanny".'

Lester was a maestro of the well-timed drink. Early on in life he had learned the importance of lubricants, perfecting the art in the watering holes of Galle Road and in Colombo's lakeside bars. 'Gin?' he asked. 'Or Scotch? Maybe Campari?'

'Oh, Lester . . .' Anjuli fluttered her eyes, and steamy possibilities hovered in the hot, intimate air for the men around her to savour.

'She'd love a gin and tonic.' Rudolf made a rough hissing sound in his throat.

'Two?'

'For me, a Coca-Cola if you please.'

'With rum, then? Local? Tanduay?'

'Just two cubes of ice please. No rum.'

'I see.' Lester turned to his son. 'You brought Coca-Cola?'

Sunny's stomach tightened. He'd only bought four bottles and each one had a very special aura: *Tina, me, Tina and me*. Thoughts ran wild in his head. He had pictured Rudolf Navaratnam as smooth and suave, easily moving from handshake to shoulder-grip and a silver Mercedes convertible on the Costiera di Amalfi, an over-tanned Cary Grant sailing high between an iced Pimm's and a second innings. Instead, here was this monstrous bat-head who got his kicks from beating his wife with cricket stumps over a pork curry, intent on crushing all hope among the young in order to shore up his lust for lost youth. Tina was a girl in a serious situation. He had to make a stand. Now or never.

'I got Coke for Tina.' He squeaked, and prayed.

She looked at him, puzzled. 'But I like Pepsi. Papa's the Coke-head in our family.' The tip of her nose wiggled.

Hector broke into a laugh. 'You can say that again. Rudolf, for all his highfalutin development economics, is the biggest supporter of Coca-Cola that the world has ever known. You know, they have a special delivery in our canteen at the bank just for him. Twice a week.'

Anjuli found that hilarious. 'He always was such a twice-a-weeker. Weren't you, Rudy?'

Mary, who had withdrawn well into her fizzy Cinzano, tipped her head to one side and took another look at Rudolf. He smoothed his gleaming hair and gave a sly smile. 'A small habit I picked up doing my doctorate in America. I used to swim twice a week, cinema twice a week, library twice a week, and I allowed myself Coca-Cola twice a week. You need discipline, you see. Otherwise you have chaos.'

Hector laughed. 'So, what happened? You are now drinking Coke all the time, no? What has happened to twice a week?'

Rudolf gave a guilty shrug. 'Well, yes, but . . . some things are more addictive than others.'

'Hector, you are a naughty one, starting this . . .' Anjuli giggled again and drained her glass of gin. She held it out for a refill. 'Twice a week. If only, no? I was thinking we should try that new cola they've brought out. Have you seen the adverts? RC Cola, the randy *newcomer*.'

Sunny went back into the house to look for Tina, who had slipped away. He found her sitting on the leather cushion that Lester had brought back from a trip to Jakarta and which Sunny used as a punchbag.

'I hate it when my mother hits the gin.' Tina pouted.

OK, just wouldn't do as a response. *My mother died when I was eight* . . . No, he knew that would not do either.

'Papa at least has learnt to stay off the stuff, but she can't stop. She's so dumb.'

'It's OK.'

Sunny wanted to make her feel better. And for her to make him feel better. Sitting there in her faded blue bell-bottoms, her arms resting on her splayed knees, her wonderfully long face turned up to him, her bunched hair almost twitching behind her like a tail, she was more than he could have ever hoped for listening to the Fab Four. And now here she was in his house. She looked plumper than she had when he first saw her climbing into her father's car. Perhaps she was a little too fond of *Halo-halo*. The stitching on one of the seams of the cushion had come undone. The white inner sleeve containing horsehair, or whatever they used in the leather dumps of the Suharto regime, looked close to bursting. The consequences could be tragic.

'Tina . . .'

'Yes.' Her nose flared a little.

'It's going to split.'

She looked at Sunny the way he had dreamt of her doing for months. Straight into his heart. But he couldn't leave it at that. She might think he was talking about her hip-hugging bells. He knew she'd noticed him staring at the creamy half-inch of elasticated fabric peeping above the tight denim.

'The humpty.' Was that a real word? Or just a remnant of Aunty Lillie's wacky vocabulary? 'The humpty might split.' He pointed to the leather seam below her thigh.

'Oh, pouffe?' She quickly stood up, almost rushing into his arms. He stepped away. He wanted to be a gentleman, despite his erratic zip.

'I sometimes punch it, that's why.'

'Really?'

'We have no Pepsi. What about 7-Up?'

'OK.'

'I'll get it then. And a Coke for your Dad.'

'Why do you hit it?'

Words were too much trouble, Sunny knew that. When they get blurted out there is no telling what might happen. Tina was looking at him now as though he was a kitten rather than the tiger he wanted to be, leaping for her.

'I don't hit it. Just punch it, see?' And dance like a butterfly, he wanted to add, thereby suggesting both sensitivity and virility, despite his glasses.

Rosa passed by with a tray of ice and lemon, trying without success to suppress a laugh.

'Boys outside, *na* . . .' she said in her high, hysterical sing-song.

Robby and Herbie were strolling up the drive, rapping the roofs of the parked line of cars with their knuckles and making karate kicks at invisible villains.

'Excuse me,' Sunny said and went to the side door. 'Here, this way, guys.'

Before he could do the introductions, Tina spoke.

'Robby. Robby? What are you doing here?'

Robby drew back and took a quick look around, checking for the nearest escape route.

'You've met already?' Sunny was troubled.

'She lives next door.' Robby reminded him icily.

'Yeah, isn't it amazing?'

'Herbie,' Herbie said to her. 'I'm Herbie, you don't know me.' His moony face broke into a smile as he added, 'Yet.'

Anjuli giggled loudly outside. Tina shrank a little.

'You didn't say there was a party.' Herbie peeked behind Sunny. 'What's happening?'

Out on the patio Lester put forward his proposition. 'You know, I was thinking that this town could do with a bit of contra-*kanos*. Not to be AA – anti-American, you know – but to provide some contrast to the B and B. The baseball and the basketball.' He still thought in terms of headlines and tended to highlight words as he spoke, seeking alliteration and abbreviation wherever he could.

'What about *Jai-Alai*?' Martin Thompson suggested, keen to show off his local knowledge.

'Cock fighting is a big thing, no? The *tupala* or whatever? Araneta Coliseum . . .' Anjuli plucked at her shimmering sari and gazed innocently at Martin.

'I was thinking of a *team* game – cricket,' Lester said.

Rudolf made an approving noise, while Hector mumbled something about a common British connection.

'No, Hector. This is not colonial claptrap,' Lester continued. 'You see how golf has been transformed internationally. Cricket might well become an All-Asian game, you know. But we need it to grow in South-East Asia, the Far East. Maybe if it flourished in the Philippines, like in Australia, India, Pakistan and Ceylon, the rest of the region might take it up. Imagine Laos, Thailand, Indonesia all hitting the Brits for a six. A true game of the South.'

'China is what counts.' Rudolf glanced at the pork curry that was being set out on the lunch table. 'Big country, China. That is what would make the difference. We should not let something like football divert them.'

'Always obsessed with China, no, Rudolf?' Hector turned to the others with a benign smile. 'This fellow just cannot understand what is going on there.'

'China will change.' Lester began to pat his pockets, searching for his pipe. 'Hong Kong is there, you know. Vietnam, however, is a different kettle of fish. This bloody war . . .'

Rudolf Navaratnam's face was swelling, as though conflicting desires were stretching it in different directions. The talk of China and the smell of pork curry was too much.

'Ping-pong.' Martin drained his beer. Everyone turned to him. Even Herbie appeared interested. Martin craned his neck, shaking it loose of its floppy yellow collar, as if to speak from a higher position. 'I heard that Imelda, the First Lady, wanted Nixon to send the US ping-pong team here before China. Now she has to make do with some Happy Valley delegation from Hong Kong. But you know, they are sure to play cricket.'

Lester was quick to cotton on. 'A one-day match?'

'Right. If we could get a team together . . .'

'We could challenge the fellows from Happy Valley. Free

booze and a bit of a bet. Those buggers will jump for it.'

Hector noticed Sunny's discomfort. 'It was Sunny's idea, you know. He wanted to see some cricket here between the juniors and the seniors.'

'But don't you see? Put together we could make a real team.' Lester beamed.

'Steve is a fantastic bowler and a mighty tonker too,' Mary mumbled through an amiable fog of Cinzano and maternal pride.

Rudolf remained silent. He seemed to be measuring each of them against some marker by which, Sunny was convinced, he would be judged an abject failure.

Lester was not put out. 'Rudolf, what do you say? Will you coach us? My friend Napoleon was in Singapore for a while. He can play – excellent catcher. We can also get a couple in from the Indian contingent in Legaspi, and possibly my friend from the Pakistan airline – PIA. He bears no grudge. Fellow is a pilot. Rumour has it, he's a pretty good spinner. He could fly in for the match.'

Rudolf seemed to wheeze; his face was now seriously bloated.

Hector came to the rescue. 'I say, Lester. Food is ready, no? Pork curry?'

'Pork? Of course. You are right. Lunch is served. Let us eat. Come, Anjuli, Mary, Tina . . . boys. Rudolf, come. Rudy, you like some rice and curry?'

Rudolf didn't need encouragement. Before Mary or Anjuli had made it to their feet, he was indoors ogling the dishes.

Rosa twittered. 'Sir, plate?' Then a crash as it shattered on the tiled floor.

'My God.' Anjuli clutched her exposed midriff. 'Rudy!'

Rudolf had his head down, cowed. He seemed to be drowning in his red shirt. 'I'm sorry,' he mumbled. '*Iskyus, iskyus.*'

'He's been so mixed up since we came here. Gets excited over such silly things. I don't know what is wrong with him.'

Rosa swept up the debris around Rudolf's feet while he helplessly looked on. 'Oh, *salamat, salamat.*'

'Move your feet, Rudy, at least give the girl some room.'

'Never mind,' Lester said. 'A plate we can drop any time, as long as out on the field we catch the ball. Isn't that so?' He attempted a boisterous laugh.

'It is good luck to break china before a match. They always used to throw crockery at the Thomians,' Hector said kindly.

'At a monastery?' Mary was struggling against her growing stupor.

'No, no. Thomians were the senior school Rudy's team played against in Colombo. Cricket, don't you know?'

The others soon crowded around the table. Herbie and Robby and Steve loaded up and headed for the seats by the pond; Herbie surreptitiously dropped some of his second-rate mescaline in for the fish.

'What about you?' Sunny said to Tina. 'Like to eat something?'

She took a plate and held it to her chest.

'Shall I serve?'

'No, don't worry.' She shook her head. 'I can manage.'

For a while there was hardly any conversation, only the sounds of mastication and the occasional low burp as the chilli hit an unaccustomed tube, or a hallucinating goldfish drowned under the lilies. Rudolf got up to help himself to more pork. Anjuli warned him. 'Not too much now, Rudy. You know what it does to your stomach, no?'

Sunny put on the Tijuana Brass Band on the new Radiola. A few minutes later, Rudolf cleared his throat. 'So, you have a bat, boy?'

'Yes.'

'And a ball?'

Sunny shrank back.

'We better see then, who can play.'

Lester applauded. 'Hear, hear. Let's do it, straight after lunch. Out in the front garden.'

Anjuli put a tempered potato in her mouth. 'My, Lester, I never thought you were such a *hotsie-potatsie* exhibitionist, darling.'

When the plates were cleared and the ice cream finished, Sunny brought out the equipment. Rudolf Navaratnam quickly took charge. 'Hector, you bat first.' He instructed Steve to bowl.

Steve was nonplussed. 'Where? There's no room here.'

Martin was evidently used to his son's lack of initiative. 'Son, just do a half, you know. Some folk here need to learn the game.'

'Will someone explain how it works?' Robby appealed first to Sunny, then inexplicably to Tina.

Her father would have none of it. 'Watch, young man. Observe the actions. Get them into your head. The rules can be constructed later.'

Wow, a real Zen master, Sunny thought.

Rudolf got Hector to stand in front of the silvania bush and then marked a spot about fifteen paces away and told Steve that this was his bowling crease. 'You don't need a run-up, just do a slow overarm like your Dad said.'

Steve did not look at all happy. He was clearly hung up on the ritual – rubbing balls, flicking hair, stamping the ground before doing the run, skip and windmill whirl with his arm.

'All right, if you have to, take a little side step.' Rudolf pointed at the paving stones along the border of the garden, at right-angles to the imaginary crease. He pointed at Robby. 'You be the wicketkeeper.'

'The wha'?'

'Stand behind that little bush and catch the ball if Hector misses.'

'But you said I should just watch.'

'Best place to watch, young man. You'll see everything you need to see. Let's go.'

Rudolf was not going to be just the coach, he clearly had ambitions to be captain, umpire, judge and possibly God.

Steve's first ball bounced, as if a little peeved. Hector didn't even have time to raise his bat. Robby only just managed to stop it with his leather boot.

'Easy, son. Easy.' Steve's father called out.

Hector missed the next couple too, but managed to connect on the fourth ball, which dribbled back to Steve.

Rudolf frowned. 'Lester, what about you?'

Lester bravely took the bat from a dismayed Hector. 'No boundaries, hey?' His laugh was hollow. He swayed in front of the bush. Sunny tried to remember how many glasses of whisky his father had drunk. No doubt Rudolf would have been counting. Why was his father not better prepared? Lester unbuckled his new, expensive watch and put it in his back pocket. The old boy was lucky. He tapped the first ball back to Steve. The second one he managed to knock into the roses. He clasped the small of his back after the stroke and used the bat to steady himself. 'You see, the eye is still there. Rosy or not. Who's next?' He was anxious to declare while still ahead with two hits and no misses.

'Me.' To Sunny's astonishment Tina took the bat and wiggled into a very professional stance in front of a goggle-eyed Robby who immediately crouched down to get in line with her bottom. Steve was too distracted to bowl anything but a mullygrubber that rolled along the ground.

'Come on, Steve, get it up.' She batted the ball right back between his pale bare feet. She then proceeded to demonstrate several textbook strokes, swivelling her round snug hips and neatly ticking the ball towards each of the fielders at different points of the garden. She cut a glorious figure.

Rudolf was impassive. After her sixth stroke, he simply said, 'Over.'

Tina turned to Sunny. 'Your turn.'

Sunny was in a state of considerable anxiety. A ball on a string was a very different thing from one launched by an ape who didn't much like you.

If Sunny had had more experience, or if he had thought more carefully about it, he could have played the way a traditional batsman would: with care, caution and natural grace. One should use the first few balls, even an over or two, to find the lie of the land, the nature of the pitch. But Sunny was reckless. Tina had shown poise and perfection. He wanted to show her something altogether more dashing.

So, when the ball came, he walloped it at the boundary.

Unfortunately, Rudolf Navaratnam's fat silver Mercedes stood right in the way.

Lester said he would pay for the shattered window. Hector offered to replace it with one from his car until the dealers could bring in the right shade of tinted glass from Hong Kong. The game was suspended.

Sunny was strongly advised to practise either with the ball back in the sock, or out in the middle of the park, far from fancy cars and picture windows. Perhaps in a month or so Rudolf Navaratnam might be willing to consider cricket again, but until then Sunny was not to plan on anything but geography homework.

Tina didn't seem to mind much about the car. Sunny hoped she might think he'd done it for her, because of her strained relations with her parents, but he didn't get to talk to her. When classes started again a few days later, she flew away to her school in the hills and Sunny returned to his dreams of destiny.

He had read about how the Zen master Awa Kenzo practised archery with his eyes closed, in the belief that if everything was calm a released arrow would find its own target; one after the other his arrows would plunge, head to butt, through the centre of a bull's eye in the dark. Sunny thought if he closed his eyes he could do the same with a bat and swinging sock ball, or indeed his life and Tina's. Attain perfection. Love. Everything. He believed in practice. It helped him think of the episode with the boundary and the Merc as a necessary event. Something mysterious and preordained; perhaps written in Aunty Lillie's book of stars.

Occasionally he managed to get Robby, and sometimes even Herbie, to join him in the park. He didn't ask Robby about how far he'd got with Tina. He was pretty sure they had something going; seeing her with a bat in the privacy of her own garden must have been what had fired Robby's interest in the game. Sunny's only consolation was that at least she had watched him put a ball through its paces, whereas Robby had only watched her.

'So?' Hector said to Sunny as they watched the Buick disappear, taking Lester to the airport. He was off to Singapore for the weekend, to cover the Commonwealth Conference as a favour for an old newspaper buddy. 'Anything planned for the weekend?'

Lester had warned him to keep Sunny off the streets. 'These demonstrations are getting bloody dangerous, Hector,' he'd grumbled. Thousands of Filipino students had been out protesting in Manila. Four had been killed. Just ten days earlier two more and a young child had been shot by psyched-up soldiers outside Aguinaldo. The Diliman mini-Republic at the University of the Philippines was under siege. None of it appeared to make much impression on Hector. Nor on Sunny, overwhelmed by longing, pining already at the prospect of a dizzy romance.

'Nothing tonight,' Sunny replied, a little guardedly. He didn't want to divulge his plans. His friend Junior was going up to Baguio to see his girl Pinky. Sunny wanted to tag along to find Tina.

'In that case, join me.'

'Where?'

'I'm going to a little meeting, over in Quezon City. You might find it interesting.'

'Political?'

'No. It is a more spiritual revolution we are after.'

'Are you a secret hippy, then, Uncle?'

Hector smiled. 'Have you ever heard of a man called Zaramazov?'

'No. Why?'

'We are exploring some of his teaching.'

'Is Dad involved?'

'Lester? I don't think so. He leaves that to his sister, no? Your Aunty Lillie, she has the spiritual touch. Your Papa prefers spirits. The blended and bottled variety, if you know what I mean.'

Hector picked Sunny up at about eight. 'Have you eaten?'

'I had a burger.' It may not have been soul food exactly, but for Sunny, in a way it was.

'Good. There won't be any food where we are going. For these meetings at Señora's we fast.' Hector spoke as though he'd picked up a new lexicon for the occasion, to match his beige Nehru shirt and pale cotton trousers.

'Fast?'

'It helps cleanse the body, while we attend to the mind.'

They stopped at a Spanish colonial villa that had black metal gates. Enormous fruit trees shrouded the garden. Sunny had not seen such an ancient house anywhere in Makati. They were let in by a thin old man wearing a tribal sash of luminous colours. Hector nodded in his usual manner and led the way up the steps. There were voices inside. Sunny followed him.

'Señora,' Hector exclaimed as they walked into a candle-lit courtyard.

'Oh, Hector.' A big, sassy voice sang out. 'Sweetie.'

'I've brought a new recruit.'

The Señora was a large, glamorous lady who lay like a bejewelled bedspread across a vast, sagging divan. 'How wonderful, Hector. A youngster.' She turned up her face and twitched her nose. 'Hmm, I can just smell that *divine* youth in him. *Gor-geous*. Come here, my sweetie.'

'Hello.' Sunny nodded politely, letting his hair flop over his glasses. There were about a dozen people – *Pinoys* as well as foreigners, men and women – in small huddles around the Igorot carvings that adorned the square.

Someone struck a gamelan, sending out small ripples of beautiful sound.

'Time, my little dears.' The Señora slowly raised herself to her feet and great folds of her voluptuous flesh fell into place. She waved a hand, jettisoning some of her heavier jewellery. 'All you pretty things hurry into the yellow room. The boys, if you are still intact after last time, go hang on to your little goolies in the green room today.'

Sunny followed Hector who was smiling sheepishly. They formed a circle with the others in a bare room.

'What do I do?' Sunny whispered to Hector.

Hector nodded his head slowly, rocking his whole body,

as though in the green room his words had to drip out one by one. 'Nothing . . . do nothing. Close your eyes. Just be. Here.' He sank down and patted the floor.

Sunny sat down and crossed his legs in a half-lotus position. He placed his hands over his groin and shut his eyes.

'Rudy.' A voice cried from the other side of the circle. 'You made it, *na*?'

It wasn't a seance, as Sunny had thought it might be. More a group meditation, but without the accompanying plucked guitar strings and burning camel dung that a younger crowd would have had to smooth the mood. They sat for about an hour – for most of which Sunny kept his eyes firmly shut, trying to keep the image of Tina's bewitching anatomy in soft focus and his own from becoming too obviously tumid in the process. From time to time there was a gasp as though someone had expired. Twice a torrent of words in Tagalog, and Pangasinan. Then someone started making tiny yelping sounds, like a dog in heat. These were the days when there was controversy over whether there should be a national language of the Philippines, and pure expression was as valued as communication. Sunny didn't dare open his eyes, hoping Rudolf Navaratnam – although he hadn't seen him, he was sure Tina's father was the Rudy who'd come in late – had also shut his eyes before he had noticed who else was in the room. Then, from another room, he heard a scream. Had Rudolf gone to vent his rage on some other young innocent?

Finally the gamelan sounded again. Hector tapped Sunny on the shoulder. 'You can open your eyes.'

'Finished? Is that all?'

'Our prayers are over. But I think the girls had more fun tonight.' He ushered Sunny towards the door. 'The idea is to let the spirit flow . . .'

Rudolf was waiting. 'So, the famous batsman has joined us?'

Sunny cringed, but then words arrived out of nowhere. It was miraculous. 'I came to watch.'

Rudolf smiled with frightening restraint. 'We believe in the essential goodness of the spirit.'

'Right.' There was a lot of goodwill around. Sunny could feel it glow in every corner of this floating villa so far removed from the Vietnam war and the skirmishes in Mindanao, the private mercenaries, the gangsters, the New People's Army and the military roaming the Philippines. He prayed it was strong enough at least to disarm Rudolf.

The Señora called out. 'Bambino, how was it for you, sweetie?'

'Fine.' Sunny twisted his hands together. 'I didn't know what to expect.'

She laughed and grabbed his wrist. 'Nobody does. That's the way, the first time. You *are* a virgin aren't you, darling?' He heard a whinny behind him from where Rudolf had been.

When Sunny got back home, he called Junior straightaway. 'What's happening?'

'Yeah, yeah. Everything's arranged. *Síge na.* Pinky says tomorrow night for the Valentine's disco. It'll be great. Your Tina will be there.'

Sunny imagined himself cartwheeling across a dance floor towards Tina. 'You got a car?' It was two hundred kilometres away, up in the hills.

'Ricardo, man.'

It was half-past nine by the time Junior arrived in Ricardo's blue Mustang. Beatriz informed Sunny that a pair of hoodlums were at the gate. He told her he'd be sleeping over at Robby's house, even though he hadn't been able to get hold of him.

'Where?' Her convent face dropped. 'Don' go someplace bad with those *bakla* boys.'

Ricardo was older than Sunny's other friends. He often wore *Easy Rider* sunglasses to hide his bloodshot eyes and his cheeks always looked bloated. He gave Sunny a tight thumb-lock when he got in the car.

'OK?'

Junior, curled up in the back, cheered. 'Let's go, *pavé. Vamos.*'

Ricardo raced the engine and they squealed off before Sunny had shut the door. The stereo was turned up high and Ricardo started thumping the steering wheel to the beat of *Stey-hey-yeh-hey-pey-hen-wolf* on a badly recorded cassette. Conversation was impossible. Ricardo in any case had limited capabilities outside the realms of lysergic acid and boiled cactus needles.

By the time they reached Baguio, a soft late afternoon light had gilded the town. There were coloured ribbons on posts and banners across the main road giving the place a sense of impending festivity. The air was cool and fresh, with the smell of pine breath wafting through. The sky was pink in places; the earth glowed a rich red. A low fat sun tugged in a raft of coppery clouds through the gaps in the hills.

Ricardo turned his car into a parking space by the Catholic

bookshop. He switched off the engine. '*Ano*, Junior? Now what?'

'Hang loose, man. Pinky has netball until five-thirty. We meet her at Al's Joint.'

'Can they do that? Call it a joint?' Ricardo broke into an ugly, sweaty laugh. 'So, who wants to be a little piggy then and snort, oink, oink?'

Sunny slipped out of the car while Ricardo took an envelope out of his shirt pocket and tipping it carefully laid out two neat white lines on the dashboard. Sunny didn't much like sticking burning leaves in his mouth, never mind stuffing powdered coconut up his nose. 'I'll see you guys later at the place. Have fun.'

At the bottom of Session Road, he crossed over and headed for Burnham Park with its pond and ducks and willow trees, hoping Tina might be floating there, waiting by some star-crossed chance, for him to appear.

There were couples everywhere that afternoon; even the ducks waddled in pairs. From time to time a gaggle of young girls, or a huddle of boys, arm in arm, would wheel out, waiting for dark when they could jump the gender gap. Under the trailing trees older, more brazen couples were entwined, their lips seldom apart. A few stray rays lit up the water before the heavy sun settled behind the western slopes. The six o'clock siren sounded across the city. Sunny stood alone and remembered a line from a song about how the light called out for more.

The interior of Al's Joint had been done up like a Chicago film set: green shades, bare floors and beams with hooks and paper hearts for Valentine's Day. All the tables and chairs had been moved to the perimeter, as though a bomb had been dropped in the centre of the room. Two spotlights with coloured cellophane wheels were trained on the dance floor and the inescapable mirror ball swung threateningly above it.

Sunny searched the faces around the room as slowly circling shoals of mirror light picked them out. There was no one he recognized except Pinky, Junior's girlfriend, standing on her own. She waved at him and he made his way over.

'Hi, Sunny.' She tucked in a bit of her blouse that had come loose. 'Where's Junior?'

'He was coming with Ricardo. I went for a walk.'

Pinky frowned. 'Oh God, not that creep. He'll never get here.'

Sunny got her a Lem-O-Lime while songs of black magic women and proud wailing Marys bounced on the hardwood floor. She flinched at 'Mustang Sally' and gave the DJ huffing behind the turntable a mean dirty look.

When three American girls flounced in with their long scarves and tie-dye tunics, Pinky nudged Sunny. 'There they are. Tina's gang.' Two older men accompanied them: black, tall, clean-shaven. 'Those two are GIs from John Hay. The Camp.' Pinky laughed. 'But they are cool. Really, you must talk to them. They plan to go AWOL. The tall thin one wanted to join the Black Panthers but I think he is *bakla*, you know? He only likes to talk. But that Winston . . .'

Neither of the GIs looked particularly effeminate to Sunny. 'Where's Tina?'

'Let's go ask.' Pinky led the way. 'Hi, Carole, guys.'

One of the GIs offered Sunny a cigarette – fresh

American Blue Seal. Sunny did a peace sign. 'Thanks. I don't smoke.'

'Whey . . .' He looked amazed. 'Pakistan?'

Sunny let it pass.

'Isn't Tina with you?' Pinky spoke for Sunny.

Carole's eyes doubled in size. 'Tina? Why, she went to Manila for the weekend, didn't you hear? Some dumb philharmonic thing. We told her Al was having a wild Valentine's, but she took the plane, like . . .' She fingered a necklace of tiny coloured beads.

'This morning?'

'Yeah. She went home.'

Pinky sucked in a corner of her lip and made a face of rubbery contrition. 'Oh my God, Sunny, I'm so sorry. What a bummer.'

Winston got hold of Pinky and pulled her on to the dance floor. The other GI asked Carole and she went too, her face thrust straight into his breast pocket. The other pair of girls bumped around their sling-bags dumped on the floor, clunking wooden bracelets together. The songs that night peddled fire and rain and hearts of gold that Sunny found very hard to take. He discovered a taste for rum and Coke and would have snorted a bucket of ascorbic acid if Ricardo had come pushing it.

'Look at the booty,' Lester said, opening his suitcase. He'd brought back two beautiful new English bats, a box of shiny red cricket balls and several pairs of gloves, pads, stumps and bails.

'That's serious stuff,' Sunny said. 'Seriously serious.'

'You've been practising, I'm sure. And we'll need the kit for the match.'

'Yes. I'll . . . get the guys going. My friend Junior wants to learn too.'

'Don't forget the girl. What's her name? Tarka?'

'Tina.'

'Tina? Yes, whatever. Anyway, she'll be a great surprise. Keep her up your sleeve.'

'So, what do you think about this ceasefire?' Hector asked Napoleon – Nappy for short – Lester's closest Filipino friend. 'You think Marcos is willing to negotiate?' Although the forthcoming match was a major concern, Hector liked to deal with bigger issues from time to time, the way his bosses at the ADB did. Sunny, who was oiling the cricket bats, looked up to see Nappy's reaction.

Nappy, a small man with a wide face that broke easily into a flamboyant smile, was always seeking to improve his skills in what was hailed as a Filipino speciality: smooth interpersonal relationships, or SIRs. 'Mindanao? I dunno. I think he is planning some, you know, *ting*. Marcos is trying to look ahead. He is a shorty, like me. We short guys know we have to sometimes step on another guy's head to see what is coming. Mindanao, Sulu – these are back doors. Very tricky. It is the Muslim *ting*. We dunno what'll happen.'

Lester eyed him and got his pipe out. 'Pan Islam,' he growled in a low voice and started to scrape the bowl. He had brought Nappy and Hector home after a round of golf to meet Rudolf and Sunny and discuss the cricket match.

'What do you mean, Lester? What pan?' Hector squirmed

as though he was being needled whenever Lester mentioned religion – any religion. It was a line that divided them: on one side was politics, opinions, facts and a reliance on basic common sense, a curious, somewhat uneasy combination of the natural and social sciences. On Hector's side was a vague stew of mysticism, religion and extra-sensory perception that should have been anathema to international banking but was, for the initiates, much the same thing.

'From Algeria to Indonesia. Nigeria to Washington.'

'What, Lester? What? You sound like you are flogging a blooming encyclopaedia.'

'Islam. World religions are like slow tornadoes. Is it not a topic at the Colombo Plan conference, Rudy?'

Rudolf was quietly sipping a Coke and demolishing a tray of devilled peanuts. 'China,' he muttered. 'In China they have driven all the religions into a concentrated force the size of a nuclear pea.'

Nappy laughed. 'Guys, we are talking about the Philippines. This is the Philippines, guys. We have all the volcanoes we want, already *na*. Marcos is playing for time. Like I say, he is a shorty looking ahead. All these demos and shooting and shouting. NPA, Maoists, Dante, Malacañang's big libido scandal. He don' like that. He'll wanna handle one *ting* at a time. You can see that from the way he handled Dovey Beans, no? In the politics, like in the bed. So a bit of peace here, a bullet there and ram, ram, ram . . .'

'Beam, Nappy. Beam,' Hector corrected the notorious American woman's name. The President's salacious affair with her was the latest scandal in the newspapers.

Nappy grinned, puzzled but amenable as ever. 'Lester, you

heard the secret bedroom tapes? Our President gunning in the bed?'

'Grunting, Nappy. Grunting. It was the big show in Singapore. Raunchiest entertainment in Noddyland.'

Nappy's eyes shone. 'They say he is like the parson who can't keep it down, no?'

Sunny found Nappy's lewd interests a little embarrassing. The first time he visited he brought Lester a small, carved wooden man-in-a-barrel that displayed a massive spring-loaded erection every time the barrel was lifted. 'Good ice-breaker for a party,' he'd sniggered. 'Everybody loves it. Our number one handicraft.'

'Never mind that. What about some looking ahead of our own? Sunny, what about this team?' Lester pulled out a tiny notebook and a minuscule pencil from his pocket. 'Let's see . . . With the five of us, the two Thompsons, Sunny's three friends, and Tina, I reckon we have a team. We don't need Desai, thank God!'

'How about an umpire?' Hector asked. 'Desai can do that, perhaps.'

'I suppose so. Joyless fellow, but at least the bugger will be sober enough. OK, let's get him to umpire.'

Rudolf, who had remained silent since his pronouncement on China, was breathing heavily. He crunched another handful of nuts. 'I say, you have actually issued the challenge, Lester?'

The lights flickered as another air-conditioner in the house was switched on.

'What do you mean?'

'Is the match fixed, is what I mean. Is there a point in

expending so much energy on this issue?' He was nothing if not economical.

'Of course, my dear man. Rudolf, they are definitely on for Good Friday. Perfect day. The Hongs will be ready to flagellate themselves before us on the cricket pitch.'

'Cricket pitch?'

Nappy clapped his hands happily. 'I asked my buddy, Gonzales, if we could use his place. He is building a driving range off the South Superhighway. Not far. Just beyond Das Marinas. Real cute area. Bays already put there *na*, for a number one grandstand.'

'Driving range?' Rudolf looked grumpier than usual. It was partly because his head sank into his shoulders when he was thinking, but the effect was not pleasant.

'Gonzales is jolly excited. All ready to mark out the boundary and level the pitch. You just tell him the measurements. Guy is one hundred per cent agnostic. He might even make it permanent.'

'Afterwards we can all come back here for a rice and curry.' Lester added as an all-round inducement.

Rudolf's face lightened. 'Curry?'

'Of course,' Lester exclaimed. 'We will have chicken curry, *miris-malu*, roast *lechon*, *lapu-lapu*. An international feast. And, if you do your job, Rudy, and we win, I will even make real Ceylon hoppers for the lot of you.'

'You can do hoppers?' The proposition of a clutch of curvaceous Sri Lankan pancakes made Rudolf break into a sweat. He mopped his brow with a large yellow duster that he had pocketed by mistake in hunger and fury at home. 'Nice and lacey?'

'Little crumpets, gossamer thin with frills on the edges, but only if we win, Rudy.'

Over the next few weeks, Rudolf came by regularly after finishing a day's dismal calculations at the office to see how Sunny and his father were getting on. He would park his car on the road, well out of range, and walk up the drive a little warily. He'd loosen his tie and try to be friendly, making precise, instructive gestures with a dark, straight open hand.

'Geometry,' he would exclaim. 'Attend to the geometry, Lester, and the rest will follow.'

Junior, Herbie and Robby came to the house on Tuesdays and Thursdays. The sound of leather on willow, sometimes mediated by a cotton sock, sometimes accompanied by encouragement – good, right – or by gnomic advice – keep your eye on the ball . . . move in, move out – began to fill Sunny's sense of that world between private fantasy and public communion.

About ten days before the match he asked his father what he thought about a full team session.

'Good idea.' Lester put away some papers; he looked preoccupied. There was a smear of blood on the rim of his collar where it had touched the bottom of his jaw.

'Saturday? Or Sunday? It's the last weekend before Easter.'

He looked surprised. 'In that case, we might have to just hope for the best.'

'You mean on the day?'

Lester tilted his head to one side. 'There's a lot going on . . . I think you younger ones are going to have to do the main thing. It is up to you people to help Rudolf pull us through the match. The rest of us will have to do as we remember. You fellows can do it. And that girl of yours, she can win it for us.' Then he added thoughtfully, as though consulting some ancient revolutionary's DIY manual. 'The surprise factor cannot be underestimated.'

On the big day, despite the aroma of curry leaves, fenugreek and yeast wafting through the house, Lester's spirits had not lifted.

At breakfast he sat staring at the morning paper. Sunny didn't have much of an appetite either; he was imagining the worst. Out for a duck, the team in tatters. A bunch of Hong Kong colonials lording it over his father's feast.

'Are you worried, Dad?'

Lester folded his *Manila Times* into a small square. He had marked out in blue pencil a small item about trouble brewing in Ceylon – a storm in a tea-isle. 'Not about the game, son.'

At eight o'clock Lester and Sunny got in the car and set off down the South Superhighway.

'What's happening? What's wrong?' Sunny asked again.

Lester stared at the road ahead. 'I think they are unleashing something that will become impossible to control.'

'Who are you talking about?'

'Perhaps it is us. We who have become warped by what we fail to do.' The car picked up speed over the white concrete surface. 'You see, we, in our generation have never really known what we should do. Wisdom has not come with the years. The government in Ceylon is a so-called left-wing coalition – socialists, Trotskyites – but the youth see only a state that does not work. So now they've taken to violence. Twenty-five police stations attacked. Forty of them dead, as far as we know. Forty young rebels.' He glanced at Sunny, his eyes glistening. 'Some of them boys not much older than you.'

The match – single innings each, limited overs – was due to begin at nine to allow for an afternoon kip, or a nip into church for the so inclined. The Thompsons were already there. Martin and Mary had offered to provide the refreshments. She'd made wonky egg sandwiches and a rum punch, while Martin had organized the midday cremation of burgers, sausages and chicken satay. He'd already unpacked a crate of San Miguel into a bucket of ice.

'Ready, mate,' he said to Lester in an effort at conviviality.

'Ready?' Lester hesitated, embarrassed.

The Hong Kong visitors came in a convoy led by Rudolf Navaratnam's Mercedes. Tina climbed out of the front. She waved at Sunny who lifted his bat, disconcerted by her skimpy tennis kit and fantastic thighs. Then Rudolf appeared, obstructing the view. He came up to Sunny while Tina shepherded the overexcited visitors out of their conference vehicles towards the bunting and flapping parasols. 'Where's your lot?'

Sunny spotted Hector creating a small commotion parking his car. 'Practising. Gearing up.'

Rudolf was tense. 'They have a couple of club players. The bowler, I hear, is a killer.'

'Oh.'

'You better watch out. He will go for your nuts.'

'Bouncer?'

'Nuts.' Rudolf repeated the word with a meaningful glance at Sunny's crotch. 'I hope you are properly protected.'

Sunny tried to be confident. 'We are ready.'

Rudolf lost the toss, but Steve Thompson came up trumps. His very first ball, pitched short, took the opening batsman by surprise. Possibly it was the sight of Tina bending over the ice bucket on the far left, but the man was paralysed. The ball hit the bails and Desai, the umpire, raised his hand and uncurled a finger: *Out*. By the end of the over a second man had been caught out when the ball dropped into the crook of Hector's arm.

Junior quickly rose to the challenge – bowling from the Bonifacio end – determined to get at least one wicket in his over. An unexpected leg-spin did the trick and the visitors were three down for just five runs. Rudolf had never looked so pleased.

The captain of the other side was a professional and had some solid batsmen at numbers four and five. They stopped the slide and steadied the game. Then they began to clock up the runs. By noon, things were not looking quite so good for the home team. The visitors reached their half-century and play stopped for lunch at 56 for 3.

Rudolf pulled his team together. 'I say, fellows, we need a bit of something in the bowling.'

'What about Tina?' Robby asked.

'She's the big surprise,' Junior reminded him. They were playing one short, keeping her in reserve.

★

Before the second session started, Herbie sidled up to Sunny. 'Forget the oldies, man. It's up to us to take over the world.' He had a mischievous grin on his face.

'Yeah?'

'I thought I'd drop a couple of Ricardo's tabs.'

'You?'

Herbie smiled smugly. 'I already have, sunbeam. I thought maybe into the punch.'

'Are you crazy? You don't know what'll happen with these guys.'

Herbie looked crestfallen. 'Valium, then? Or Seconal?'

'It's OK, Herbie. Don't do anything. You don't know Mary's punch. There's enough rum there to pickle the hen that laid the eggs she put into her sandwiches backwards.'

'Yeah?' Herbie tried to understand. 'Are they *balut* sandwiches or something?'

By the barbecue table Lester was talking to Hector and Nappy about the news he'd heard of the events in Colombo. 'Mrs B. our lady prime minister says it is an insurgency, backed by, I quote, "big money, diabolical minds and criminal organizers", unquote.'

'Diabolical, eh?' Nappy shook his head. 'Sounds a bit like our Marcos here, no? The language?'

'You know, she made a good proposal in Singapore at that Conference. Turn the Indian Ocean into a nuclear-free-zone. All the old Commonwealth nuclear groupies were miffed by her speech. It is an idea I liked. But who can push it now, with this going on in the backyard? The young wanting to fight; the old wanting to fight back. What happened to Gandhian non-violence?'

'What, you now turning into a peacenik? A little old, *na*, Lester?' Nappy laughed.

Hector stepped in. 'Why? Why do you say that? You think growing old is about sending the young to die?'

'Hey, just joking only.'

'No joke there.' Hector snapped. 'Everyone will rush to aid Ceylon now – China, Britain, the US. Nobody wants an insurrection. But these are just youngsters. What do these kids know? Little red droppings of Mao. Some dross from Moscow. What will happen to the country if a whole generation is wiped out?'

Lester sighed. 'I called Ananda to ask for the story, but he says it is impossible to get any more information. Curfew. No one allowed anywhere. Even Rosenblum's line – the *Times* man – was cut mid-flow.'

Then Rudolf joined them. 'Bad business this. Hector, we might need you to bowl.'

It was a mistake. When they restarted with Hector, after lunch and the statutory siesta, he was thrashed. Sunny fared no better. He even dropped the easiest catch. Junior came back and just about held the visitors at bay.

Rudolf called Herbie. 'Time to try out your googly, boy.'

Herbie smiled in a worryingly beatific way. 'Goodle-dee, google-bee, google-lee.'

Herbie took his first couple of paces towards the crease and was mesmerizing. It was impossible to work out what he was going to do. Herbie himself seemed to be spinning while his face stayed in one place. The ball had a magic all of its own. It did the impossible: bounced, spun, veered and swerved and lifted the bails off the stumps from beneath. The batsman was flummoxed. Herbie giggled. Junior jumped and even Lester seemed to cheer up.

Herbie was unstoppable. The wickets tumbled: bowled lbw, caught by Nappy, caught by Robby . . . In less than an hour the visitors were all out for eighty-nine.

Everyone on the home side was cheering. Even Mary Thompson whose son's star had dimmed. '*Fantashtic.* How does it feel, Herbie, to be so *fuckin'* good. Oops.'

'Wild.' Herbie's face split into one of his biggest smiles. 'Wildest trip ever.'

'Have some raisin bread.' Lester patted Herbie on the head.

After the break, Sunny went out to face the killer. Rudolf loitered at the other end. He caught Sunny's eye and lowered his head in a mixture of pity and encouragement. The bowler looked almost a foot taller than Rudolf and twice as fierce. He was a giant who worked in the prison service in Hong Kong. Angrily weighing and rubbing the ball, he walked halfway back to the northern windswept street of his Lancashire home town for his murderous run-up.

Sunny began to doubt his resolve and cricket started to lose some of its charm.

The first ball was well wide. The second Sunny managed to nick past the slips. He survived the over with no runs, but no injuries either.

In the second over Rudolf began to score. Sunny stayed on the defensive while Rudolf gained glory again and again. Then at twenty runs, he fell. Junior came. He hit a boundary, got cocky, and fell too. Steve did better. Got up to thirty before he was lbw'd. Sunny's score was low, but he hoped that when Tina came in as the last man, they'd make a lovely pair for a brief but brilliant innings. But first Hector was put in. He missed the first two balls; fortunately they missed the wicket too. 'Take a deep breath and think of your leader,' Sunny urged him.

'Zaramazov,' Hector hollered and belted the ball past extra cover, making three. Then Sunny hit a single. The next ball he played ended in a catch and he was out.

Lester took his son's place. He survived five balls and made one run, then he was out. Nappy came and Hector went. Then Martin in quick succession. Herbie was hopeless. He had no idea who had the ball and by the time he worked out where it would come from, it had smashed the stumps. '*Bahala na*.' Robby took his place, looking very vulnerable in a buttoned-up polo shirt. Finally, after Hector fell, Tina made her entry.

Her bare legs shining behind the strapped pads may have sent the wicketkeeper, the slips, the gully and the short fine leg into a reverie, but they never got near the ball. She smashed it to the right, she smashed it to the left, she cut it, she clipped it, she banged it right out of the field. And Robby, much to Sunny's envy, gave her every chance to show off her incredible prowess, taking a paltry single each time he was on the receiving end.

By quarter to six they had reached eighty and were chasing ten to win. The reclaimed swampland had few trees and hardly any birds. When night drew close there were none of the shrieks and caws, the cacophony of parrots and cricket-mad crows that accompanied the end of a match in Colombo or Galle, Karachi or Jaipur. The visiting captain called out to Desai, the umpire. 'Getting dark?' Desai looked at the sky, searching it for signs of flapping wings.

'No birds, eh?' Martin Thompson observed. 'Bloody Japanese. After the invasion, nothing survived.'

Rudolf muttered something about the sparrows in China.

The umpire examined the ball and then chucked it to the wicketkeeper. He caught it.

Desai pronounced his judgement. '*Acha*, enough light for the last over.'

'Come on, Tina.' Sunny yelled without thinking.

The very first ball she hit for a gorgeous six. There were only the ten of them, plus Mary and Anjuli and a small scattering of the curious who had heard of this peculiar passion play, but the cheer could have been that of a hundred thousand. Tina held her bat up in the air like the sword of Boadicea.

They roared.

The bowler bowled.

She missed.

The next ball, she clipped perfectly – past square leg. Two runs. The fourth did nothing. The fifth ball she snicked past gully, but only made one run. A man appeared from nowhere and stopped it with a slide.

The last ball, an even score, but Tina was at the wrong end. Robby stood at the crease, trembling. He pushed back his visor as though he'd have preferred baseball, or jousting with dragons. His face was as white as the bowler's. The run-up could have been on chariots of fire, the ball flew. Sunny's bat in Robby's hands met it, shuddered, and sent it straight back with Robby running right behind it. The ball slipped past the bowler – the killer – who wheeled and flipped back. He was flat on the ground, thumping it. Tina and Robby crossed at the halfway point. Their fingers reached for each other, brushing in a swift kiss, as they sped towards each other's crease. They made it.

'By a nose, eh?' Hector beamed.

That night was the saddest night of Sunny's life in Manila, despite the victory. Everyone was in the house by eight o'clock. Both sides, plus a few hangers-on. Tina and Robby were the champions, toasted and fêted, a couple to rival Ferdinand and Imelda in the celebrations in Urdaneta.

Lester slapped Sunny on the back. 'Good show,' he said.

For the moment he seemed to have put the troubles of Ceylon – like those of Pakistan, the emerging Bangladesh, Mindanao and the rest of the Philippines – out of his mind.

Sunny opened beer, Coke, 7-Up; poured wine, water, gin and whisky. Rosa fluttered about with a tray of glasses and a bowl of peanuts. Beatriz, in her pinny, danced in the kitchen to a tune of her own.

Herbie, Junior and Robby sat cross-legged by the pond with Hector. They lit joss sticks and talked cricket like converts. Tina, on the patio, was having a ball with the visiting team who were all agog, now that she'd not only bared her legs but also her shoulders.

At ten o'clock Lester in his big white chef's hat got the hopper pans going and the food was served, drawing one or two of the Hong Kong foodies away from Tina's delectable flesh to the spiced meat of the table. 'Eat, my friends,' he grandly declaimed. 'Let us tonight, at least, forget the rest of the damn world and be a little happy. *Para bailar la bamba,*' he sang as Trini Lopez spun on the stereo.

It occurred to Sunny how much their lives had changed since his mother died. She would not have countenanced such frivolity. He asked his father for a special egg hopper, done hard. Lester turned the *thatchiya* – his hopper pan – expertly in his hand. 'There's one over on the table for you, son.'

Sunny was too late. Steve was already gobbling it.

Herbie came up. 'Hey, Sunny, relax, *lang*. Man, you look like you really need a bit of happiness, no? Come with us to Baguio tomorrow. You heard about the big *Pilipinas* Woodstock night? The Family Affair? Ten thousand heads will rock . . .' He peered into his psychedelic shirt pocket. 'If you like, you can start the trip now.'

Sunny didn't want to listen; he didn't care about Herbie or the contents of his pocket. He was reeling with the knowledge of the stupid mistakes he'd made and the chances he'd missed. He looked for Tina and saw her on the other side of the room next to Steve. She had a small silver valentine on a chain around her throat. He saw her touch it as she caught Robby's eye.

After that one and only Makati cricket match, everything in Sunny's life – and in the Philippines – began to change. In August, two grenades exploded at a political rally on Plaza Miranda; *habeas corpus* was suspended. The newspapers were in trouble. Advertising budgets were cut. Lester became tense and moody. He moved on from the PR agency and took up a new job in corporate communications with a big commercial group.

Hector was appalled. 'You've got the wrong ascendant, Lester. Why do you want to be a Marcos crony now?'

'This country has been good to us, Hector. We must be generous.'

Lester had his problems and, at sixteen going on seventeen, Sunny had plenty of his own. Robby's family had decamped to the south-west of France for the summer and hadn't come back. There had been no word from him. Tina disappeared at a gallop before Thanksgiving: Anjuli Navaratnam had decided Manila was unpropitious and had bullied her husband into finding a job in America. In the new year, Ricardo overdosed on sweet strychnine and drove his car into Subic Bay; Herbie was sent into rehab. Junior lost at hurdles and several other athletic and emotional challenges. Then after a month of earth tremors, floods and explosions, on 21 September 1972 martial law was declared. Even the editors of the *Manila Times* and *Philippine Free Press* were arrested. At the end of that year came the real bombshell for Sunny.

He was up on the flat roof above the patio, trying out the last of Herbie's stash that had been solemnly bequeathed to him, and watching the sun collapse behind the skyscrapers of Ayala and Buendia. He was learning to be content on his own.

Hector came up the drive carrying a bottle in his hand. 'Lester?' he called out. 'You left this at my house last night.'

Lester was settled into a large wooden armchair on the patio below Sunny, reading the paper. He still assiduously read whatever was printed. 'That's yours, Hector. Your bottle.'

Hector stopped by the potted plants and examined the bottle in his hand. 'Polish vodka, *men*. I don't have this Polish business.'

'You do, Hector. I gave it to you. Nappy brought it. I don't keep vodka in the house. You know that . . .'

Hector came up to the patio, walking slowly, shaking his big greying head at the bottle.

'Irene?'

Sunny hadn't heard his mother's name in a long time. He rolled closer to the edge of the roof.

'If it weren't for that bloody vodka, I might have known what she was trying to do. I could have stopped her, but that damn stuff knocked me right out.'

'It was not your fault, Lester. She was brooding, wanting the impossible. The time had passed for those kinds of dreams. If she'd really wanted to be a performer, she would have gone when she had the chance. She made the choice to end her life, not you . . . Lester, you know if it had not been that night, it would have been another. That Alphonso's pictures made her think she was already a star. That was the problem.'

It had not been something wrong with her heart. It had not been an accident. Sunny tried to imagine how she had got to that point. Was it drink? Pills? He remembered looking at her hands in the coffin and how odd they seemed then. *Had she slit her wrists*? It slowly dawned on Sunny that no matter what Hector said, his father was to blame. She had killed herself because he had robbed her of her future and failed her at her most vulnerable moment. Up on that hot, flat, ugly roof Sunny heard the sound of her piano in his head. Then the hammering of his father's useless typewriter.

CHIN MUSIC

1973

IN SEPTEMBER 1973, Sunny arrived in London to become a student of engineering. Each day turned colder, darker, as his first true autumn closed in. Manila, those bittersweet years of wavering adolescence, faded into a dream.

Engineering was a sadly uninformed choice. Although he had always liked playing with machines, and had a reasonably systematic mind, Sunny had yearned to follow Tina to America and study something like flower power. His father said that England was a more wholesome place and refused to discuss it further.

Sunny had appealed to Hector.

He shrugged. 'What with Woodstock and now Watergate, America is impossible, Sunny. You see, your father is becoming keen on more traditional values. Adolescence has never been part of our culture. In England at least he knows you will have the benefit of a society that has a firm grip.' British institutions at that time, he seemed to believe, were rocked only by the odd scandals of a kinky Conservative. 'Besides, you like *The Avengers*, don't you?' Hector added.

Sunny considered Cream, cows on album covers, floating zeppelins and figured England might be worth a try. Even Jimi Hendrix, the demigod of the electric guitar, had gone to London to get experienced. And Tina, he knew, was not for the uninitiated. Engineering happened to be the first offer that came out of a random mailshot.

His father's last request before Sunny left Manila was, not unnaturally, to do with words. 'Will you write?'

They hadn't talked much for months. Sunny sometimes wondered if his father had guessed what he'd learnt about his mother, but he never broached the subject. His reply was pointed. 'I don't think I'll be much of a correspondent either.'

Hector was there. He was always there. But Hector too had diminished in Sunny's mind. He had kept too much back. Surely, Sunny thought, I could have been told the truth by now?

'Perhaps you'll send some pictures then,' Hector suggested. 'I got you a camera.' He presented Sunny with a new Rangefinder. 'Voigtländer. Very good make.'

London turned out to be a playground of slapstick politics, economic hiccups and constantly replenished cold rain. The IRA tried to make him feel at home with popgun salutes made by men wearing socks on their heads, but shooting in the air seemed to him like pissing against the wind. Sunny ignored all of it and took his cue from those around him for whom Ceylon was only ever a cup of tea, and Manila a type of envelope.

He started out housed in a rabbit warren off Cromwell Road in West London. Although there were other students living in the building, there were no Filipinos in the vicinity at that time. No hint of the Little Manila that would blossom in Earls Court thirty years later, no *sarisari* mini-supermarts, no *pancit* restaurants, no *kayung-kóng* bars. Nor any Sri Lankans, as they were now known. At least Sunny didn't see any among his fellow students, although he did find a small Sri Lankan restaurant tucked down a tiny street.

After the initial excitement of arrival, and being on his own in a great city, he began to feel isolated. Where was the famous 'my generation'? He made friends with a couple of Malaysian students – Anwar and Karim – and Lydia from Mauritius, but metropolitan life had none of the huggy togetherness, the hippy debauchery he had imagined from the English pop lyrics he'd memorized in Makati.

'How about a game of bridge tonight, Sunny?' Anwar would tap him on his shoulder every few days. He was a budding business specialist who liked to stick to what he knew best.

Sunny would feign study overload. 'Brunel project, man.' Or, 'Ruby bloody Tuesday. Materials deadline.' Anwar didn't think it was odd.

Lydia's idea of a wild time was a romp through Kensington's museums. She was studying meteorology and liked to measure old rocks. So much for hedonism.

The combination of frost, fog and the enforced proximity of undesirable strangers in his overcrowded house made Sunny more introspective than ever. It ought to have been conducive to developing more of an affinity with his subject – the study of the inner workings of inanimate objects – but the lectures were soporific. Apart from London's famous underground, he had hoped that he might be inspired occasionally by outstanding feats of the industrial imagination. The Britannia Bridge of Anglesey, or the Aswan dam. Maybe gain an insight into Windscale. Experiences that would set him apart from the froth-heads of the Vietnam generation. Instead, what he got was a closer perspective on the screw, the bolt and the widget – all examined without the slightest hint of a pun that had been the hallmark of his father's wordplay.

After the move to England his contact with Lester became entirely pecuniary. A father's cheque repaid with a son's silence. Hector wrote to say that Lester was turning into a recluse and that a letter would make a real difference. He described how Lester spent long hours sequestered in his office and ignored most of his former friends. He had reduced his socializing entirely to corporate functions, and in those tended to speak only to praise Marcos's New Society. He had begun to recommend martial law as the solution to all political, social and even domestic problems.

Sunny sent Hector a postcard of fat men drinking whisky but nothing at all to Lester.

Swathed in scarves and scratchy wool, he snuffled from Barkers to Harrods, to Harvey Nick's – the only experiences that came close to blowing his absolutely chilled mind. By the time he found the legendary Marquee and the 100 Club, they were cancelling gigs. London's lights were beginning to dim due to wildcat strikes and an impending three-day week. Anwar huffed and puffed and declared he was going back to KL until British heating standards improved; Karim, the sweeter, toothier one, tried to make do with a cuddle from Lydia. The one time Sunny thought he might take a photograph, his camera froze.

Then, a couple of weeks before Christmas, he met Ranil.

Sunny had seen him often, ducking into a house down Penywern Road. He looked like an overgrown schoolboy in his awkward mac and grey flannels that were inches too short, but he had a friendly face. He frequented the Bestways corner shop where Sunny acquired his milk and munchies and studied the same crowded noticeboard next to the door. One afternoon, standing in the queue, Sunny decided to come out of his shell.

'Christmas, huh?' He glanced at the packet of mince pies in the other man's hand.

Ranil looked blank at first. 'Theology?' It sounded as though he was issuing a challenge.

Sunny tried again. 'Christmas?'

'Oh, yes.' Ranil looked surprised to find the mince pies in his hand. 'A little treat. Come and join us. Flat 7, number 3, over there on the right. Overseas student, aren't you?'

Sunny nodded. 'From Sri Lanka . . .'

'Me too. Sort of. That's to say, my dad is. Ranil is my name.' He extended a hand. He had wide searching eyes, a seafarer's nose flattened by the wind, and the broad face of a man happy to turn the other cheek.

'Did you say us?'

'Yes. A few of us are getting together. Eat, drink and sing, you know.'

'Sinhala?'

Ranil laughed in a distracted sort of way. 'No beach *baila* tonight, I am afraid. Carols. But we will have mulled wine. You know it?' He paid for his mince pies. 'Remember, number 3. OK? Come when it gets dark. Do.' He dipped his head politely.

There was a glow in the sky. The old drunk on the other side of the road, a dreamer from Port of Spain, was teetering to carols of his own, his brown homburg ruined by the drip of too many winters out alone.

Sunny hurried back to his room and wolfed his samosa with the gas fire burning at max. He kicked off his shoes and crouched close, not so much for the heat – for that he needed an oven, not a one-sided toaster – but in the hope that the grease and the smell of cheap spice would be sucked in and spewed out of the broken chimney pots to dissipate with the rest of the winter's burnt-out days. Sunny sealed the oil-stained brown paper bag in plastic and popped it in the cheap metal waste bin.

Sunny climbed the steps and rang the bell for flat 7. A sash window, two floors up, opened. Ranil peered out.

'It's me. Sunny.' He stepped back down on to the pavement.

'Who?'

Sunny realized that he hadn't told Ranil his name and that now it was dark. 'You remember, we met earlier.'

'Oh, the samosa man.' Ranil disappeared. A minute later the front door opened.

Ranil's room was long and narrow and painted an austere shade of grey. Inside there were two men and a woman in a fug of warm alcohol and mince pies. Choral music rose from a small, oblong cassette player.

'Good tidings, huh?' Ranil introduced John, Matthew and Rachel. The packet of sacramental pies lay open on the floor between them. They all wore soft, suede desert boots.

Sunny was handed a mug of spiced wine.

Ranil's friends were also studying theology. They had never met an engineering student before, but found Sunny's garbled stories about the Easter rites in the Philippines more riveting than anything he had to say about widgets. He described thin men with wispy beards carrying crosses from station to station while flagellants whipped themselves over each shoulder and crawled bleeding and wailing along the streets.

'You have actually seen a crucifixion?' Matthew shook his head in a very Herbie-like wow.

Although he'd never been to see Ricardo's friend who got nailed in Pampanga every year, Sunny found it easy, after quaffing a couple of cups of warm wine, to embellish the tale a little. 'The nails go in here.' He showed them the centre of his palm. 'You see stigmata, you know.'

Rachel's eyes widened. 'Really?'

John and Matthew acted like a pair of narks.

'Oh, yeah.'

'Far out.'

Ranil seemed to want to adopt Sunny. He had an uncanny knack of making him feel he belonged. 'You must come home with me, up north. You must have an English family Christmas.'

Having read Kerouac, Sunny was keen to hitch-hike. Ranil laughed. 'With a face like yours, my friend, we'd be on Finchley Road until at least the Day of Reckoning.'

They took the train instead.

Somewhere near the heart of England Ranil leant across with a question. 'You like London?' The Intercity table between them was littered with Mars bars and the *News of the World* – Ranil's antidote to an overdose of course work.

'It's OK.'

'A bit lonely?'

'Not really. There are lots of people in London.'

'You have a girlfriend back home?'

'You mean in Manila?' Sunny thought of Tina. 'We lost touch. What about you?'

Ranil pulled open his blazer as if to make room for a swelling heart. 'There's a girl I know. I've known her for years. She's just finishing school. Then, maybe, she will come down to London.'

'To do theology?'

Ranil's face was radiant. He laughed again, bobbing his head. 'Yes, maybe. You'll meet her anyway. We all get together over Christmas.'

At Runcorn they sped over a river of ink, a bridge falling into darkness. The horizon disappeared and a grey grain obscured everything. The train rattled in a void. Sunny shifted in his seat, wondering what lay ahead. It had been a long time since he'd been with a proper family, and he had never been this far north before.

Ranil's home was in Oxton, Birkenhead, which he explained was a world away from the great city of slave ships and sugar, the Liver birds and the famous mopheads. 'We are on the other side of the river. We have docks though, you know, and a park just like Central Park in New York. Only a hundred times smaller. It was the prototype. An experiment.' He had a child-like smile that often preceded his quick, short laughter.

His father, Ranil said, had arrived from the town of Galle in old Ceylon to study medicine at Liverpool, and had never left the banks of the Mersey.

'A doctor?'

'He's actually an undertaker. He failed, you see.'

'Oh, really?' Sunny was slowly beginning to see how in this world one thing led to another.

Ranil tried to stifle a laugh. 'You could say we have a family interest in the afterlife.'

Ranil's father was at the door the moment Ranil rang the bell.

'Hallo, hallo. Come in, son, come in. And welcome, Sunny, welcome. You are very welcome here in our house, Sunny.'

Tifus was a round jolly man with a wide, open face. There was no obvious resemblance between father and son, except in the tendency to laugh at unexpected moments. Sunny shook his small, soft, plump hand. 'Merry Christmas, Mr . . .'

'Tifus. Just call me Tifus. Should be Titus, you know.' He chortled. 'Damn fool in the church mistook, you know, the tea for an eff.' Another laugh burst out.

'Church?'

'The christening, you know. A long time ago now, I know, but I like to explain these things right at the beginning. To lay your mind at rest. Early training. Very important to lay the mind to rest, not just the body. Ha, ha. Now, to more important matters. Have something to drink? Tea?'

A pale woman in a striped woollen dress appeared from a doorway behind him, wiping her hands on a small checked towel.

Ranil strode across and kissed her cheek. Like Tifus, she was much shorter than her son.

'I am Ranil's Mum.' She didn't look quite English, but neither did she seem Sri Lankan. 'Delora,' she added with a hint of acquired Scouse, and extended a pair of thin arms to greet Sunny.

A pot of tea was brought into the sitting room and they sat in front of a large TV kept on low, like an open fire. Tifus plied him with fig rolls and Garibaldi biscuits while Ranil gave an eloquent lecture on the limits of knowledge and the metaphysical aspects of living in London. As Ranil expounded, Tifus fell into silent awe.

Sunny listened with admiration too. Ranil had a way with words that he wished he could emulate without in any way bowing to his father.

On Christmas Eve, Ranil suggested they go to a pub in New Brighton. 'You'll see, you know . . . the talent. And they have music and that sort of thing.'

'Santa Claus?'

'Oh yes, a lot of red noses.'

The phone rang. Tifus took the call. His voice became serious and businesslike. Delora raised her hands in despair. 'Tifus always has a call before Christmas. It's the excitement, you know, old men getting into those tight red costumes. You can count on at least one fatality on Christmas Eve. And, you see, Tifus likes to give the staff the whole of the holiday period off. So he has to go himself.'

As if on cue, Tifus put the phone down. 'Yes. I must be off. It's not just the excitement, sometimes it is the pressure of memories that mount up at this point in the year. You can only take so much, you see, before you pop . . .'

The two boys left Delora in front of the TV and took the train to the waterfront of what was once Britain's industrial anchorage. The water was up and stippled with the tall lights of Liverpool. An icy wind whipped around the floral pavilion decked out in holly and a few spare strings of hopeful Christmas bulbs.

At the pub, Ranil shouted to him above the sound of popsicle tunes. 'I called her, but she couldn't come out tonight.'

'Who?'

'You know? Clara. The girl I was telling you about.' He seized his lemonade. 'Remember?'

Sunny looked around at the girls on the dance floor in their fluorescent white thigh-high boots and tried to imagine this Clara and an overexcited Ranil drinking Babycham and discussing Schopenhauer over the strains of the Osmonds.

'Where does she live?'

'Just down the road. She's like the girl next door, you know?'

Ranil said his parents had known hers for about ten years – ever since Tifus had buried her nan. He'd done a good funeral and cheered them up with jokes about waiting rooms and the hereafter which her father, in particular, had enjoyed. They'd met for a seasonal drink regularly after that but Ranil had not noticed Clara until last summer when, after his exams, he got a job in the surgery next to her house. 'It's like something that has grown between us. Love grows, Sunny. Right? You'll see when you meet her.'

As Ranil had promised, there was a big Christmas party at the Veeraswamys', another Sri Lankan family living it up on Merseyside. They drove to the house in Tifus's estate car. 'Kill two birds with one stone.' Tifus laughed. 'You see, this Renault is a fine family car. But, in an emergency, you can snap the back seat down and slide the client in, no problem.'

Sunny looked over his shoulder, just to make sure the back was clean and empty, and huddled deep into the discount winter coat Ranil had insisted he buy at the Army & Navy Stores in Liverpool.

'I wouldn't half like a Benz though. You know, for us Ceylon boys that is still the tops, no? Unless we go for the *topey-top* like Jaguar, Bentley and all that impossible business. And Benz do one that would be perfect – in fact, they use it as a hearse in Germany – but you know, Sunny, people here are a bit funny about German cars. For the older folk, the war was not so long ago, you see, and they are my main clients after all. I don't like to make them restless. Especially after the final exit.'

Everything had a roundness to it, the road, the grass verge, the wall of the municipal pissoir, the sky above it, the halos around the street lamps, the branches of the trees beyond, life itself. Sunny looked at Tifus's round head, set low on his shoulders like a baby's. It trembled slightly and lifted as the rumble of another laugh reached up into it. 'Sunny, you ever see snow before?'

'I'm hoping for my first white Christmas here.'

Tifus laughed and his small hands shook on the steering wheel. The car snaked a bit. 'I remember my first time. I was so excited. I had not even seen frost, you know. Never been up into the hills back home.' He glanced at the rear-view mirror. 'You see, I come from a very humble family.

We never moved out of our backyard. Ever. Imagine that, eh? Even with the sea just there.'

Delora tugged at his sleeve. 'Keep your eye on the road, Tifus. There is ice.'

'Yes, yes.' He patted the steering wheel. 'Snow will fall, I'm sure. You'll love it. There's never snow in the Philippines, is there?'

Sunny smiled in the dark, thinking of Herbie snorting. The alternative Manila of the arctic fox. 'No. It is like the dry zone in Ceylon. Anuradhapura or somewhere.'

'You say Ceylon still? Not this new business, Sri Lanka? Good old name. But you see, Sunny, I have never been to the dry zone. We never went bloody anywhere.' He paused as they came to the crossroads. 'This Philippines is Catholic, no? Ranil mentioned something about crucifixes.'

There were pine woods ahead tinged with a warm sodium glow. The indicator blinked on the dashboard.

'Yes. The only Catholic country in Asia.'

'I must tell you about my friend. My teacher, actually. He also became a real friend. He went there, you know. To this Manila.' Tifus slowed the car. 'Later, when we get inside. I'll tell you later.' He parked carefully, on the road but with two wheels raised up on the kerb above a frozen puddle.

Sunny followed him and the others under the mistletoe and into the redbrick house, imagining the sea route from the mouth of the Mersey to Manila, a merchant ship carrying a cargo of cricket paraphernalia for the Makati XI, circling the globe and drawing his disjointed life back together, healing rifts, smoothing the furrows of anxiety, the knot in his head, turning Tifus's old buddy into someone he knew.

The Veeraswamys had a red carpet in their spacious hall and a small unbalanced chandelier of pointed candle lights and tangled glass pendants hanging from a meat hook. Tifus laughed out loud as he shook hands. 'Put on weight, huh, Veera? Too much Christmas pud, I bet. Better measure you up one of these days.' He chortled and turned to Mrs Veeraswamy. 'Just joking, my dear. Just joking. This champion of yours will see us all out. You can be damn sure of that.'

Veera, a confident portly man in a giddy blue waistcoat, smirked happily. He had a gold front tooth. His wife was much the same comfortable shape as him and sparkled with a diamond nose-stud. She was clearly very fond of powerful scents, although hers did not entirely overcome the smell of chilli paste and hot frying oil lacquered in her hair. She ushered them into the living room. There were too many people for introductions to be made. Sunny found himself a perch by the fireplace from which he could observe the crowd. Ranil was quickly sucked into a bevy of well-powdered Wirral ladies who wanted hear all about London and the Christmas lights on Regent Street and how they compared with Blackpool and what would happen when the country's power supply was turned off. Delora joined them while Tifus bounded from one group to another, laughing and raising his glass to good health and longevity.

Despite the winter frost outside, the strained English accents, damp wool and farty tweed inside, the scene with its babble of lubricated conversation was oddly familiar and comforting.

'Well, what do you think of England, young man?' The question came like a gunboat salvo from a stout, cheery man who smacked his lips approvingly at a dark drink in his hand.

'It's cool.'

'Winter, eh? Discontent?'

'I mean England is OK.'

'This weather toughens you up. You can go places then.'

'You mean, like migrate?'

'You've tried Guinness?' He raised his big tall glass.

'Looks impressive.'

'Good for the soul.' He puffed out his chest and brushed some flecks off the lapel of his green cardigan. 'Like adversity.'

'Yup.' Sunny began to see why Ranil may have felt compelled to study theology, having grown up with so much spiritual enrichment around. 'I better go get some then.'

A bar had been set up in the dining room. Mr Veeraswamy was pouring whisky and ginger ale into a fine piece of cut glass. He gave Sunny a sideways glance. 'Ranil's friend, no? Like a jar, or something?'

'Can I try a small Guinness?'

'Small? I don't know about small. Big is the thing with Guinness. Heavy. By the way, are you a cricketer?'

Sunny winced. 'I've played a little.'

'Bowler?'

He shrugged.

'This is the business for it. You see, people think to be a really fast bowler you need to run like a lunatic from the back of beyond. No, sir. You do not need a huge run-up. The speed comes from rhythm, wrist and internal energy. Guinness is the oil for the engine.' Veera clenched his podgy hand into a fist and moved it like a piston.

'Heavy, you said.'

'Precisely. You need weight. The velocity comes from

turning that weight into motion. Our Ceylon boys are too skinny to be really fast bowlers. How can they play first-class cricket if they just blow away in the wind? What I say is give them stout. They need a bit of beef on those skinny bones. And weight. You ever been to Nigeria?'

Sunny raised the glass of brown boiling clouds and took a sip.

'Wait, hold on.' His interrogator from the other room appeared. 'You must wait for it to settle, young man. This is a drink that teaches you patience.' One hand held his Guinness steady while the other fumbled around in his trouser pocket.

Sunny put the glass down and thought longingly of the simplicities of Coke, 7-Up and calamansi juice. Then remembered his father's maxim about never rushing. A reverential silence enveloped them as they stood around the quietly seething stout. Conversations in the other rooms welled up and broke apart. Sunny heard the rise and fall of 'Nowhere Man' and tried to formulate something interesting to say. Perhaps he could talk about widgets.

'Now.' The expert bowed, exposing a flaming orange neck.

Veera unhooked his thumbs from his flamboyant waistcoat and pumped the air with his fist again. 'Ha. Yes.'

Sunny took a sip of the thick, dark-brown creamy liquid. It was like the nicotine he used to clean out of his father's tar-guard; a ritual he had been addicted to until Lester took up the pipe. A rich, seductive, sniffable syrup of slow death that had to be mopped and scraped out of a stubby black cigarette holder with toilet tissue.

Ranil came into the room and grabbed Sunny's elbow. 'Come on. I want you to meet her. Excuse us.'

At the top of the landing, Tifus stepped out of the lavatory. 'Boys, how's it going?'

'Fine, Dad.' Ranil eased past.

Tifus placed a hand on Sunny's shoulder. 'Sunny, I was thinking about your Manila.'

But Ranil was in a hurry. 'Come on. She's in here.'

Tifus laughed. 'All right, all right, boys. Later.'

Sunny followed Ranil into one of the bedrooms, a kid's room. The hall light picked out a couple of youngsters by the window. Incense curled out between them in a feeble attempt to disguise the stink of burning weed and charred mould. Ranil stood in the doorway peering, until young Veeraswamy Jr – a sulky fourteen-year old – told him to get in, or get the fuck out and close the door.

Ranil withdrew. 'Maybe not.'

'Clara?'

'Someone said she was in there.'

They went back down into the kitchen where Mrs Veeraswamy was ladling chickpeas into a Pyrex bowl. She had hitched her maroon sari up so that the brocade on the hem didn't touch the floor. Her bare ankles, strapped in glittering plastic, looked like those of a mannequin. 'Ranil, be a good boy, darling, and run and get me the Crisp 'n Dry from the cupboard outside.'

'Oil?'

'I forgot to fry the onions to put on top. Run, Ranil, will you, dear?' She placed a frying pan on the stove. She moved in a slightly awkward, robotic way as though everything must run according to a predetermined order. Her omission of the onions was clearly proving traumatic.

Ranil returned gripping a bottle of Crisp 'n Dry in one hand and the arm of a thin, pale girl in the other. 'Oil,' he said to Mrs Veeraswamy. Then, a little more coyly, he turned to Sunny. 'Hey, this is Clara.'

Sunny looked at her and a warm tingle ran through his body. Blood began to swirl in his head and the air in his lungs emptied. He put his hand to his chest and stared at her as though he was seeing through her. Her clothes – a white cheesecloth shirt and white jeans – had a kind of transparency that was more ethereal than sensual. Her skin was barely distinguishable: a smooth milky surface puckered only to form the petals of her sensitive lips, a thin but promising nose and a pair of very dark eyes.

'Hi.' Sunny felt as though even that single syllable might blow a hole through her.

She smiled shyly, her lips barely parting. The tips of her teeth, just visible, seemed to him pure as snow.

A moment later Mrs Veeraswamy let out a bloodcurdling scream as her frying pan ignited. Flames whooshed upwards. Ranil was transfixed. Sunny pulled Mrs Veeraswamy back. Clara shouted at him. 'Quick, wet the rug.'

'What?'

'Wet it.'

Ranil looked aghast as Sunny poured his Guinness on the floor. Clara used the sopping kitchen rug to smother the flames while Sunny threw the contents of the washing-up bowl over everything.

Their reactions were swift but perhaps a little drastic. The flames would have died out without doing much damage.

And it was perhaps unfortunate that Mrs Veeraswamy's silk sari ended up so unflatteringly wet.

Veera peered in and saw the rug on the stove and the signs of a flood. 'What the hell happened here?'

'This cooking oil is like petrol, no?' Mrs Veeraswamy pointed accusingly at the bottle Ranil had brought in.

'Oh, oh.' Veera stepped back. 'Where did you find that?'

'Outside in the store cupboard.' Ranil muttered.

'The one with the Everton sticker?'

'Yes.'

'Was it on the shelf with the chrome polish and the Turtle wax? The big yellow sponge and the WD40?'

'Yes. And the bleach and the Ajax. Everything was there.'

'Oh dear.' Veera glanced away. 'I am afraid I haven't sorted that cupboard out yet. I think that bottle better go back. It is not for cooking. With this oil crisis looming, you see . . .'

Mrs Veeraswamy was steaming from behind and above. Suddenly she exploded. 'Where's my Crisp 'n Dry, dunder-head?'

Veera shrugged. 'OPEC?' It was hardly a hoard but Sunny reckoned that every litttle bit helped.

'My cranberry sauce and castor sugar?'

'All in the bag, my dear, all in the bag. You know, it has been a bit of a rush today.'

Mrs Veeraswamy snorted and bustled out of the kitchen, trying to hide her damp bottom with a blue and white tea towel commemorating the Royal family.

Sunny glanced at Clara; the tip of her nose had turned a faint pink.

*

'So, tell me. What sort of a place is this Manila? Like Colombo, is it? Better than England? This bloody country is getting into such a mess, no?'

'Nothing like Colombo. Hotter, drier, richer, poorer. Like some place between Hollywood and Mexico.'

Sunny tried to explain the history and the cultural influences that had been drummed into him during countless school sessions of Manila orientation.

Tifus listened attentively at first, but then became absorbed in a buzz of his own. 'I told you about my friend, didn't I?'

'You were going to.'

'He is my friend, but he was my teacher first.'

'Where? Here?'

'No. Not here. Back home. Galle, you know? He was a new young teacher and he thought I was bright enough to do well. Such a good fellow. He gave me private tuition for my senior school examination. Free. My family could not afford anything like that, you know. We are a very humble people. He treated me like a little brother. He got me a scholarship. I came to England because of him. We kept in touch for a while and then . . . lost touch.'

'What happened?'

'When I was studying here, we still exchanged letters. But then change of tack and all that, everything went . . .' He blew a raspberry out of the corner of his mouth. 'You see, I felt ashamed when I had to give up on medicine. Then, a few years ago I heard he had gone to Manila.'

'To do what? Is he still there?'

'I don't know. I suppose he must be. There can't be many Ceylon boys there, no? Hector Ekanayake is the fellow's name.'

'Hector? Uncle Hector?' Sunny's voice rose. He began to tell Tifus about Hector, his Mercedes and the scene in Makati, forgetting for the moment the complicated feelings he had about his former life.

Tifus shook his head in amazement. 'A Benz, eh? The bugger has a Benz. Not an estate car, no?'

'He's had one of those too. He changes his car every two years.'

'Every two?' Tifus shook his head again.

Sunny went on to tell him about the Navaratnams and their Mercedes and the cricket ball he'd hit through the front window.

'Buggeroo.' Tifus erupted into one of his high-pitched, hiccupping laughs. 'Smashed the glass? Navaratnam, did you say? Ha. Fellow must have been livid.' He was most intrigued by the depiction of Urdaneta. 'So, this village is really a private compound for the loaded?'

'Yes.' Sunny explained about the high fencing, the gates and the security guards. Tifus listened intently, eyebrows arching towards each other in studious prayer. Veera passed by with some crisps and Tifus called him over. 'I say, Veera. Come and listen to this. You'll like this idea. Tell him, Sunny, about this Uruda-net business.'

Sunny repeated his exposition on the islands of the wealthy and the foreign in Manila, while Veera listened politely.

'Oh, yes. Yes. Tifus, they have these compounds all over the place, you know. Kingston, Jo'burg. Many places. We should do it here. A bit of fencing, you see, will pay phenomenal dividends.' He hooked his thumbs into his waistcoat pockets and patted the sides of his tummy lightly.

'So, what happened to Kingston then?' Tifus looked stumped.

'Experiment. Take Manila. Rich place, no? Am I right?'

'In parts.' Sunny remembered the slums of old Tondo where Herbie went hunting for his poppy seeds and dragon tails. The sour water, the garbage that overwhelmed the small wooden shelters; the deprivation that people had to live with and die in, halfway to nowhere.

'In twenty, thirty years we'll have them all over Liverpool. In fact, I am thinking about doing something in that vein myself, around here.' His gold tooth glimmered. 'If you want to invest, Tifus, this is the time to do it. The dark days are coming, Tifus. Very dark days indeed.'

Tifus's round face clouded over. 'What do you think, Sunny? Should I give up the coffin lark? Go into security today instead. Follow our Swami Veeraswamy . . .' Then he broke into his happy smile. 'I should ask Hector, I suppose. My old teach, eh?'

The spring term back in London was not easy. Sunny couldn't focus on anything. As the days grew lighter, he got gloomier. Every move he made seemed to be a catastrophic mistake, the most serious one being his choice of subject. He tried to speak to his tutor about it but got no comfort. The older man squinted at him. 'Mr Fernando, there is no need to get emotional. Draw a line and carry on. You could become a man your country would be proud to honour. An engineer trained in this department is hard to beat.' The tutor's knuckles tapped the message on to his grey Formica desk.

In desperation, Sunny borrowed Ranil's books on liberation theology and took an evening class on decision-making for personal growth. He began to suffer from headaches.

One evening Ranil brought over a thermos of herbal tea. 'You know, Sunny, if you are having these migraines, maybe you shouldn't read so much. It is sometimes better to empty the mind, you know, and start afresh.' He poured some of his foul brew into a mug. 'Drink this. Then listen to some madrigals. They can be very calming.'

'Ranil, I hate engineering.' Sunny had no one else to complain to. Anwar had given up on the UK; Karim and Lydia had no time for anyone but each other. 'I can't do it any more.'

'So, don't. Your life is not your life.' He sounded like a Confucian sage – *a horse is not a horse.*

'Whose is it then?'

'I mean, your life is more than this.' Ranil made a grand gesture to include everything in the room.

The following week Sunny quit his degree. He found himself a bedsit around the corner from Warwick Road and enrolled on an Accountancy and Finance diploma at a private college. Just enough to persuade the immigration officer at Lunar House to renew his student visa for another year. That was all that mattered.

He continued to meet Ranil regularly for a drink near Gloucester Road. Sometimes he'd invite him back for a takeaway from their favourite corner shop, a couple of samosas and a chicken tikka; occasionally a curry at the Ceylon restaurant opposite the tube.

Sunny's new course mates were all misers and without Ranil he would have turned into a full-time loner. Capital Radio was his only other life-saver. It allowed him to be a new kind of Londoner: in touch without anyone to touch. When the experiments with phone-ins started he was completely hooked. For most callers the advice on the radio was the re-heated 'Hey Jude' line. *Go out, man, and get her.* Who? Sunny would cry in response and run through the possibilities. It didn't take long: Tina? Lydia? Sometimes he'd want to shout out of the windows, or dunk his head in his washbasin of a thousand cracks.

Lydia, having split up with Karim, had moved to the other side of Hammersmith. Sunny met up with her again, by chance, at the Commonwealth Institute where he liked to go to look at texts on kinship patterns.

'It is good to see you, Sunny.' She took his hands in hers and squeezed them as if to check for fractures.

'You want to catch a movie?' *Jaws* was on at the Odeon across the road. The frights were good and jolted the two of them closer together; she even trembled in her seat and his passion grew, but it wasn't enough to sustain a romance for very long. Her kisses proved exceedingly sharp, and a little vinegary, while his exuded a fast-acting anaesthetic; within a couple of months they were both looking for a way out.

'This is not working for me, Sunny. I need to *feel* something more.' She stopped and chewed her nails. 'You understand?'

Ranil, meanwhile, steamed on from religion to philosophy. He embarked on a doctoral thesis on the resurrected muse and received an uncommonly generous scholarship. It allowed him the luxury of a two-room flat off the North End Road.

'I need the space to think, Sunny. Think.'

'Yes, Ranil. I can see that.'

Sunny, stuck in a cycle of obligatory fails and retries with his accountancy exams, remained in the same bedsit. He got the landlord's permission to redecorate the room and went for red woodwork and yellow walls.

'Buddhist colours?' Ranil asked cautiously when he saw it.

'You disapprove?'

'No, not at all. Each to his own.'

He noticed the photograph that had finally been brought out into the open again.

'My mother,' Sunny explained. 'She died when I was very young.'

Ranil stared at the portrait for a very long time. 'She certainly had a pianist's hands.'

'She needed something more . . .'

'Inspiration?' Ranil sighed as though he understood.

After a couple of years of drudgery and odd jobs, Sunny managed to gain his certificate and wangle a position as an accounts clerk at Harpo's, the new department store that had opened nearby. Harpo's accounts section, like most large ones in London at that time, was an enclave – all the South Asians on the payroll could be found there: junior clerks with circumscribed prospects, an aptitude for mathematics deemed to be their only useful genetic disposition. Sunny felt comforted by the thought that Ranil, at least, was dealing with accounts of a greater magnitude, weighing good against evil in his spartan room. He'd ask him about Nietzsche or the concept of Free Will over a Guinness and then let the stream of incomprehensible words wash the week's accumulation of double-entry figures out of his head.

Since Lydia there had been only one other affair. Patsy, a marketing executive for an American firm, who was staying at a Knightsbridge hotel. She had asked Sunny for directions to the Norwegian Embassy. He walked her to the square but the Embassy was closed. She was exuberant, as only a visitor can be, and they'd gone for a drink and after that, with dizzying swiftness, back to her hotel room on the second floor. She'd tuned in to a country programme. 'Honey, I just love the rodeo.' She'd wrapped both her hands around his head and got down to it with real gusto. Sunny felt like Superman and woke up the next morning with more eagerness in his flesh than he had felt since puberty. But she had wanted breakfast in bed first and became enraged that the eggs were hard-boiled. When Sunny started to get ready to go to work, she threatened to jump out of the window. 'You can't leave me now. Look at this chicken shit.'

He'd had to call in sick and stay with her for days. Each morning, in the confusion of funky horseplay and unreliable room service, they managed to miss the opening hours of the Embassy and ended up back in the pub and then the bouncy bed. On the fourth morning his back seized up. When she'd hollered for him, he'd hesitated. She got furious and dumped the breakfast in the loo. 'My flight is at twelve-thirty,' she snapped and chucked him out.

Then one weekend in 1979, soon after Maggie Thatcher swept into Downing Street, Ranil asked if Sunny would come and help him paint his flat.

'Why? Because Callaghan lost?'

'Clara is coming to London.'

'Clara? To live with you?'

'Good grief, no. But I need to paint this place before she comes over.'

'What colour?'

'Why, white of course.'

Sunny imagined Clara entering Ranil's room and disappearing. The invisible muse. Nothing left but a wrap of cheesecloth floating in the air.

'She's got a job here. Isn't that marvellous? At last, we can get started. It was impossible with her waltzing off to secretarial college. Utter madness.'

Ranil's plan was to show Clara his newly decorated flat, then go for a drink at the pub.

'What about a meal, at least?'

'You mean at the flat?' He ate only bread and cheese there, occasionally a slice of ham that might have accidentally found its way into the fridge. It was a place of frugality designed for solitude and high thinking, not romance and, heaven forbid, never anything so vulgar as sex.

'How about the Ceylon restaurant?'

'No, not Sri Lankan. One's ethnic roots is almost the last refuge, you know.'

'Thai, then? That might be good. The Busabong on Fulham Road?'

'A bit dear, isn't it?'

'You wanted to go out places, didn't you?'

'London, Sunny, not Siam. Not to be stupidly extravagant. Anyway I wouldn't know what to order.'

'Oh, come on, Ranil.'

'Will you come too?'

'OK. I'll book a table for three.'

★

Ranil had arranged to meet Clara at Earl's Court tube, nearer Sunny's place than his, because he thought it might make a more cosmopolitan impression. He had offered to collect her in his car – a grey Citroën 2CV – but, he told Sunny, 'She is insisting on making her own way.'

He arrived at Sunny's twenty minutes early. 'Let's go. Come on.'

'The station is only two minutes away. Have a coffee.'

'No. She might be early. Can't have her hanging around there with all those odd types about.'

'OK, OK.' The landmark constants could be scary: the drunk Calypsonian, a Mr Veeraswamy lookalike leering in his brown suit; the giant bearded busker with his shrill penny whistle; the tethered dogs; the muscle-bound twins in their busted leather jackets preening by the off-licence, one always ducking and combing his hair with an elbow up in the air, the other usually striking matches off his unshaven chin.

When they got to the station Ranil stood at the entrance with his hands clasped behind him as if to banish the damp grime and dull light, and through his sheer presence transform its dingy interior into a sparkling metropolitan hub. His lips moved as though he was arguing with a secret contractor.

'What are you doing?' Sunny asked him.

Ranil looked surprised, caught out. 'What? Nothing. Nothing.' He glanced at his watch and rocked on his toes as though he wanted to spin the earth a little faster. Closer to the moment when she would emerge, floating on a cockle shell up the sooty stairs, illuminating the dark turbulence around them and the underworld beneath with her inner wintry glow.

'Ranil, what happens now?'

Ranil pulled his crumpled mac tight around him. 'When she comes, we drive over to the flat. Then your Busabong business?'

Sunny felt a tremor under his feet as a tube train pulled in thirty, forty, fifty feet below. There were screeches, whistles, the clamour of a carriage retching its guts out. He remembered the alarm and the excitement he'd first felt arriving in London: the promise of metropolitan glamour. The stench of parboiled lives, unwashed clothes, piss and vomit, the eeriness of travelling underground and surfacing in the middle of a zoo. The sudden light. He felt all those dissonant feelings rising again, as though all his protective layers had been unpicked and left him bare to the bone.

Ranil gasped. 'Oh, my God.'

Clara appeared: a luminous face under a dark woollen hat and then a long burgundy coat clutched close around her as though to draw some colour from it. A bell rang underground and the air misted in front of her. She held her head at a slight angle, as though she was listening to someone at her shoulder, until she saw Ranil. 'Hi.'

Before Sunny could say a word, Ranil caught her elbow and swung her out on to the pavement. The wind whistled down through trees shuddering to the rumble of tube trains and HGVs. 'Clara,' he paused to scowl at a couple of layabouts and steered a path through the rubbish outside the chemist. 'Shall we go to the car?'

Sunny couldn't move for a moment. He clenched his cold fingers and banged his head. He hadn't managed a single word of greeting. She wouldn't have known who he was, standing like a moron behind Ranil. In a panic he grabbed a carnation from the station flower stall. 'How much? How much?' Without listening to the surprised flower seller's answer, he dumped a handful of coins on the green baize and hurried after the others.

He was out of breath by the time he caught them. 'Welcome,' he panted, trying to regain some composure. He held out the pink offering.

She took the single stem and held the scentless flower to her nose. 'That's nice.' She watched the car heaving as Ranil pushed and pulled at the temperamental door. 'So, where are we going?'

'My place.' Ranil managed to wrench his door open. He crawled in and opened the other doors from inside. Clara got in the back; Sunny sat in front. Ranil raced the tiny engine and manoeuvred the car out. 'OK,' he whooped and let her go, the way one might release a spaniel in a city square. The car lurched out to the main road, swerving, sniffing, stopping and then shooting out into traffic. Clara clung to Sunny's seat as hers shifted under the acceleration. 'Sorry,' Ranil yelled over his shoulder. 'I must have not done the lock underneath. The seat comes out, you see, for picnics.'

Ranil's flat was chillingly austere. The walls, the ceiling and most of the furniture – table, chairs, half-empty bookcases, cupboards – were all plain white. The carpet was a muffled grey. The only colour was provided by a big brown grizzly sofa.

Ranil directed Clara to it. 'Please, sit.'

Clara nudged the sofa, then sank into it, clearly relieved

to be on something immobile. 'Very nice,' she murmured. 'Ranil, your flat is very clean.'

'Ah, yes.' Ranil shuddered, thrilled that she'd noticed. 'Just painted, actually.'

'Really?'

The whiteness of the room added colour to her skin. The old sofa might have given her some shape too, if she hadn't been wearing such a dark jumper and chocolatey velvet jeans. Only her hand stood out, disembodied, the skin slightly reddening in the barely heated room. She turned towards Sunny but her dark eyes revealed nothing.

For a long time now Sunny had wavered, unsure of what to do and where to go. His life had seemed pointless. Sometimes he'd think of his father losing his mother – how the two of them had lost faith in each other and perhaps themselves – and wonder which came first. In his life he had never felt he knew anything for sure. There was only a hollowness that swallowed hope too soon; never anything to hold on to. Sometimes he felt like a rudderless boat heading nowhere with no one on board. Now, facing Clara in Ranil's room, his feelings of despondency began to lift. Something was growing, feeding off her. He averted his eyes and stooped down to straighten his socks; he leant a little closer, hoping to catch some brief quaver in her voice or her breath, maybe a hint of movement in her soul. The smell of cold winter air warming seeped out of her clothes and made his head spin.

Clara slipped off her shoe and raised her leg up on to the sofa. She hooked the foot behind her other knee and wiggled it. Sunny looked up and discovered that she was watching him. He held her gaze and forced his tongue to move in his mouth and somehow make the sounds of human speech.

'You've got a job here, in London?'

She remained very still. 'Yes, a small company. They do stationery.'

'That's wonderful.'

'Not really.' She paused. 'I do some typing.'

'But it is a job. I meant that it's wonderful to get a job these days.' Truly. Surely. Honestly.

She asked what he did. Sunny shrugged and mumbled a few words about the department store. 'A back-room job. Accounts.'

'You get discounts?'

'Yes.' A door opened. 'Fifteen per cent for staff.' He knew it wasn't Shakespeare, but for him the conversation was intoxicating.

Ranil, who had been completely spellbound until then, started chuckling. 'Sunny is such a materialist. Not only does he work there, but he spends all his free time roaming around that crazy shop.'

'Fifteen per cent in a department store is a lot better than ten per cent off a load of waste paper, Ranil.' She looked genuinely impressed.

Sunny imagined her among the butter cakes and Chelsea buns of the food-hall bakery, his hand guiding her as he flashed his staff badge to clear the path, fifteen per cent at a time, with the bearing of a . . . stallion.

Then she tightened up as if to draw in her resources – oxygen, light, the moisture within. 'Sometimes I think I need everything, but I can't afford anything.' She opened out her thin, pale, glowing hands and turned to Ranil. 'Then, I look at a room like this and think, maybe I need nothing. Like you, Ranil.'

At the restaurant, Ranil floated in a state of blessed contentment. Sunny ordered cocktails.

'Cocktails?' Ranil queried.

Clara and Sunny exchanged glances, as though they might already have shared a couple of naughty Mai Tais.

'Speciality of the place,' Sunny explained, trying to hold back an utterly pointless laugh.

Ranil frowned. 'Thai?'

Clara picked up the menu and mouthed the names of the dishes as though each diphthong held the taste of ginger and sweet basil. The left corner of her mouth had a tendency to lift more than the right, making her look almost impish.

Sunny tried to pull himself together, and suggested chicken, prawns and the *kaeng masaman*.

'Noodles?' Ranil asked.

'If you like. Or fragrant white rice might be nice.'

'Fragrant?' He could tell she liked the word too.

The food ordered, they settled down with the long straws of their absurdly colourful cocktails. The glasses, packed with ice and memories of hotter climates, were decorated with glacé fruit and tiny brollies made of toothpicks and coloured tissue: pink, orange, green. The drinks went down fast and were quickly replaced.

'Ranil, do you remember that chippy we used to go to?' Clara twirled one of the little umbrellas, making a rainbow spin between her thumb and forefinger. 'On the hill by the corner? You could see the sea.'

'Wallasey?' Ranil took in half a glass in one suck. His shoulders dropped and he smiled. 'Jimmy's.'

'Did you ever imagine then that we'd end up in a place like this?'

'Aw, Clara . . . d'you wanna chip?' Ranil started to raise his hand but it flopped heavily back on the table. He rolled his eyes as though the useless limb belonged to someone else. She giggled.

Sunny took the cocktail decoration out of his glass and shredded the flimsy paper. Clara and Ranil shared things he had no way of reaching. Jimmy's? What did Jimmy's have? Cod? Haddock? Skate? Fat soggy chips? Wrapped in what? The *Liverpool Echo?* What could the sea possibly look like from a grease pot in Wallasey? Nothing like the sea from Galle Face in Colombo, or from Roxas Boulevard along Manila Bay. He remembered the sunsets, the luscious, swirling, sexy sky.

Clara ignored the small pile of debris accumulating between her knife and Sunny's fork. 'I miss the water. Being near it.'

Sunny experienced a rush of unexpected loyalty. 'What about the Thames? Brighton isn't that far. And Southend?'

She smiled at him as though to shield him from a world he could never understand.

Ranil snorted. 'Not the same thing at all. There is no sense of freedom. You need freedom.' For a moment he sounded like Lester before martial law had changed him. 'And anyway we have had industrial-strength pollutants to lace *our* sunsets.'

The food arrived and the young Thai waiter tried to explain the contents of each dish in tentative, puckered English.

Clara picked at her food like a bird, tasting a little bit at a time. She said it was delicious, but Sunny was not placated. He wanted to make up for their lack of a shared heritage of Mersey chips, industrial sirens and frigging Woodside foghorns.

He picked up a plate of prawns and passed them over. 'Try these. At least it's seafood.'

She spooned them on to her plate, skewered one with a fork and nibbled it. The prawn still had its boiled tail, which stuck out of her mouth like an exploded cigarette. She pulled it off and licked the sauce from the bright red fan and then from her fingers. Her face coloured as the fresh chilli drew heat from somewhere inside her. 'I like these.' She closed her eyes and tore the tail off another one.

Ranil scooped up a huge helping of the *masaman* and grunted. 'I'm not sure about prawns.' He looked with drunken disdain at Clara's plate. 'They are such a low form of life.'

Sunny was incensed. 'Higher forms of life are what you prefer then? Chicken, lamb, cattle? Why not go all the way up the food chain? What about people, Ranil? Human beings?'

'OK, all right. Easy. I am just not a seafood person, tha's all.'

'Chips with battered fish, huh?'

'What?'

Clara intervened. 'Can you pass the rice?'

Sunny wanted to hurl it across the table. A massive storm was building up in his chest. She must have sensed it, although he was sure the metaphysical head case next to her hadn't. She held out her hand for the bowl. They were connected by the gilt rim of the porcelain for only a moment, but it was enough to discharge the fury.

'Thank you.' She helped herself to a spoonful of scented rice.

Sunny knew he wanted too much, he knew it couldn't be, it shouldn't be. Somehow things had fallen into the wrong places, but there was nothing he could do about it. Not just then.

Ranil stared at his food and ate with the kind of intensity with which he sometimes talked of divinity and revelation.

Clara began to describe her impressions of London. She was living beyond Archway, sharing a small flat with Holly, a girl she'd known at school and who had moved to London a few months earlier. She said it didn't feel like the London of her imagination, but it did seem close to it, as though she might find the other place if she walked just half a mile down the road. She said she felt she was near something very big, bigger than anything she'd known. 'Sometimes I think I might be able to hear the real city if only the buses would stop for a bit.'

'Yes.'

'I can walk over to Waterlow Park. They've got ducks and birds of all sorts there.'

'Migrants? Temporary visitors?' Sunny tried to find some common ground.

The waiter came and asked if they wanted to order more food. Sunny looked at Ranil and couldn't stop himself. 'Prawns?'

He wouldn't be baited. Clara clammed up after that. For dessert, the waiter suggested rambutan but it could have been monkey testicles for all Sunny cared.

'I think I'll go home now.' Clara said when they'd finished. 'I should get back.'

'I'll drive you.' Ranil rose unsteadily to his feet.

'No. It's OK. The tube is fine.' She put her coat on and wrapped a scarf around her neck.

'I'll drive you back through the park. Hyde Park.'

'No, Ranil. I want to take the tube.'

It was clear that any expedition with Ranil would be risky. 'We'll walk you to the station, then.' Sunny chimed in, feeling stupid but gallant.

She softened and touched him. 'Yes, that'll be good. Thank you.' They walked in the cold night air swaying gently, each with an arm through hers.

Over the next few months the three of them would meet up from time to time in Kensington, or Chelsea, or Fulham. Clara liked to explore new areas. Ranil was content to let things drift until the moment, as he put it, was ripe.

Sunny tried to focus on his second-level part-time course without any notable success, and then let things drift too, as was his natural inclination.

In the spring of 1980 Sunny received an envelope addressed by his father's secretary – Miss Esmeralda Ramos – whose hand he had learnt to recognize from the annual payouts sent by Lester. It contained a twice-folded blue aerogramme addressed to him in Urdaneta. On the sender's line was Robby's name and an address in East Finchley. Sunny couldn't believe it. Robby wrote with the familiarity of someone for whom ten years or so was of no significance. He said he was living in London and had been to a Sri Lankan restaurant in Hendon where he had eaten egg hoppers like the ones Lester had cooked after their big match.

It made him want to get in touch. Sunny imagined Robby with his mouth full, his keeper's paw around Tina's waist. Robby went on to describe the pubs of Tufnell Park as though they were the inns of paradise. Sunny found this unsettling, as though he was eavesdropping on someone else's conversation. He hadn't been to Tufnell Park, Hendon or East Finchley, but from Clara he had a rough idea of the area.

Robby had not given a telephone number. Sunny toyed with the idea of writing to him via the Makati post office with the help of Miss E. Ramos, or turning up on his East Finchley doorstep with a suitcase, but then decided on a postcard of Big Ben sent first-class direct. He suggested a rendezvous at the Half Crown in South Ken.

At twenty-five Robby had become quite rotund and a little bow-legged, as though he'd been crouching behind Tina for longer than he should. He sat down with his legs wide apart, nurturing his belly like a pregnant woman. Stubble had grown along his lower jaw as if to compensate for his false womb, or his prematurely receding hair. He wore black in a cool, carefree sort of way.

'*Kumusta ka, paré*?' His eyes looked to Sunny for a familiar response. '*C'est moi*, Robby.'

Sunny took his hand, unsure whether to clasp or shake or return to the arcane rituals of their adolescence. 'Guinness?' He wanted to show how deep he was into the local culture. Robby preferred cider, his most recent discovery.

'I was amazed, man, to get the Big Ben postcard. Amazed.'

'Me too. A letter after so long.'

'Yeah, you know how it is. I never used to write letters. But then last year everything all changed and I discovered . . . many new things.'

'You mean, like cider?'

He laughed, proudly shaking the modest scrub on his chin. 'Health. Not easy these days with all the fucking scares we get.'

Sunny passed him his cider, bemused. 'So, how come you are in London? What are you doing here?'

'Following the hard path of love, *paré*. These days you must stick to the one you find first. If you understand . . .'

'Oh yeah. Love the one you're with . . .'

Her face came back to Sunny then, like a familiar refrain, looking back over her shoulder as she walked up to the chalked crease. Her bare legs shining behind the hot pads of a batting fantasy. 'I see.'

'We have a small company. We do lingerie.'

Sunny saw ivory lace garters beneath her kneepads. 'Both of you? In East Finchley?' He could understand it, yes. Tina's teen passion.

'Mostly mail order. We have a shop front on the high street for seasonal wear. But our speciality is the *exotique* in our catalogue.' Robby fluttered an eye. 'You know, like the *barong* materials. We do a fantasy range with banana and pineapple fibre from the Philippines. Murder to wear. You remember what it feels like? *Piña*? *Jusi*? That stiff harsh material. But some people just love the idea.'

'So, you go back to Manila?'

'We have a good supplier.'

'And Tina? How is she?'

Robby looked perplexed. 'Tina? You mean from Makati days?'

'I thought . . .'

'She went to America, didn't she?'

Seeing Robby again made Sunny realize something about his life. He had always seen himself as existing in a special world of his own making. People who entered it and left it only *seemed* to do so; they were shadows on a window which became something more only if he wanted them to. They were there, but not really there. It had never occurred to him that he might appear in the same way to other people: an image in a lens. Someone who went away and never looked back. He had not understood before that they each had the power to be wherever they wanted to be.

Robby gave Sunny his number in East Finchley and they'd meet up every now and again, but it was never quite the same as the old days. Robby was too busy with his business and his partner, whom he preferred to keep to himself.

The fact that Robby had changed made Sunny feel as though he was the only one incapable of moving on in life. The ghost of Tina still haunted him. Lost love, lost opportunities. Robby reminded him of it all. One time he brought up the subject of cricket. 'You play the game here?'

Sunny made a face. 'It is not so easy in this country.'

Robby laughed. 'The home of cricket? Not easy?'

'It's a team game. I don't know how to get into one here.'

He told Robby about the guys upstairs, at work, who were dedicated cricketers and spent all their summer weekends in some green and pleasant county field. Somehow he couldn't see himself in their team, not even in the same field. 'It's a very exclusive game here.'

'Like everything, *na*?'

Sunny shrugged. Over the years he had come to understand that England ran on eccentric notions of privilege. With the new Conservative government getting into stride it looked set to become more so. Was old Veera in Birkenhead right? Was it only a matter of time before Makati-style villages sprouted here too, separating rich from poor with rubber truncheons and high-voltage wires? Perhaps even guns one day.

At the end of July that year, the summer of 1980, Ranil suggested a picnic by the river. 'I'll ask Clara and some old college buddies. Why don't you ask your Filipino friend to come along?'

'Robby?'

'Yes, Robby. We can go to an island in Teddington.'

The prospect of Ranil, Robby and Clara together filled Sunny with anxiety.

He was pretty low because of his work. His section head was becoming more demented by the hour and the sight of his desk almost made Sunny physically ill. It was not a good time. A stupid mistake he'd made with the accounts for the first quarter had affected the whole section; his colleagues were not pleased, especially the three exiles from Makerere – the experts – who had to redo the ledgers. Coffee breaks were grim and the Jaffa cakes he'd taken in as recompense hadn't made much difference.

On the day of the picnic, the sun bloomed with a soft

lazy light. Pretty fuchsias, their pink slips showing, swayed over the walls of Redcliffe Gardens and the smell of lavender drifted over the bleached larch. Bees swooned between slowly opening buds and tumbled down warm yellow trumpets. In the blue sky a plane traced a line towards the warm south.

Ranil was painstakingly cutting feta cheese into ragged cubes. 'I got a cooler. If you look in the fridge there are two ice packs for it.'

Sunny got them out, as well as a whole tray of sliced meats covered in greaseproof paper.

At eleven o'clock precisely, the buzzer went. Clara was on the steps with a rucksack on her back. She wore a pale scarf around her head with small, beaten gold disks attached to each edge.

'Hi. You guys ready?' She smiled. Her face seemed to float up in the clear morning light. She pulled off her scarf, and shook her hair loose.

'You got the chicken?' Ranil yelled, putting the final touches to his Greek salad.

'Lots.' She looked at Sunny. 'And what about you, Sunny? Did you bring the drink?'

'There's another guy bringing wine.' Sunny tried to sound nonchalant, but there was a sharp pain in his gut.

Ranil parked in a sodden field of cow parsley and urban debris. Robby, who had been picked up at Turnham Green, was first out. They unloaded the car and set off, carrying cardboard boxes, the hamper, the cooler, carrier bags, Clara's rucksack and the back seat of the 2CV in a procession that rivalled *A Passage to India*. Ranil's island lay like Sindbad's whale in the dark water with a bridge, as he had promised, to its green forehead. 'We must face south,' Ranil declared and spread the blanket.

Clara stripped to a strapless buttery top and started applying cream to her arms.

'I brought cider,' Robby announced. 'Anyone for a glass?'

'Lovely.' She slipped off her sandals and rolled up her jeans to rub more cream on to her legs.

Ranil turned to Sunny. 'Those two can look after the food, while we go look for the other chaps.'

The water was dark despite the summer sun. The river eddied and seemed to flow in both directions. Ranil marched on ahead. When Sunny caught up, Ranil shook his head as if to clear it. 'Strange girl, you know, Clara. Sometimes I really don't understand her. When I first mentioned the picnic, I couldn't get a smile out of her. Then when I said we could have a bit of a do, with you and the others, she perked up and offered to make chicken drumsticks. Next thing she goes all quiet again. How is a fellow to know what to do?'

'Yes.' Sunny didn't know either.

Three figures appeared on the path ahead: John, Matthew and Rachel, Ranil's old college mates. 'Hey, you made it.'

Although clueless about Clara, Ranil was good at maintaining his friendships. Sunny just couldn't manage it. Even Robby had had to seek Sunny out.

Clara peeled herself off the car bench as they returned. 'Oh, hallo.'

Robby, who had been lying on the ground next to her, stood up too.

'There you are.' Ranil beamed. 'Robby.'

Wine was opened and passed around with the cider. The newcomers started a conversation about voices in the wilderness and the iconography of world religions.

Robby opened the Tupperware, while Clara removed the foil from her chicken dish.

A warmth spread across Sunny's shoulders. 'Your recipe?'

A patch of skin near her throat had burned a foxy red in the sun. 'I learned a bit from Mrs V., you know? Our lady of Birkenhead.'

'She taught you to cook?'

Clara picked up a celery stick. 'I used to go over and help with her ironing as a sort of Saturday job and she started teaching me a few things from the Kama Sutra.'

'What?' He saw her naked limbs entwined above her head. The celery in her mouth. Steam. Her nipples popping out.

'Just teasing. God, Sunny. You are getting as intense as Ranil.'

'I'll never forget that Christmas party.' He struggled lamely for something to say.

'You've never come back, have you? Up North?'

Sunny told Clara that apart from the trip with Ranil, and one other works outing, he had not ventured much beyond Euston Road.

'Come up to Archway then. I can show you Waterlow Park. Robby lives only a little further on.'

Sunny looked around and saw Robby lying on the ground between Matthew and Rachel, his head propped on a green wine bottle and his knees bent. Occasionally his whole body would shake to one of his unfathomable jokes. Clara was not Tina, but she put thoughts in his head that he wanted to chase.

'Like to feed the birds?' Sunny stood up and offered his hand to pull her up. They walked down to the water's edge, each holding a handful of brown crusts.

Two coots had found a still patch of water. Sunny threw some bread to them and they gobbled it up.

Clara threw some too. Sunny looked at her. A feeling of extraordinary happiness flooded him as he stood there with her, breathing as the wind might do over the unfurling petals of a wild flower on some distant mountainside. When the bread had all gone, the birds squawked out a few complaints and then drifted out into the current. After a few seconds in silence, Clara turned to go. It hadn't lasted long, but Sunny treasured their moment together.

The rest of the summer slipped by uneventfully. Then, when the leaves in Kensington Gardens began to turn, Sunny finally decided to brave the upper reaches of the Northern Line. He arranged to meet Clara at her flat. Ranil was out of town inspecting Durham cathedral for a footnote in his thesis.

Sunny had dithered because he didn't know what to say, or do. There was no one he could ask for advice. Ranil no doubt had her wedding ring on deposit. Robby probably had her ringed and unringed, clothed and unclothed, every other day.

The door opened.

'Sunny. So early.'

The hallway was narrow and had been turned into an architectural puzzle of locked doors. Clara opened one with a *Star Wars* poster stuck to it, revealing a flight of cheaply carpeted stairs. 'This way.' She bounded up, two at a time, in rainbow socks.

At the top she held back yet another door with her bum. 'It's not as big as Ranil's, but you can see trees out of the window. Well, some twigs anyway.' She laughed with her head tilted to one side.

'I brought you these.' He gave her the bag of shy cashews he'd bought instead of flowers or chocolates.

'Lovely. How about some tea? Or would you like something else? Cider?' She cleared some magazines and newspapers off the fake maple coffee table.

'Can I take you out for tea somewhere? What about this park you mentioned? Do they have tea rooms?'

'Waterlow?' She wrinkled her nose. 'I thought we could go for a walk in the woods instead. You'll find it quite different. Wilder.' She straightened and smoothed down her jeans.

'Wild would be nice.'

'No tea rooms there, so have it now?'

'OK.'

While she filled the kettle, Sunny checked out the bookshelf by the armchair. Thomas Hardy seemed to have more than his fair share of space.

'Hardy fan?' He asked as she came back in with two Disney mugs.

'Those? No. They are my flatmate's. She's a teacher.'

'Out today?'

'Half term. She's gone to her folks.'

'Liverpool?'

'Birmingham.' She placed the mugs on the table. 'Sugar?'

'No thanks.'

The conversation was not sparking the way he had hoped it would. There was too much he wanted to say. He couldn't quite focus on her, but he could see her ears were pushed forward by her hair. Closer. An inner ridge of her right lobe shone. It was a sign that she was ready to hear him out. He couldn't stay silent. 'I wanted to talk to you.' It came out in a whisper.

'About what?'

'Marriage,' he blurted out.

'Pardon?'

He took a quick sip of scalding tea, hoping his tongue would be burnt off. 'I wanted to know what you thought about marriage because there's this person – friend . . .'

'You want to marry someone?' She looked amused.

'No, no. I was talking, thinking I mean. What do you think about marriage? As an institution, I mean.' This was no good. Outdated. There was no way of retrieving the situation. There was no way of finding his balance now. He sounded like a fusty Victorian.

'These days, Sunny, I'm not sure if marriage has much meaning.' A loop of her hair swung down in front of her as she bent to pick up a magazine. She tucked it back behind her ear. 'Just a piece of paper, isn't it?'

Sunny was on a raft in a river, being taken in a completely different direction from where he had wanted to go, downstream to white water and sharp rocks. He watched her fingers straighten and her hand cup as she brushed some crumbs to the edge of the table. He reached out to help her.

The telephone rang. She strode over to the desk and answered it.

Sunny sank back into his chair.

'Robby? Hi.' She smiled exquisitely. 'Sunny's here,' she pressed the receiver close. She told Robby that they were going to Queen's Wood and could meet him by the old paddling pool.

When she put the phone down, she turned to Sunny with a happy smile. 'He's got a free afternoon. Isn't that great? I was hoping we could all meet up.' Her face was full of light.

'Me too. Who knows, Ranil might be paddling in this pool of yours as well.'

She laughed. 'Top up?'

They walked to the tube station and through it into a road of tall Edwardian houses and then a small slipway down to the woods. The ground was completely covered with leaves. The tarred path, the broken wall, the iron railings at the edge didn't alter the sense that this was the habitat of birds, squirrels, foxes and phantasmagoria. The sun gleamed lighting small spots, circles and shafts between the trees. Clara put her arm through Sunny's and snuggled up for warmth. She pointed out the allotments with their gremlin sheds and plots of autumn vegetables, a spade stuck into a mound of black earth by the gate.

'This way. Come on, let's find Robby.'

'Do we have to?'

That stopped her. She looked genuinely puzzled. 'What do you mean?'

'Nothing. Just joking. Let's go.'

Robby was sitting on the low rim of the pond in his beret, gloves and scarf. He had a parcel for her. 'Wicked silk strings, our latest range.' He laughed. 'Going like hot cakes in Crouch End.'

In December that year, Ranil told Sunny that he had a message for him from Tifus. 'He really wants you to come for Christmas. He is expecting a visitor he wants you to meet.'

'Who?'

'He says a friend of his whom you know from the Philippines is coming.'

'To Birkenhead?'

He had, of course, aged. His hair had thinned and whitened, making his face seem a little darker. Or perhaps it was the effect of northern light. He hoisted himself out of Tifus's recliner. 'Ah, the prodigal son.'

Sunny shook his hand. 'I never expected to see you here.'

Hector kept Sunny's hand in his as he spoke. 'You young fellows never look back. You forget everyone, everything. I thought it was high time you were reminded.'

'But what are you doing here?'

'Seeing old friends, Sunny. Old friends. You do that as you get on. You have to refresh the memory, Sunny, otherwise it all shrivels up. You know, the last time I saw young Tifus here, he was trying to learn his arithmetic.'

'A fine teacher, this Hector.' Tifus beamed. 'Coached me through the exams, opened the world for me, you see? Arithmetic, English, everything. *Tcha*, if only he was here to help me when I got to the university.'

Hector's face fell. He let go of Sunny's hand and rubbed the bottom of his jaw. 'I'm sorry, Tifus. Perhaps this name of yours didn't help in medical school. But you know, you have found your own vocation.'

Tifus tapped his head. 'Yes. Ho, ho. Yes. I can count them in and count them out. Haven't lost a single one so far . . .'

'Tell me,' Hector interrupted him, as though he were still a teacher, controlling the conversation in the classroom. 'Tell me, Sunny. How about you? How are you? I hear you are also a bean counter?'

'Not by choice.' Sunny realized the excuse sounded a little weak after all these years. 'I too did a diversion.'

'You know, your father misses you. He'd like to see you.'

Sunny ignored the comment. He wasn't ready to get into all of that. Instead he asked Hector how long he was staying in England.

Hector didn't press the point. He was a gentleman. 'This is my pre-retirement cruise. Next year, 30th of September 1981, I shall come to the end of my time with the bank. So I am looking around to see what I might do next. I've never been to England before.'

'Liverpool is your first stop?'

'No. I was invited to Manchester. An odd conglomeration there – academics, consultants – have caught the whiff of a truffle or two at the bottom of our little Asian institution and hope I might lead them there. I might be a guide after I retire.' He smiled.

'Guide, mentor, tutor.' Tifus shook his head in admiration.

'Guide, philosopher, friend.' Hector corrected him.

Hector had taken up residence at the nearby Bowler Hat Hotel. He told Sunny he very much wanted to talk to him and find out what he had been up to in London.

'You never wrote, my boy, except for a postcard.' The disapproval was mild.

'Writing was my father's job.'

Later he relaxed a little and told Hector how Robby had turned up in London.

'The wicketkeeper who made the winning run? How is the young fellow?'

'In the rag trade.'

'Doesn't surprise me. Always very dapper, wasn't he?'

By the time Hector was ready to go back to his hotel that evening, he and Tifus had got through the best part of a bottle of Teacher's. Hector said that he couldn't eat; he was fasting that day. 'No solids, only liquids.' Delora had made what she called her special sardine sarnies so that Hector wouldn't be tempted by a hot meal.

That night Sunny found it hard to sleep. Although the heating had shut down, he was sweating. He kicked away the blanket and the candlewick bedspread. He kept seeing Hector and his father drinking; his mother with her wrists slit. How could she have done that?

The next day Tifus offered to take Hector for a drive. 'Sunny, you come with us too.' He wanted to show his mentor the country lanes, the grand houses of Hoylake and West Kirby, the view of the sea, the river Dee and the dappled outline of distant Welsh hills; the northern world he had inadvertently exchanged for his south coast Ceylon village. Tifus had a route mapped out, like an old sailor, full of tales of shipwrecks, tragedy and sudden exits. He'd veer to the left to bring them near the gate of a famous skipper who had sailed the herring seas without mishap but died inflating a lover's dinghy at the sailing club; then up a hill to show the garden of a mansion in which a professor of physics had tried to fly, da Vinci-style, for his paramour and failed spectacularly; next down a lane to a gothic manor in which a retired QC had expired *in flagrante*.

'You have certainly seen it all, Tifus. I'd never have thought so much happened in these quiet cul-de-sacs.'

'Our last moments are full of surprises, my friend, teacher and guide – except I'm the guide now, eh? I tell you, you'd be amazed at the number of clients I have had who conked out on the job. You'd think there's more to life than popping one's cork, eh, Hector?'

'Clients?'

'I try not to be the first to think of them as completely gone. I am not a doctor, Hector, as you well know. I just was not cut out for that business. The name was not the problem. You see, the medical profession is used to discriminating a disease from a person. I just had no heart for it. I am more of a tailor. Sometimes I think actually maybe I am only a valet.' He made a point of pronouncing the T with a gleeful grin.

When they reached West Kirby, Tifus parked down a small side street. 'Would you like a little stroll? While I'm here I'd like to drop in and see Mrs Woodhouse. Have to keep her spirits up, but the three of us, I am afraid, might be a little much for the old thing. There is a nice little tea room at the corner. You can go in and have a cuppa, if you like.'

'Yes. Let us have tea, Sunny, and not frighten his old flame.'

The two of them set off down a lane. For a while they didn't say anything.

'So, how is Dad?' Sunny finally asked.

Hector took in a sharp breath of cold air. 'He misses you.'

'We each have our own lives.' The truth of this was obvious to him.

'Do we?' Hector paused. He looked at Sunny, as he used to, challenging him as an equal despite the gap in their age. 'Your father is not a happy man.'

Sunny stiffened. 'And my mother? Does he . . .'

'Your mother's death was hard for you, I know. But it was hard for him too, you know. She was a very special woman. He loved her.'

'He neglected her. Frustrated her. He let her die. He killed her, didn't he?'

Hector stopped. 'It was not like that, Sunny. Your mother was a wonderful, talented woman. Your father is a good man. He is not a weak man. He tried to find his balance. But the two together . . . Something didn't work. Love needs something more.'

Sunny found Hector's words hard to take, here in the cold sunshine of a rocky town perched on the tip of a peninsula so far from the heart of their two lives, their three or four lives.

'What does it need then?' Sunny asked. 'This love?'

Hector stopped. They were in front of the tea shop. The glass door had a wrinkled lace curtain pinned to it. There was no one inside. 'The right time. The right place. Luck.' He pushed open the door. 'I am a little cold. Let's have something to warm us up.'

A timid blonde girl guided them nervously to a table by the window.

'Perhaps we could be nearer the heater?' Hector asked.

She was nonplussed. Hector repeated his request and she pretended to understand.

He smiled and chose a place by the radiator. He sat down and took off his hat. 'Two cream teas, my dear. And I'd like some of those round little bready things.'

'I don't think they have cream teas here. That's Devon.'

The young waitress was completely lost. She began to twist her apron with both hands. Hector picked up a small handwritten card from the table. Right in the centre was the speciality: cream teas with scones. He pointed to it and indicated two with a small smile of triumph.

When she had gone, Hector resumed. 'Lester is now a senior vice-president in the corporation. He has done well.'

'As a corrupt crony capitalist?'

'No, Sunny.'

'I thought these days everybody over there is.'

'Not him. It is a legitimate company which does some very good things in a difficult world. Promotions for all kinds of social welfare programmes. You should go and see him. See what he does, talk to him. Show him you are still his son. He would love to see you.'

The tea came. Two scones each on separate plates with a disc of heart-stopping cream and a saucer of arterial jam. Hector looked at the presentation with a critical eye, but did not say anything to frighten the waitress.

'He never told the truth.' Sunny couldn't explain what he wanted from him, or from Hector. He couldn't see beyond the apparent deceit to what had been before. The fog wouldn't clear. 'The point of his profession was to tell the truth, wasn't it? Isn't that what a reporter has to do. Otherwise what's the point? Why did he move into PR?'

'It hasn't been easy for him. She was not an easy lady, your mother. After you came along . . . their lives changed.' He sipped his tea and seemed to sink into a torpor. When he next spoke, he was barely audible. 'Sometimes unrequited love is all we have.'

Sunny didn't answer. Hector was not the right man to talk about love. He had never married; he had never come close to it. There was never anybody else in his life. He seemed to be someone who wanted to be either completely alone or in the company of a great very many, involved in a collective spirit. Sunny remembered the happiness he'd exuded in the Señora's house in Quezon City, communing. He could be an uncle, but not a father.

'Do you still go over to the house, like before? Walk around the same block in Urdaneta?'

Hector smiled. 'Yes, but a little slower. I drop in for a drink most Fridays, if he is there. Lester is, I suppose, the busier man.'

It all came back to Sunny then. The hot nights and the tungsten light of the street lamps. The basketball courts, the soft footfalls and his father trying desperately to keep up with his teenage son – a new life growing too fast out of his hands. Meeting Robby again hadn't brought his memories back in this way. Robby had come with too many new connections, his new world had rinsed out the old.

'There's Tifus.' The café door opened. 'Tifus, come and have one of these *scones*. We have cream and some very red jam.'

Tifus pulled up a chair and sat down. 'No cream, Hector.

It's a killer.' He picked up the top half of a scone. 'Is this not stale?'

'Have the jam, Tifus.'

'Not strawberry.' Tifus sighed. 'I don't like this commercial jam. I'm a marmalade man myself.' He pulled out a little jar from his pocket. 'Home-made, you see?'

'Good God, man. You carry a jar of marmalade with you?' Hector's eyes bulged.

Tifus's skittering laugh bounced off the walls and rattled the china behind the counter at the back of the café.

'Hector, you are a funny man. Very funny. Mrs Woodhouse always gives me home-made marmalade. She has an inexhaustible supply. Come, shall we go? I want to show you our beach.'

On the winter beach, by the red rocks, in the car and back in the guest room of the house, Sunny thought about Manila. About his father, his childhood and his adolescence, a past that had slipped away like so much loose change. He didn't know how it had happened.

The next day Ranil said that he'd arranged to meet his friend Drayton at a wine bar across the water. 'Come with us. Clara can show you the wigwam afterwards – the Cathedral. It is very special.'

The wine bar was empty. Ranil waxed lyrical about the wigwam, the Philharmonic pub, the Everyman theatre and the multitude of visitor attractions of this most famous seaport of the British Empire until eventually Drayton arrived.

He was lean and hard, with a whole history of substance abuse chronicled in small dry gutters down his face. His long

matted hair was tangled into the knotted mane of his ancient Afghan coat. 'All right there? Ranil, man.' A wrecked grin wrestled with his serial addictions as he flopped into a chair. 'Hey, Clara, wow.'

He turned to Sunny. 'Gorra ciggie?'

'Sorry.'

Unfazed, he pulled out a pouch of Golden Virginia and grappled with a roll-up. He licked the Rizla paper carefully, as if it might have been a razor, then lit the cigarette. He inhaled and spoke with the smoke trickling out of his mouth, as though he was a minor god of sacrifice. 'So, you all live in London, den?'

'Sunny is in Earls Court. I live near Hammersmith and Clara lives in North London.' Then something snapped in Ranil's head. 'But when we get married, Clara and I might move back here.'

'What?' Clara's empty glass dropped and bounced off the table.

Sunny caught the glass – that innate talent for fielding finally flowering.

Ranil's face had shrunk. 'Won't we?'

Clara's had turned livid: a colour never seen before, even in the skies of Liverpool where the wind and the petroleum burn. 'Ranil, are you off your head?'

'Hey, wot? Liverpool's ace, you know. Load of right-wing crap . . .' Drayton's roll-up had gone out.

'Marry? Ranil. No way, never. Wherever did you get such a daft bloody idea?'

Not only Ranil's face, but the whole of him seemed to shrink.

'Clara?' He uttered her name as though it could right the world.

'I don't know what you've been thinking, Ranil, but we've only ever been friends. Right? That's all. Good friends. Not marriage potential.'

He was watching her but he seemed unable to hear. Great puddles collected in his eyes.

Drayton picked a few strands of stray tobacco and loose hair off the table. 'Look guys, there's some stuff here you've gorra sort, and there's some stuff I gorra sort too. I have to meet a guy at O'Connors. Just back from Marrakesh. Maybe I'll see you later, right? Tar-ra fer now.' He got up and did *namaste* with his scarred hands to Sunny before making a rapid exit.

'I need some air.' Ranil got to his feet and rushed for the door.

'I can't marry *him*.' Clara was incandescent. 'You know that.'

'Robby?'

'What?'

Sunny swallowed hard. He should have learnt from Ranil's example to keep his mouth shut.

'Why did you say Robby? What has Robby got to do with anything?'

He shrugged.

'Robby is gay. You know that, don't you?'

Sunny blinked. 'Right. I see. Actually . . .' The whole evening, the whole day, was becoming overrun by surprises. His head began to reel.

'He must have told you. His partner? Coming to London

was all about it, surely you knew? Weren't you in bloody school together?'

For one mad second he decided this was the moment to divulge his own feelings. Then he thought better of it. This was not the right time. Not the right place. They should walk down to Pierhead like in a song, stroll below the stars and the Liver birds and let the spirit move them to speak of things both deep and dear. He knew he was not the best judge of timing.

When he'd first met Robby in Manila as a kid, he'd been impressed by Robby's knowledge of women. He seemed to know the ins and outs of female anatomy like nobody else. With Robby there had never been any of the cock-a-hoop finger wagging of his Colombo classmates, he didn't moon out of windows like the American boys in Makati, lighting flares out of their arses. Robby was the guy who had a scorecard with the name of every prom queen in town on it. He was wild about girls, Sunny had thought . . .

They didn't go to Pierhead. Instead they went in search of Ranil. He was sitting on the freezing steps of the Catholic Cathedral, hunched in his mac, his big black shoes bobbing like lost boats.

She went up to him. It could have been a play, Sunny thought, in which he had forgotten all his lines. She bent over Ranil, illuminated by a street light. A few minutes later they came back together and headed for the car.

Ranil drove slowly down towards the Mersey tunnel, letting the town famous for its beat and sound, its language and loquacity, slip by in the dull whine and creak of a straining 2CV.

On the other side, Ranil paid the toll, took the flyover past Cammell Laird's and headed for home. He dropped Clara without another word. From her house the journey was too short to offer any chance of a post-mortem. In any case Sunny didn't know whether they should rake over what had happened or let it pass into oblivion.

Tifus came out of the sitting room. 'So, the revellers are back. Had a good time, Sunny? I thought you fellows will be going to the clubs. Great night clubs, no? Dancing à gogo and all that?'

Ranil hurried upstairs, muttering that he had a headache.

'Always the boy has a headache. Thinks too much. That's his trouble and he never exercises his neck.' Tifus lowered his head, then rolled it from side to side. 'You see, you must rotate the head and clear the linkages every day. It is very important. You must do it, Sunny. Make it a habit.'

'Tell me,' Hector leant forward. 'How do you manage in your London, Sunny? Can you cook like your Dad?'

'Yes . . . sort of.'

'Pork? *Oorumas*?'

Sunny shrugged. 'There's Clara. She makes a mean chicken tandoori sometimes when we all meet up.'

Delora came in and sighed. 'That girl, she's going to be one heck of a wife one day. So chic, so smart. And can even cook.'

Sunny turned back to Hector. 'I've been thinking. I will go and see him. I don't know why but, somehow, it seems possible now.' Something in his constellation had shifted in the confusion of the previous night.

Hector nodded without showing any surprise. 'Remember

the good times?' He reached inside his jacket pocket and produced a small square photograph of Sunny as a boy, handing Lester a cricket bat. Already two inches taller than him.

'Next month,' Sunny said to Hector. 'After the January sales, I can take some time off. What do you think?'

'The sooner the better, Sunny. When the time is right, you have to act fast.'

In spite of Hector's urging, Sunny didn't feel like rushing his return to Manila.

He met Robby the day before he was going to book the tickets. He wanted to ask him what had happened between him and Tina all those years ago. Was that only a batting partnership after all? If only he had known then what he knew now, life might have turned out so very differently. Or would it? He told Robby about Hector and the decision to go back to Manila.

'Are you going alone?'

'What do you mean?'

'What about Clara?' He paused, and then added, 'And Ranil? They'd both love it.'

'I am going to see my father, Robby. After seven long years . . .'

'Maybe we should go together. I ought to go and sort out a new supplier. The guys in Cebu are no good, and we really want to resuscitate the Filipino tart line. Can you wait until end of Feb?'

Sunny compromised. He postponed the trip for a week so that they would overlap and have some time together.

It was a mistake.

Three days before Sunny was due to leave, Hector called him at work. 'Hallo, Sunny?'

'Yes.' He recognized the low, grave voice immediately. He knew what was coming. He was too late. He had left it all too late. Stupidly too late. He was always too late. He knew it. His father, his mother, Aunty Lillie had all complained that he was never on time for anything.

He was cold. The temperature had dropped. The office was never comfortable. He moved the fan heater closer with his foot.

'I am very sorry, Sunny.' Hector's words dribbled down the line and grew faint. 'So very, very sorry.'

'What happened? What has happened? Tell me.' Sunny wanted more words. Clearer words. He wanted to hear a voice from his youth, Hector's voice, if not his father's. Silence would not do. Not any more. He knew what had happened, somehow he knew, but he wanted to hear where, how, why. He wanted to be told the truth.

'Your father was driving back from Farmers Market. There is so much traffic now, Sunny. It is horrendous. You won't believe it . . . He must have been trying a shortcut. As he was coming off Aurora Boulevard, some kid in a sports car crashed into him. Smashed . . . I am sorry, Sunny, your father is dead. He died almost immediately.'

Sunny flew to Manila on the next available flight, in a rush now that it didn't matter. Hector arranged for Aunty Lillie to come from Colombo. They were all like zombies at first. In his absence Lester seemed all the more maddening, pulling them together for nothing. A dead man in a strange land, pulling strings for no purpose.

Aunty Lillie had grown thinner and sharper. She stroked Sunny's cheek as if to measure its fatness, and tutted to Hector. 'Tut, tut. Just look at this boy, Hector? Look at him.' She didn't seem to notice her nephew was no longer a twelve-year-old.

Partly to assert himself, partly for his father's sake, Sunny told Hector it would be better if Lillie stayed out of the way. Perhaps in Hector's house.

'I think that is a very good idea,' Hector replied. 'You know, the dear girl would like you to do whatever you think is best. She has her own special arrangements for the next world and you are, after all, your father's son.'

'Not my mother's?'

Hector bowed. 'I'm sorry. Perhaps it is a mistake to see such things as mutually exclusive.'

'Anyway, I think my father should rest here. He shouldn't be buried next to my mother.'

Hector understood. 'Nappy will handle everything. You remember Nappy? Very reliable.'

The funeral was small, swift and efficient. Manila had changed since Sunny's early days, but Nappy helped him to find a place for Lester close to the things that he had grown close to, true to the Makati spirit he had so admired. They kept religion out of the proceedings. Only right at the very end did Sunny cry. Hector put his arm around his shoulder. He wept too.

Nappy and Hector managed to ensure that there were obituaries in all the papers Lester had liked to read. After the funeral, Aunty Lillie tried to sound caring. 'Will you come back home now?'

Hector cut in. 'At least he saw you, Sunny. I showed him the picture I took of you in Liverpool. He was pleased to see how you'd turned out.'

'I was stupid not to have come back sooner.'

The silence stretched out, profound, unfillable. There was nothing anyone could say.

Later, Hector took Sunny to the bar of the Peninsula Hotel in Makati. He told Sunny more about himself then, with a San Miguel in his hand, than ever before.

'You know, Lester was my oldest friend. We knew each other a long time. We go back before college days. I've known him longer than our Liverpool friend, Tifus.' The sun had not yet gone down in Makati. The sky was deep red, bleeding into the glassy skyscrapers and the trees that had grown old and heavy in their wake. Sunny noticed that there was more of a haze at the end of the day than there had been when he'd lived there. Hector sipped his beer. 'He was a clever man, your father, but he didn't always see what was close by. His eye was always on things too far ahead. Do you know what I mean? He always believed that I had no passion. I suppose I have tended to be more interested in inner peace. I never chased things as he did when he was young. He learnt from me to calm down, you know. To be patient. But that was later, when he played the part of the great angler, when things went wrong and he had to find ways in which to cope. At the time he met your mother, he was a different kind of person – actually we met her together at the cricket club before the war. Did you know that? It was the time Bradman visited Ceylon. His last whistle-stop tour. 1948. I saw him, you know. Yes. We shook hands. I was no cricketer, as you well know, but we all went down for the party. You remember Rudolf? Rudy. He was there. Anyway the cricket lads were all with the big man Bradman – he was already a legend, you see. But Lester found a much more interesting proposition that evening in your mother. Irene was there with your Aunty Lillie.'

Sunny tried to picture it: his father and his mother, Hector and Lillie as youngsters, flirting while the king of cricket was interrogated by bowlers and catchers, dingos and cadgers on the other side of the room.

'I thought Lester would go over to the Bradman congregation. He was always on the lookout for a good story. He had a flair for words, as you know. But he didn't. Buggered up my pitch instead. I didn't dare say what I wanted to . . .' Hector waved a hand over his beer.

'What?' Sunny wanted to hear more, but Hector seemed to retreat. A kind of peace soothed the lines around his mouth. He ran his fingers down the lapel of his dark jacket.

'Lester often regretted not doing more with his writing. Irene tried to encourage him. She was almost more upset by him squandering his talent than by her own constraints. She felt she was frustrated by circumstance, whereas he had the chance to do something and just . . . didn't. It was a shame . . . You know, Lester did blame himself for her death. He took it all on himself. Even when you abandoned him. After that he felt he had lost all connection with his past, his present and his future. He'd say he didn't know why he couldn't see what was there before him. It wasn't the drink, you understand, Sunny. It was more like a blindness, a blind spot. He wanted the world, you know, to find the world. Sometimes he said he had only Rosa holding it all together for him.'

'Rosa? What do you mean?'

'Besides me, there was no one else close to him at the end. You see, Sunny, you find only part of the world in yourself.'

But for Sunny even that small part had been too elusive. And now, at the age of twenty-six, after his father's death, finding that inner core, his true self, finally seemed possible.

There wasn't much of an inheritance – Lester had invested in a lot of dud companies and had been embezzled by the same crooks who'd systematically plundered the rest of the Philippines – but there was enough for Sunny to give up his job at Harpo's and try for a more satisfying life. Sunny gave himself six months to explore what he could do for himself. He found the Voigtländer camera Hector had given him when he'd first set off for London and felt better for holding it. *My mother could have been a star; my father should have been a writer. I will be a photographer.* He wrote the sentences in a little black jotter he had started to carry around with him.

At the beginning of May, Robby called to say Ranil was leaving London. 'He's ditched the Ph.D. Needs the inspiration of a new place to discover the meaning of life, he says. He's off to Nepal to work with a Jesus charity and write poems out of mountain air. Absolutely *lóco-lóco*.'

They met up at Max's, a wine bar, not far from the French Institute in South Ken that Robby frequented. Ranil and Robby were already sipping mint tea when Sunny arrived.

He collected a coffee and sat down. 'So, what's in Nepal then?'

'I need to separate out the dross, Sunny. Our time is too short. The scholarly stuff, all this context rigmarole is becoming very tedious. In poetry I find something closer to what I am looking for . . .'

'But why Nepal?'

Ranil smiled. 'The mountains are there. The first and the biggest. They mean something.'

'For Hillary and Tenzing maybe? But for you?'

'We must all do what we have to do.'

After Ranil left London on his great quest, Sunny bought a small manual SLR camera, a Pentax MX, an extra telephoto lens and a black leather jacket. Also a load of how-to books. He discovered that great photographers sometimes stumbled into their calling. Robert Capa had a lucky break: no professionals to go to Trotsky's speech, so he went, and captured the expression of a revolutionary in a single frame. Sunny wondered if he could invent a different persona for himself, just as Capa had, and find a new world.

To begin with he was obsessed by death, loss, things coming apart. He took hundreds of pictures of wilted flowers, gravestones in Westminster, the flotsam and jetsam of Victoria Station and the sweet slurry of the Thames at twilight. The cameras, the jacket and the growing pile of elegiac images on his bedsit table gave him a curious confidence. He felt able to call Clara from time to time to suggest a walk, sometimes in her woods, sometimes Hyde Park, where he would crouch and artfully shoot the odd duck or deformed pigeon. He'd zoom in on a burka or Burberry, trying to catch the line of one of Robby's finer basques underneath. He even found that his eyes had improved and he didn't need his glasses as much as before. The optician said his body was adjusting; he thought it was more to do with his state of mind.

Clara always seemed pleased to see him and they talked as friends do without revealing what might lie dormant in each other's minds. She still worked at the same stationery company, but was now PA to the Managing Director – a workaholic called Gumbo.

'And you? You like the freedom from the store?'

They were in the café by the Serpentine, drinking weak afternoon tea and sharing a jam doughnut. Sunny cleared his throat. 'I need a bit of time to work things out.'

'You'll stay in London?' She wiped the sugar off her fingers with a tissue.

It had not occurred to Sunny to go somewhere else. 'Having finally got my permit to stay, unlimited, it'd be crazy to do a Ranil now.'

'Was that difficult?'

'Luck. I just had to hang on. I don't think it will be quite so automatic in the future with all this xenophobia in vogue.'

Out on the water, a duck went under arse-up. Sunny didn't have his telephoto lens, but he went for the picture anyway. He was getting fast at this sort of impromptu shot, winding the film as the camera came up, hitting the green light for the aperture and focusing in one swift action and then the click of the shutter. As it opened again he saw he had caught Clara too in the frame, her eye turning, the curve of her brow, the hint of pink from her nose. He loved her and said so as the duck, in the distance, righted itself.

'The camera or the duck?'

'You,' Sunny repeated. 'You.'

He had never thought it would be so easy. The right words, at the right time, in the right place, were like a key turning in a lock. His heart, and hers, opened.

Her smile that day, by the Serpentine, was unlike anything he had ever seen before. Warm and wide, it drew him in. He felt moisture on his lips as he kissed her, then tasted on hers the sweet residue of sugar and syrup. He took her hand. Her pulse was strong and fast and seemed to him to spell out both her feelings and the ones rushing through his own veins. Her plain peach jumper glowed.

'What do we do now?'

She touched his lips with hers again and tightened her hand. They kissed again. Across the water big, bold trees shed their foliage slowly in the breeze.

All the thoughts and anxieties that had plagued him for years seemed to evaporate. Each second bloomed into a star inside him. He pulled off his scarf and tugged at his collar. He pushed his leg against hers and the table slid a little between them. He pushed it and moved closer putting his hand behind her and pressing her towards him.

'Wait.'

'Why?'

'Christ, you've waited so long, Sunny . . .'

Sunny took her hand to his mouth, then smothered her face again, then her neck and her throat. The chair on the other side of the table toppled over.

Clara giggled and pulled him off. 'Sunny . . .'

'Should we celebrate? What would you like? A concert at Albert Hall? Dinner?' The words tumbled out.

She stared at him, searching his face. 'I like Italian . . .'

'There's a fancy restaurant in Beauchamp Place.'

'I like to eat Italian naked . . .'

'Spaghetti or tagliatelle?'

She pulled in her lips. 'Fettuccine, actually, with just a dab of butter.'

'I think I can manage that.'

They walked through Kensington Gardens, past the roses and a corridor of rhododendrons. Late-flowering shrubs nodded as they twirled past, hand in hand. Sunny's heart was racing and he wanted to run and throw confetti into the ponds. 'Hey, slow down . . .' Clara stumbled as he pulled her along.

'Don't you want to just shout out loud?'

'What?'

'Anything.'

'I'm hungry.'

Sunny laughed. 'We'll go to Safeway. They have loads of pasta.'

When they got back to his room he discovered the bruised foil wrapper he carried in his wallet had cracked open, drying out the rubber inside. While Clara filled the kettle he checked the sealed packet he kept by the Weetabix, but that too was well out of date and no good.

'One thing I forgot,' he said. 'I'll nip out and get some fresh milk for tea.'

'It's OK. I can have it black.'

'No, no. I need some milk. I'll be back in a minute.'

At the corner shop he picked up the milk and a selection of Durex, and on the way back, the last rose – a pale pink

– from the flower stall. 'No red? Why no red?' Would it do?

When he reached the door of his room he hesitated. The hall, the doorknob, everything seemed cold. He swallowed hard and opened the door. She was still there. 'Is the water boiling?'

Clara's job was nine to five, but in the London of 1981 even stationers liked to cultivate an air of hyperactivity. Often she had to stay late typing reports, reorganizing and unpicking the mistakes of the day. She and Sunny couldn't meet every night, and arranged their rendezvous like secret agents.

Friday-night conversations revolved around Holly, her flatmate, whose boyfriend lived in Sheffield.

'Your wild woods or my mean streets?'

'Holly is already on the coach.'

'OK, I'm on my way.' The scent of eau de toilette and fabric conditioner at Clara's was infinitely preferable to the lingering beef stir-fry that steeped the sheets of his bedsit, no matter how hard they sweated.

In the new year Holly landed a job as deputy head in a school in Doncaster. She left at Easter.

Before he moved in Sunny said, 'Maybe we should get engaged?' He made it sound like a joke, but it was a genuine proposal. He had a desire for order, the ritual of legitimacy. He placed his hand on her back. 'And get married? What about it?'

'No, Sunny. I don't think we should.'

'Why not?'

'You know I don't believe in that kind of stuff.'

'You think your parents won't approve?'

'What have they got to do with it? It's not like we have to please someone else to please each other. I just don't want to end up like them.'

'What do you mean?'

'Stuck, rather than together.'

Sunny thought about his own father and mother, who had ended up being neither stuck nor together. Clara's parents, Beryl and Eric, seemed to have managed much better. 'That's a little harsh.'

'They are trapped by promises they can't keep, but can't break either. After I left, they should have too. They'd each have been much better off on their own.' A thin groove deepened down her forehead, dividing one temple from the other. She mashed her fist up against her lips. 'You know she'd get so fed up with Dad, she'd throw pies at him.'

'Don't be silly.'

'She did. And he did too. They'd go mad.'

'What pies?'

'Chicken. Steak and kidney. I don't know, maybe cottage pies. Sunny, what does it matter?'

'They seem happy enough now.'

'It is like a game they don't know how to stop.'

Sunny didn't think so, but he didn't know how to explain what he saw as important. He wanted the two of them to be part of something bigger, something that went beyond the individual. Somehow to be able to survive the inevitable wobble that came with time. It wasn't a game. But he knew that if he tried to describe it to Clara, he'd sound too much like an old-fashioned fool.

Sunny didn't bring up the subject again. He quickly learnt

what needed to be talked about, and what was best left unsaid. When he saw her brushing her hair, there was nothing much more he wanted, other than for the moment to last just a little bit longer.

'You do know this is real, Sunny, don't you?' Clara fished a grey, steaming ball out of a bowl of Chinese soup.

'Wontons?'

'I mean everything.'

'Yes.' Everything was real, from wontons to futons. More real than ever before. The walks and rambles, the theatre, films, and exhibitions, the embraces, the kisses and the surfeit of fettuccine. He'd never thought he'd live like this. Every time they saw each other, a rush of blood would knock them into each other's arms, and he'd wonder how he'd become so lucky.

He joined a photography club in Jackson's Lane and began to build up a portfolio of city portraits: St Paul's seen through witch hazel, the black British Museum, old chestnuts. He found a curious satisfaction in trees and buildings. 'It's like haiku,' he said to Clara. 'Serendipity.'

She had discovered tantric yoga and became obsessed with serpents. She got Sunny to practise chakra-lifting and eating pasta in different positions. Her firm had diversified into art materials and Gumbo had made her head of stock control. She began to bring samples of cartridge paper, crayons, acrylics and oils back to the flat and make Tibetan mandalas – intricate patterns representing spiritual and sensory evolution. She urged Sunny to do so too.

'I'd like to go to India,' she said one day between a *kun-*

dalini starburst and a quick stir of a Mrs Veeraswamy chickpea recipe.

'Where in India? Big place, India.'

'Maybe the north. Follow the Ganges. Go up into the Himalayas and find a yogi.'

The muscles in Sunny's chest tightened. He saw Ranil seated high on the rim of Kathmandu valley, in white robes and *chappals* instead of his mac and school shoes, intoning the lines of his latest erotic verse drama, waiting for this moment. Was she still thinking of him after all this time?

'Why not south? You get sea and art. Buddhism too. We could go to Sri Lanka.'

She put the lid on the saucepan and patted the centre of her tummy. 'We could . . . but do you really want to?'

'Actually, yes. I've been thinking. I don't know what it is like any more. So much must have changed in the last few years . . . and there's roots and all that.'

'You think we could do India as well from there? I have a connection too, you know. On my mother's side. Her grandmother had an Indian . . .'

'Sure, sure.' His mind was racing. He remembered Clara's mother telling him, 'Many of us have kith and kin around the world, Sunny. It's the seaport in us. Sailors and storytellers, that's what we are. We like to reach out to the rest of the world. One of my own forebears was from India. But this doesn't mean that we're all the same, does it?'

'Is August a good time? I can get two weeks,' Clara added.

'Can't you get an extra week?'

'Gumbo would throw a fit. You know how he hates giving any time off.'

The very next day, Sunny got hold of some holiday brochures from the Ceylon Tea Centre in Haymarket and tried to wean her off the idea of India and the Himalayas. He found a Sri Lankan travel agent, Boris, who offered a cut-price deal absolutely totally guaranteed, but which would double in price if they stopped over in India. 'There's no time to be going back and forth,' Sunny told her. 'Anyway, I found a yogi with a beach practice for you.'

While Clara went into a controlled breathing exercise, Sunny made the bookings and fixed up a couple of hotels. Top of the range in Colombo and a bit of dive, down the coast, that Boris said had the cheapest aromatic oils. The Sri Lankan tourist board had recently started advertising. He could see the beach in his head, and the two of them cavorting, carefree.

Clara saw the news first and called out. 'Colombo is burning. It's on TV.'

The sky was grey on the screen. Dark smoke spiralled out of the place that Sunny could recognize as the town of his childhood. This was not news from elsewhere. These were not atrocities committed in a country of some other world. This was a part of him destroying itself. There are no boundaries in our lives, he thought. There are no borders except in our minds. Who were these murderers? When the BBC reporter described the killing and burning, and spoke of rabid Sinhala mobs hunting out Tamil families, Sunny shook his head, ashamed. He couldn't understand where these monsters had come from. He felt sick.

'How can they do it?' he asked Clara. What could make a person throw kerosene over another human being and set fire to him? Watch his skin crinkle and burn? How could they hear the screams, see the flames wrap around a writhing man, smell the burning flesh, and then do it again. Anger? Money? A warped fantasy? Was it the corruption of culture and identity, or plain political thuggery? Vicious barbarity had erupted during the Partition of India. It had been visited upon Vietnam and Cambodia. He knew that. The Nazis had perverted the nature of man. But this was an island he had known. With people – victims and perpetrators – who looked just like him. An island where he and his mother and his father had been born. Surely people should know how to be better by now.

Each day the smoke grew thicker, and the images sicker, the wounds deeper. He heard of a minibus full of Tamil passengers being burnt; of thirty-five prisoners in Welikade being massacred; of political gang masters leading attacks, burning houses and shops and bussing gangs from district to district. Maniacs and morons were in control.

Sunny watched things slowly fall apart as his father would have done in Manila back in 1971 when his old world – his Ceylon – had exposed its inner brutality and shifted his ideals for ever out of reach. Then, despite ten thousand deaths and heaps of bodies that clogged the rivers, there had been no pictures shown, hardly any news. The true enormity of what had taken place was slow to emerge. Now, in 1983, decapitations, bomb blasts, mutilations, were being flashed across the world. Corpses could no longer be so easily hidden. Not even in mass graves. And no one could be untouched, untarnished by the savagery unleashed.

★

Sunny didn't want to talk about Sri Lanka again. Or any other place. Not even with Clara. All the world could go to hell, as so much of it was bent on doing. They agreed to cancel the tickets. In August, his Manila was in the limelight with its own bid for blood. Benigno Aquino was gunned down on the airport tarmac when he returned to oppose President Marcos. His death too was captured on film. Everywhere, it seemed, there was a greed for gore.

Clara saw the wisdom of the east in a new light. She dumped all her yoga books at Oxfam and meditated more on the things that mattered around her: the tensions and struggles of a society under stress, and Sunny's gradual withdrawal.

Sunny buried his head in his darkroom, in images that had nothing to do with the news of the day, be it cruise missiles or political assassination. Mrs Thatcher escaped in Brighton; Mrs Gandhi didn't in Delhi. He began to think that biology, life on earth, had more to offer a person of his disposition. He bought a new macro lens and began to study the traumas of smaller creatures: spiders, moths, the Beelzebubs of lichen groves.

Then, early in 1985, Robby threw his own little googly. 'We are leaving London,' he said. 'We want to open up in Paris. Spice up Montmartre like we did Finchley.' His face broadened into one of his huge, carefree grins.

'You can't.' Sunny was devastated. Robby was all he had left of his *merienda* years. That in-between time which had come back to him like an unexpected spring.

'What's the problem, old *paré*? Things change. We have to move on.' He turned to Clara. 'That's life, right?'

'I think it's wonderful. We can visit you. Maybe your incredible hunk will be happier to meet us in gay Paree.'

Robby grinned. 'Oh, no. That mystery must remain. *Au revoir.*' He blew a kiss.

Robby knew how to handle life – what to hang on to, what to let go, what to give, what to take. Clara knew too, and Sunny reckoned even Tina must have done in her own way. Ranil certainly knew what was important to him. Sunny wondered whether his mother had ever known – or had she always turned the wrong way? Lester hadn't really known how to handle anything. As for Sunny himself, how could he possibly know?

A DUCK'S EGG

1986

MICHAEL SUVAN EASTON-FERNANDO was born to Clara on the 25th of February 1986, at the Whittington Hospital off the Archway Road. The birth was said to be easy – although that was not how it looked to Sunny.

The Filipino nurse who was around most of the time had a thin wire plugged into her ear. '*Ano*, Bibi see!' She moaned every time he asked her anything. She kept a scorecard of all the dilations on her ward and every now and then she would squeal and cheer. Late on the night of the birth, Sunny learnt it was not to do with an extra centimetre at the cervix, or the glimpse of a nearly born peeping out, but rather the news coming out of Manila on her radio. Cory Aquino was being sworn in as the newly elected leader; Ferdinand Marcos was on the point of reinstating himself against her. Something was about to snap.

'We have twins,' she announced at one confusing moment, and Sunny developed palpitations to match Clara's. 'Twin Presidents, *ay naku*.' The nurse cooed and giggled. 'You know Mister Sunny, how they will both fight for Malacañang now.'

But she was wrong. The age of peaceful revolutions had finally dawned. People power. Easy births. Everything was painted yellow. Marcos was swiftly evacuated.

At the time, Mikey's birth was the biggest thing ever for Sunny and Clara. Adrenalin, anaesthetics, angst. Breaking waters and epidurals. The world was changing and this was the momentous event that needed to be appreciated by all. Sunny called Clara's mother. 'It's a boy. Five pounds twelve and no hair.'

Beryl repeated the details to her husband Eric. Then she consoled Sunny. 'He will grow, Sunny. Don't worry, he will grow. How is the new mother?'

'Clara is fine. Everything is fine. The NHS is wonderful.'

He also called Tifus and Delora.

'Good show,' Tifus whooped. 'I love the sound of a baby. Take it from me, it may seem like yowling now but that is the most fantastic music you will ever hear, Sunny. The best.'

Clara's parents visited soon after Clara and the baby came home. Installed in a nearby hotel, they were pleased but wary, in at the deep end sooner than anyone had expected.

The name Michael went down well. Beryl was delighted. 'If you had been a boy, Clara, that is exactly what we would have called you.' There was a lull. Sunny could see her father had questions brewing behind the immediate adoration.

'So, Michael what?'

'Hyphenated.' Clara replied.

'Pardon?' Eric glanced at Sunny, puzzled. 'Not Fernando?'

'We are not into that kind of thing, Daddy.'

'But what about the baby?'

'He will have what he really needs. Not just Sunny's name.'

Sunny didn't entirely agree, but tried not to let her dismissal of old conventions niggle him. He reached for a bottle. 'Gin and tonic? Ice and lemon?' He knew when a drink was required. There were some things he had learnt very well from his father.

A lifetime earlier, when it had been first confirmed that Clara was pregnant, Sunny had set about looking for a house with a third bedroom, a photographer's attic and a view of some empty London sky. The last of his father's money was going to provide the first instalment of a proper home for the old man's grandchild.

He found the place in Hornsey, not far from Clara's flat but oriented north rather than south into the city. There was a view of Alexandra Palace and the sky above. The estate agent said it was a good time to buy: prices had stalled briefly in the aftermath of the riots further east in Tottenham, but Clara was more persuaded by the elderly Turkish lady who was selling up. She showed an intense interest in the unborn child and gave Clara packets of herbal medicine and childcare advice every time they met. She'd look over Clara's bump with an almost familial pride. She left the carpets for free, because she thought the yellow polypropylene in the hall would cheer the baby and wanted to leave her furniture too, a Parker Knoll suite with floral patterns and a pine kitchen table, at next to nothing. 'What for furniture, where I'm going? And you, I think soon you will have no time for anything.'

Settled in his house, Sunny had assumed that they would teach the baby to speak, bringing him into a world of bowdlerized English; but it was Mikey who was teaching them a new language. For months that quickly turned into years they were incapacitated and could only speak to other flummoxed first-timers who like themselves lived in a sleep-deprived sub-world of elemental urges and umbilical plugs, who understood that conversations had to be punctuated by sudden squawks and burbles, kutchi-coos and pipi-poos flying between caged playpens and tilted high chairs.

Sunny had never thought he would go back to engineering – that is to say to the business of applied science and construction design – but that is precisely what he found himself doing. The house had been renovated in the early 1970s by a Struwwelpeter devotee – every imaginable child-unfriendly, baby-unproofed surface, texture, plane, corner and device had been imported into the house. Danger lurked everywhere. 'It is not easy,' he confessed to Clara. 'I'm not handy like your dad.'

Eric was a civil engineer who had been at the same firm for all of his working life. He said he had been good at drawing but preferred to build things. Doodling and fooling around was not for him. 'I like to put my time to good use, don't you?' He had said pointedly to Sunny at their first meeting. 'I like to read, of course. History and biography particularly. There is a great deal to be learnt outside fiction.'

Between the snuffles and the colic bubbles, Clara came to the view that she could not go back to work full-time when her maternity leave was over. 'Gumbo says I can reduce my hours if I go into the new budget team, but the money will be less.'

Sunny shrugged. 'If you are happy to crunch numbers, that's OK. We'll find extra income.'

Clara abandoned her sable brushes and sank into baby baths and wax crayons; Sunny took his camera and photographed mother and son, finding in each frame an escape from the mundane. While she clucked, he clicked, thinking about the other couples they'd met at their antenatal classes, and after Clara's postnatal sessions. There were a lot of babies in the neighbourhood, and a huge desire among their parents to retain the baby-glow in glossy reproductions. Not many of them had the time or know-how to do really big, heart-plucking, high-quality pictures of their bundles of joy. The other mothers they met at the park seemed befuddled by any technology not directly linked to the life-support system of a Maclaren buggy. And their partners were apparently all too busy pedalling furiously between alcoholism and workaholism to discover any real pleasure in a viewfinder. 'A perfect opportunity,' Sunny explained to Clara in a rare moment of lucidity.

He put a card on the bulletin board outside the children's library with a pin-sharp photo of Michael, bright-eyed, rising like a fish to the surface of his mother's attention. A brilliant lure. He framed the card with paper tassels giving his telephone number and the prospect of the best baby pictures in the world.

His first client arrived while he was still pressing the thumbtacks into place. She was one of the librarians. A pleasant young woman with a freckled brown face and a lopsided afro. She was unusually dedicated to books, even for a librarian, and always had one open in her hand. She would read as she date-stamped, stacked returns or carried newspapers to the stands. When she left the library to go home she would read her way to the bus stop holding a torch to the page.

She came up with a huge tome and coughed behind him. 'I would like a photograph. Yes.'

She didn't look like a mother, although Sunny was beginning to realize that they came in all shapes and sizes and habits, and sometimes seemed most unsuited for the job.

'Great.'

She flicked a page over and took a quick glance. 'You do cats, yes?'

'Babies are what I've been concentrating on.'

'She's a kitten.'

He wasn't sure whether he should be diversifying so soon. On the other hand, the kiddies section in the library was a very busy one and she looked quite influential, even if she was probably not directly connected to the NCT coffee network.

'OK. Where?'

'You know that Palm Court with the Sphinx in Ally Pally? Do you? I'd like a picture of Kimmie there. She so adores the Sphinx.'

The following week he managed to do two alpha kids. Requests trickled in after that, providing a modest turnover. He put adverts in all the branch libraries and in the windows of newsagents as far afield as Muswell Hill, Southgate and Edmonton. Black and white was the key. Everyone had their colour snaps, but a classic black and white 8x10 made new parents feel that they were still upwardly mobile despite the burden of fast fattening progeny, soiled nappies and shambolic wardrobes reeking of ammonia and Sudocrem.

One evening, just before collapsing into a brief snatch of sleep, Clara sniffed at her baby's eggy head and murmured that someone at the infants' club had been talking about video cameras. Everyone had gone potty over the idea of capturing the first walk, the first words, the first birthday. She looked at Sunny, her tired eyes briefly flaring at the possibilities. 'Maybe you should do filmings for special occasions?'

'I am a dream merchant, my dear. I give them dreams about the future, glamour retouched. They look at their baby in my glossy pictures and they see *Vogue* around the corner. The video business is . . . documentary. Any fly on the wall could do it.' He laughed.

But it made sense. Not many people wanted to spend money on another Japanese gizmo. Sunny took Clara's advice and invested in a state-of-the-art camcorder. He found he was quickly in demand. Every week there was some kid speaking her first words, or rising to his feet and taking those first astonishing steps. He'd get calls and repeat calls. Emergency calls. 'Goldilocks is playing the piano! Come, quick.' Those who had their son's first steps on video were hooked. They had to have the hands-free walk, the Eureka rhapsody, the monkey-moment with the TV remote, the precocious delight in a note of Beethoven or the tinkling of The Byrds. He gave them raw footage, edited highlights, life stories. He was cheap and available at almost any time, day or night, like Govinder in his corner shop strewn with emergency supplies of milk, cigarettes and loo paper.

Mikey was a model child, and Sunny practised on him, learning the speed and accidents of growth; using them to make the images by which childhood would be remembered for ever in the middle terraces of outer London.

*

In time though, as Mikey's third birthday approached, Sunny began to feel that baby pictures might have been another of his misjudgements. Business slowed down. Camcorders dropped in price and his customers began to do their own thing. It was also becoming clear to Sunny that something more important was going on around him, that he should be out on the streets, not in the front rooms and cluttered kitchens of north London. Even the day of the famous fatwa passed him by almost unnoticed; he was busy photographing a birthday party in Finsbury Park. He realized, too late, that 1989 was the year for political photography, not portrait pieces: Bradford, Tiananmen, Prague, Bucharest. And Sri Lanka, where beauty had been criminally debased, year after year, with a death toll nobody could have imagined. He knew from looking at the reporters on the screen, the panned shot and the quick zoom, that he was missing something vital. He had a son but had run out of adrenalin.

Clara's new job was not working out the way she had expected either. 'I can't do it any more,' she complained one morning, scrabbling around for her flat black shoes.

'Do what? The budget?'

'Leaving him. Mikey looks so forlorn.' She began to excavate a pile of plastic toys in the hall.

'Leaving him with me?'

'You are so preoccupied all the time. You don't talk to him.'

'How do you know? Does he tell you that? We talk a lot.' He saw one of the nunnish shoes behind the rain-hood of the buggy and handed it to her.

'Where was that?' She looked at him as if he was the culprit.

'Just here.'

She slipped it on. 'You only talk to get him into a picture. You are not really talking to him, you just tell him what to do. How will he ever learn anything?'

She was right. He didn't like chit-chat. How could he talk to the boy? What did a little person like that have to talk about? Sunny thought of his own childhood. He knew nothing and saw nothing in those early years. He had no images from the year dot to four, except for a bit of sunlight. A leaf on a red step. The hedge he used to put his hand into. A ball. Skin. The grey felt hammer on a piano string he did not want to hear. Big things happened even in those days: the Prime Minister of Ceylon had been shot dead not too far away from where Sunny was playing the lone Spitfire against a carefully imagined Luftwaffe, but it made no impression on him. There was no photograph in his head of that event. Only perhaps a vague memory of a shout from the kitchen. A worried conversation as darkness fell and Lester had ambled from one room to another, trying to find the right words with which to fill the front page, the correct point for a full stop. Sunny thought of his mother checking the scales, becoming increasingly unsure of everything.

'It was only after I started at Harpo's that I was able to listen to piano music again. I borrowed recordings of Beethoven, Chopin, Debussy from the library and worked my way down to Ravel and Tchaikovsky. My mother must have played their compositions every day when I was a child, but I don't know . . .'

'You must remember the *Nocturnes*.' Clara closed her eyes, as if even she could hear the notes. She was exhausted.

'All I remember are those pupils of hers, taking over her piano. And then, at night, the clatter of my father's typewriter drowning everything out.'

Clara responded with something between a sigh and a snore.

Sunny took another sip of wine, and felt himself becoming too talkative. 'She told me once – I must have reached the magic age of seven – that her piano had seven octaves and if she could find the right sequence in which to play the notes, she'd have the key to open any heart. Sometimes I see her fingers move in the photograph. Then everything becomes a blur.'

He wondered whether he'd find her, or hear her music, if he ever went back to their actual house in Colombo. He glanced at Clara. She was fast asleep, her thin stretched eyelids barely able to keep her dreams in.

'Give up the job if it is making you so tired and unhappy. I can do something more than baby photos. I could go into photojournalism. News.'

'How can you do news?' Clara asked the obvious question. 'You never know what's going on. You hardly even read the newspaper.'

'You were never a mother, until Mikey came.'

'That's different.'

'My father was once a journalist. I watch TV. I know there is a picture I will one day take. Our lives cannot be for nothing.'

'One? What good would one picture do?'

'A perfect picture, where the whole world holds its breath.' The phrase echoed in his head. For a moment he felt that was all he needed. It might not change the world, but it would make all the difference to him. It would allow him to believe that somehow everything moves for a purpose. And that for once he might get something absolutely right and remove the doubt that never stopped growing inside, slowly, inexorably distorting everything in his life. He wanted it not only for himself but also for his son.

'All I know, Sunny, is that we need to feed Mikey. We have to feed him every day.'

The watchmaker's shop opposite the kebab joint was on the verge of collapse. Mr Stan Ladek, the owner, had been cramped in it for years, growing awkwardly into whatever space his body could find. He had enormous hands with overgrown knuckles and stubby, square fingers that looked as though they might have difficulty gripping a crowbar, never mind a pair of tweezers. But, invariably, there were tweezers peeping out of his fist, or a jeweller's miniature screwdriver twinkling under his anglepoise. He would often have an eyepiece lodged between his right cheekbone and his brow, but with the growing proliferation of electronic watches there was less call for his miniaturist skills; his days were numbered. Sunny first met him when he popped in for a replacement watch battery.

'What's that?' He frowned. His shoulders were hunched and his immense balding head rushed downward to a small vanishing chin.

Sunny showed him the dead battery.

'Battery? No batteries. I don't keep batteries. Why would I keep batteries? For real time, young man, you must put energy in manually and measure its release. Wind and watch it unwind. Or use motion, kinetic energy, to build up . . .'

'Yes.' Sunny nodded. 'Yes, those are the watches.'

'Timepieces.' He glared. 'My father *made* them. I am still learning only to mend them.'

'Was this his shop?' Sunny imagined a lineage back into the nineteenth century.

'Pardubice,' the old man replied. His free eye brightened. 'He had a shop in Pardubice. Czechoslovakia, you know? Everybody else was at the factory. He made a watch that you could wear in the spring. The spa. You know spa? What it is? Not the shop. The spa.'

'Yes. Spa.'

'Could have made him a fortune.'

'It didn't?'

Mr Ladek looked at Sunny with a strange protective kindness growing over his face. 'No. And now, I don't even have that little blighter.'

Surrounded by old watches and small clocks, submerged in a sea of clicks and ticks, Sunny felt time stand still, as though Cartier-Bresson himself had captured them in his magic box.

Mr Ladek watched him without a word. Then, as though making amends, said, 'I've tried to make one like it.' He opened a drawer and pulled out a silver timepiece. 'The problem is the heat. Tepid is fine. But in a hot spa, the seal will go.' He snapped a colossal finger.

'Is that the only problem?'

'Oh, no. No. But it is the present problem. The time has come for me to devote myself to perfecting this. It will do much more than tick in a teapot. It will undo time for me.'

'What do you mean undo?'

'It is a suspicion I have.' He looked down at the dial on the table. 'I think it is possible for some restitution. The time is close, I think, for me to give up this place and find some . . .' He was suddenly at a loss. He plucked absently at his braces. 'You know, this Havel's velvet business. Who could have believed such a thing was possible? That a revolution would come from juveniles whose heads had gone soft with pop music? That you could go back to the beginning with such youngsters? You are a young man. That is very good.'

Two months later Stan Ladek had sold the lease to Sunny and returned to Czechoslovakia. 'I was born there.' He quickly blew his nose on a voluminous red handkerchief. 'I would like to see it again before I die. I'd like to hear my real name again, as it was. Stanislav . . . Why? I don't know. Perhaps it is the foolishness of the old and lonely.'

The lawyer was a friend of Stan's and did all the paperwork. Sunny trusted him. The lease was long enough, he said, for anyone to get started, even selling second-hand cameras.

Clara pulled at her mouth with her fingers, slowly pinching each lip in turn. 'I must say I never saw you as a shopkeeper.' She glanced around the kitchen. The windows needed cleaning. There were cracks around the door frame.

'I am not a shopkeeper. This is more like being a teacher. I will be helping people create better photographs. Using skill, rather than just technology.'

This alarmed her even more. 'But you have to be able to sell cameras, don't you? You're not giving evening classes.'

SNAP was to be the name. 'Hopefully it might quicken the heart a little. Someone will see their dream machine and feel *snap*, there is the answer. Then they'll snap it up – their bargain.' Clara wasn't bowled over, but Mikey loved the word and kept repeating it. Sunny liked the modern urgency of the name and the way it contrasted with the stillness of a photograph freezing a moment. He put up a sign and distributed leaflets around the area. Clara relented and helped organize a mailshot to his old customers. Within a week Sunny had sold two cameras: a reliable, solid Pentax Spotmatic and a ridiculously expensive Nikon that he had never quite got on with.

'See.' He showed Clara the cheques. 'The beginning. You can give up that grumpy Gumbo.'

'I'm not so sure.'

'Maybe we should try for a second baby. A brother or sister for Mikey? Do you think . . .'

'We can't afford it.' She hung up her long grey winter coat. The shiny lining was ripped around the sleeves. Two of the marbled buttons were missing.

'You need a new coat.'

'Not yet.' She pulled a loose thread off the cuff. 'I can wait for the sales.'

Sunny started scouting around Holborn for second-hand stock and picking up mail-order bargains that he could pass on with real, valuable advice – a few choice historical anecdotes – to the growing arty community of their up-and-coming neighbourhood. It wasn't exactly a lucrative business, but it was a reasonably honest and pleasurable one. He took fewer and fewer pictures for the sake of the shape, the line, the pattern of the image, and more and more simply to check out the equipment. There was more satisfaction to be found in the turn of a knob, the pressure of the button, the click of a shutter, the smooth flip of the internal mirror, than in composition. His attention completely shifted from the end result to the mechanics of photography.

When the Gulf War started, he realized he had no desire to be out in a desert capturing the effects of a falling bomb. He preferred to stick to things that he was beginning to understand – the history of optics, steel, precision, the story of light, smart lenses. He wanted to shield Mikey's childhood from the bullying world around and tried to concentrate on domestic survival skills.

Clara tried parenting manuals but preferred intuition. She'd read out a passage or two of some Dr Quack and then toss the book into the bin. 'Don't do this, don't do that . . . You'd think we were all born with bullet points up here the way they go on.' She abandoned everything to urges in herself. She'd say she knew what her child needed, dismissing the cowpats of the over-opinionated, much in the same way as Sunny ignored the instruction pages that the new breed of camera producers offered in a dozen translations of gobbledegook.

Social life was agreeably non-existent. Nothing had weight, nothing mattered but the chores, the schedules, the trappings of the moment. To him it was like taking a photograph, when the world is reduced to a measurement of light, a balance of shape, an existence in the space of a mind – not quite in the skull and not quite outside. Like composing or playing music, or football, or cricket. Solving an equation or riding a bike. Finding a solution for one thing, while excluding everything else. In a sense their lives were settled, but he knew something was not quite right. Not just out in the world, but in himself. And in Clara. And between them. Something had gone, slipped out along with the baby oil and the bath water. The bond they had forged was being worn away by the grit and grain of passing days and piles of plastic toys. Very occasionally she would try to sketch Mikey sleeping; it seemed to frustrate her more than assuage anything. Sometimes a blustery red bill would arrive and induce a panic, but Sunny kept his mouth shut. Words had been no good for his mother, and in the end they had failed his father.

Their annual holiday was always brief and British: up to Liverpool to see Clara's parents and then a few days in Wales. The motorway journey this time was easy; an audio tape of *The Secret Flight* kept Mikey hooked until Chorley and after that he slept the rest of the way. Clara offered to drive and then fell asleep too. Both of them were fighting a losing battle against a school-borne cold. Sunny gripped the steering wheel and tried to stem his growing sense of inadequacy. He was not even providing vitamins for his unconsecrated family.

Beryl, Clara's mother, looked on Mikey as the saviour of her dotage. 'You'll be a doctor when you grow up, Michael, won't you, buttercup? Look after your Granny when the time comes.' She had aged since Sunny had first met her. Her strong jaw seemed to have lost its way in the drapery that had been drawn lower each year. She tended to emit her words through clenched teeth, not out of anger but an early training in elocution. Eric, a little hard of hearing, usually ignored her remarks. 'If you don't move your lips, my dear, I can't even guess what you are saying.'

Beryl quickly got Clara and Mikey up into their rooms with Lemsip for her and Calpol for him. Eric offered Sunny a coffee and said that in his opinion the air in London was very poor indeed.

'You see, you don't have the north wind, do you, to blow out the cobwebs? And all those tall buildings, they are designed to keep the bad air in the city. Actually, bad planning goes back a long way. You've read Pepys? You'll see the trouble there. Now, Paris, on the other hand, has the right profile. The place could be cleared of an Asian flu epidemic within days. No high-rise buildings.'

'How's the Chunnel?' Sunny asked between sips, thinking of the road, the lights and the wheels. Eric was working on a ventilation component for the Channel tunnel project.

Eric pulled at his chin and waggled it. 'Ah, yes, you are quite right. You should have been an engineer, Sunny. Getting the air moving is the real trick. It has not been easy. There is still some concern about staleness. How about a stroll in the garden?'

The Easton garden was a jumbled-up affair. Quite at odds with the measured, precise world of Eric's professional life, unless one saw it as a permanent construction site, the equivalent of a laboratory where he experimented with wild ideas about wind tunnels, excavations and techniques of earth moving. The sheer magnitude of the disruption to an otherwise unremarkable plot of land suggested that Eric, rather than Beryl, was behind it, but the truth was that both of them vented their frustrations on the garden. It hadn't always been so. In the early days, Clara had told Sunny, their garden was almost Elizabethan in its graceful artistry. A small raised rectangle with borders of pansies and bright evergreens. A little overgrown in places, but colourful. There had been a slight slope to the lawn that wouldn't have caused much consternation even for a game of croquet, but as the couple rushed towards their silver seventies, hunting for bizarre comforts to compensate for the history of broken crockery, the alteration had been radical. The slope had turned into a mountain of scrap, bits of building debris had been melded into miniature promontories, holes were dug, filled and dug again, ponds overflowed. There was even a miniature swamp. The two of them – Beryl and Eric – didn't seem to notice the pandemonium. They only ever saw one bit at a time – a flowering bush, a sunny paving stone, yellow autumn berries – and appeared perfectly happy with the skimble-skamble hazards they'd created out of the thin air of a carefully veiled marriage.

'Dad, why are we here?' Mikey asked when they had finished tying the last of the tent's guy ropes.

'What do you mean?' Sunny wasn't sure if this was one of those grand metaphysical questions that occur out of the blue to some kids.

'Why are we here?' Mikey donned a grubby fleece and

flicked back the hood. He was eight years old. It was the summer of 1994.

'You mean on this earth? Or in Wales?' They had a pitch on Shell Island, with a good view of the sea and, given a judicious bit of parking, protection from the evening gales.

Clara popped her head out of the inner compartment where she was untying the sleeping bags. 'The campsite is a lot cheaper than the other places on offer.'

Sunny tested a peg. 'Why we are here is a big question.'

'No, Dad. I don't mean why are we *here*. I mean why do we *come* here? We are not Welsh.'

Clara squinted as she moved out into the sunlight. Sunny wondered if she was going to tell Mickey of his unexpected conception not far down the coast, below a sky full of swallows, but she seemed absorbed in something else.

He remembered the farmhouse where Clara was sure it had happened. The slate of the fireplace solid, like a sea of painted ripples. Cool despite the crackling flames. The hearth about three inches thick and made of one stratified piece set into the stone walls at each end. The front edge had been rounded and made safe. The mirror-like surface, the blackness of the rock, had absorbed all his inner uncertainties as simply as charcoal pulls poison from bile. Something more than mica had been metamorphosed there. The slate understood pressure; it could take the spin of the earth and make something beautiful out of it. When he had entered Clara's warm naked body, he'd felt the air press them into one shape, as it did the hills around them. She said later that she felt something come into being there. Something unstoppable like a balloon released underwater, rising up to the surface, lifting her into a new world.

What ties a person to a place? He thought of his father finding a home in a fantasy. Makati. Almost a whole life spent somewhere else. His mother giving up her place on earth. Who has a claim on any place? The loudest, the nearest, or the most recent?

He looked at Mikey. The boy was waiting for an answer.

'I like to come because the sea and the mountains answer something in me. They call it *hiraeth* here. That's the word for it.'

'What does it mean?'

'I can't explain it. A kind of longing for something that goes to the heart of everything . . . You'll understand one day. You'll recognize the feeling.'

Mikey wrinkled up his nose. He wasn't convinced. He was a tall lad for his age and when he was unsure of anything his whole centre of gravity would shift; he'd move his head back as if he was afraid. He would look like he was about to topple and Sunny would want to reach out and catch him, steady him, reassure him, show him that the world was of our own making and that there was nothing we should fear in it, nothing that could not be righted, made good. The movement was something he might have picked up from his father, but to Sunny it seemed more to do with the boy's age, his generation, the tenderness we all begin with.

The sun slowly sank through a bank of bluish clouds furled on the horizon. Then a quiet circle of pale western light spread over the water. Sunny had a pan of pasta boiling on a small gas Primus outside the tent. He opened a Coke and shared it with Mikey. Clara had gone to the shower block by the main gate.

The sea was calm. Beneath the surface millions of shells were being swept towards the shore, being crushed as they had been over the ages. Sunny thought about how he had ended up here, in the same place as them, but intact. He wanted to tell Mikey about it, but saw that the boy was looking at the sky in wonder.

'Will we see stars?'

The sky was clear; the clouds had been pulled right down below the horizon. 'Yes, we will see the stars tonight.'

'How many?

'Millions. Like the shells on the beach.'

'Which do you like more? The stars or the shells?' Mikey's upturned eyes were like young scallop shells, filled with everlasting light.

'I can't choose.' It was the combination he liked, and being able to appreciate both.

The boy nodded, on the brink of something. 'I like it here too,' he said. 'I don't know whether I would really want to be up there like in a cruiser.' He twisted his mouth and pulled a face. 'But I don't know. It might be really good to be, like, *in* the stars.'

'Well, you know, in a way we are.'

Sunny had told his father once how he had no wish to go anywhere, least of all outside their world. He meant the earth – he thought Apollo was a waste of money. Lester had assumed he was talking about the domestic world he had extended for his son from Colombo out to Manila, and was dismayed. 'You need to know what's going on,' Lester had said. 'It is important that you expand your horizons. Don't dwell on the problems of the past.'

After Mikey went to sleep, Sunny warmed himself with a whisky and stared at the multiplying stars.

'It's good to be out here,' he said to Clara when she joined him. 'Isn't it?'

She huddled into the soft velour folds of her dressing gown and mumbled a kind of sleepy agreement.

'Do you think we should move out?' He poured a drink for her.

There was no immediate response. Then, she laughed lightly. 'I thought you said it was good here.'

'Out of London, I mean. Maybe we should move somewhere a little less cramped.'

'The country?' There had been a lot of Sunday articles about the flight from town to country recently.

'I was thinking that Mikey has known only London.'

'And here. And the other places we've been. Liverpool.' She sounded surprised. 'You saw what happened to the damson pair?' A couple – parents of one of Mikey's classmates – had decamped to Norfolk and re-camped swiftly when they found village life more circumscribed than city life, and damson jam too much to take by the pint.

'Yes. But what about Liverpool? Or this side of the Mersey, where you grew up? Wouldn't you like it?'

Clara went very quiet. Her breath misted the air. 'Would you go back now to your Manila to live? Or Colombo?'

'That's different. That world has gone. The past was very different. I couldn't go back.'

'You think Birkenhead has stayed the same? Merseyside?'

'Maybe it has got better? You could be in Wales in less than an hour.'

'I am not going back. Sorry, but that is just impossible.' She didn't wait to hear any more. She dumped her cup into the pail of washing-up water and crawled back into the main sleeping section of the tent. She unzipped a sleeping bag and, a few seconds later, zipped it up again.

Sunny wasn't sure what to think. He wanted more than he had. Something more. From her, from himself, from the place in which they found themselves.

In the morning, the sun shone in through the small mesh window on to Clara's half-covered face. Her hair seemed to whiten in the early light even as the skin on her upper cheek reddened, warmed by the rays. He noticed a brown mole below her left ear that he'd never seen before; perhaps it had grown bigger. The fine down on her neck appeared to have grown too. A cornfield in silk. As he slipped out of the sleeping bag, she moved an arm under the yellow corded edge. Her lips, swollen from slumber, were slightly open. He watched her breathe; the creases in her face rippled. He wanted to kiss her as he hadn't done in years, but he didn't want to wake her. There was peace to her sleep that seemed more valuable than the tug of a homeless thought, any fleeting moment of desire.

In the other compartment Mikey was in as deep a slumber; his young body completely engrossed in growing. Sunny stepped out on to the grass.

Clara's preference to stay in London surprised him. He

had always thought she would be the one who'd want to leave the city and that he would be the one who would want to stay. He didn't really know any other place in Britain; everywhere else would harbour such uncertainties of belonging, race and class. There was nowhere that could be said to be his. Birkenhead, where they had some connection – a reason for being there – was the only possibility. That connection though was something rather more for her; not a link but a web constructed by others. Not only her family, but also Ranil's family, the Veeraswamys, the whole mob would be there, weaving an inescapable net out of the past. It wouldn't do. He could see that. All those simmering memories of petty parental rows and pointless bickering. But then, he wondered, what is it we are weaving for ourselves between Alexandra Palace and Archway? A safety net for Mikey? For ourselves? Clara liked to keep in touch. Didn't that inevitably create a web?

He remembered what the owner of the cottage where Mikey had been conceived had told him. 'My husband could never leave Wales, you know. He says it is too beautiful. That is the trouble with being born in these parts. You can never leave, you know, until the day you are called, and even then they say you only go into the next valley.' She'd untied the carrier bag she'd used to cover her head and had shaken off the rain.

'Ah, but I hear your country is very beautiful too. A lovely island you have, is that not so? Never mind, you are most welcome here. We need folk to come. There are not so many of us being born here any more. Never mind the foolishness people talk these days. We all need some healing and this is a good place for it.'

A place of healing was what Sunny had been seeking all his life.

He went back to the car and got out his Pentax and an old Hoya 150 mm telephoto lens. He wanted to make a composition again, feel the peace of a scene captured on his own terms.

Mikey was growing fast. Sunny could sense it. Something frighteningly adult in the way he flinched. The monologue in his head had started. That moment when the world and you are no longer one, but you are in one place and the world is out there, a world on which you keep a running commentary. Animals don't do it. Infants don't do it. It comes when you become aware that the commentary is yours and you are talking to yourself. Few manage to break the skin that then forms and return to childhood. Soon, Sunny felt, it would be impossible for Mikey to hear anything he said; his own voice would slowly drown out his father's, until he learned, too late, that he could no longer hear those who were nearest.

'Daddy.' He had come up behind Sunny. 'Daddy, what are you looking at?'

Sunny lowered the camera. 'Nothing.'

'The sea?'

'Yes, the sea, I suppose.'

'What's there? Are you taking a picture?'

His instinct was to deny it. He was trying to do the impossible, capture a sense of things passing. He had to make a conscious effort to overcome the desire to hide in silence. He swallowed hard. 'Yes, a picture. I wanted to make a picture of that boat in the middle of nowhere. The sea is so . . . unpredictable.' He wished he could say something more meaningful.

'Can I see?' Mikey wanted to see the same thing his father had seen. A patch of sea, a sail brought up close through the magnifying lens.

'Be careful.' Sunny knew he shouldn't have said it. He restrained himself from putting the camera strap over the boy's head. Mikey did it himself. Then he lifted the camera to his eye, holding the barrel of the Hoya in one hand and the light metal body in the other. He let his weight drop to one leg; his elbow rested against his body as he squinted through the viewfinder. He had learnt all this by himself. Sunny had never shown him how to hold a camera. He had never thought to; he wouldn't have known how to.

The boy turned the focus ring. 'There's two,' he said. 'Two boats.'

Sunny took the camera back and looked again. The boy was right. There were two boats going in the same direction. 'Do you want to take a picture?'

'With that?'

'What about yours?' Sunny had given him a small black box Yashica automatic for his birthday. He hardly ever used it. 'Did you bring it?'

'Oh-oh.' Mikey made a face, stretching his mouth and lowering his lip the way Clara did. 'I don't know where it is.'

'Is it in your bag?'

'Mummy will know.'

'I'm sure she will, but it is your camera.' Ownership, care, concern. The mantra bubbled in his head.

'I'll *be* a camera,' Mikey said suddenly. He put a fist to his eye and looked through the aperture he made with his fingers and thumb. He clicked his tongue and shut his eyes. 'There. It's inside now.' He pointed to his head. 'I've got it.'

'Good. You've got it, all right. But if you had your camera and got it in there, then you could show it to us too.'

'You've got it too.'

'Yes, but what about other people? Mummy? She's not seen it.'

The breeze lifted. It seemed to have given Mikey something; he was more talkative than usual. 'She'll see it when she comes out.'

'It won't be the same.'

'The sea will still be there.'

'The boat – the two boats – might not.' That was the point, Sunny wanted to say. With the camera you had a description of what was in front of the lens, sometimes even of things not there, of absence. It was not like words, with which you must always construct, or reconstruct, or like Clara's paintings, which were things in themselves. The image on the film was light, just as it was when you held your breath and time stopped. That was all and everything.

Mikey was waiting for him to continue; Sunny couldn't find the words. He wanted to say: a real photograph is as true as it gets. 'The picture on the film is of the moment,' he said in the end. He knew this didn't mean much to Mikey. The moment, at his age, was not of great significance; for him, there was the prospect of an abundance of them. A seagull swooped on to the beach below.

'There, get that, Dad. The bird.'

It flapped away before Sunny could focus. He was too busy thinking about his son and how he himself had so easily stepped back from his father.

'Taking pictures?' Clara had emerged from the tent. Her dressing gown billowed in the breeze, her hair was in tangles.

'Not really.'

'Missed.' Mikey tried to hide his smile.

'What time is it?' She braced herself against the wind, fast and steady; she seemed to grow stronger before her son.

'I don't know,' Sunny said. On that bare small island, for a moment, it seemed not to matter.

The next day they climbed up a hill to see the view of the river merging with the sea.

'This river, where does it start?' Sunny asked Clara.

'Lots of little ones go into each other. There's no one starting point.'

The idea intrigued him. As they stood on the side of the hill, staring down through the branches at the wide pewter-tinged estuary that absorbed the rain seeping out of a hundred hills, drawing water from a thousand hidden springs behind them, around them, and below them, it came to him that perhaps we ourselves begin and end in a similar way. Yes, our bodies begin with one cell and perhaps end only when the last of the billions we've grown has been extinguished. But our minds, our conscious selves, like the story we make of our lives, must be something more. A deep but temporary unity – a stretch of river – fed by a network of tributaries.

Clara gave Mikey a chocolate bar. Sunny watched him carefully unwrap it and nibble a piece. The boy was lost in thought, his own private torrent of thoughts. Sunny wished he could say something but it was hard enough to hold back the tears.

On the last day, Mikey spent most of the morning exploring rock pools. He was looking for fish with his little net while Sunny looked for fossils, bits of calcified past to give him a sense of the shape of the world. Clara was up on the dunes, engrossed in her watercolours for the first time in ages. Sunny had a collection of shells and sea gems in a plastic bag – ringed clams, faded molluscs, whalebone and tiny bleached cauliflower sponge heads – but he was beginning to despair of finding anything that could really compete with the slivers of live flesh Mikey was seeking as he crouched on the rocks, poking the green handle of his net into the water. He looked content on his own, as though he needed no one. The gulls in the air were no freer.

Up on the cliff bells tinkled. A line of people materialized, chanting and hopping like puppets with strings up to heaven. Sunny heard the '*Hari Krishnas*,' and '*Ram, Ram*,' and thought of Ranil up in the Himalayas. He wondered if Ranil had been to this beach before, as a child growing up in the north-west of England. Like Clara, he might have sat among the same dunes, come down to these same rock pools to collect shells and soak up the sun. They belonged to the same world.

Clara, her picture finished, came up to Mikey and stood beside him, stirring the water with her bare foot. He looked up to her and held her hand. A mother and her son. Sunny heard him talking to her but couldn't catch the words. The sea wind had picked up.

GROUND GLASS

1994

IN HIS Christmas card of 1994, which featured the three wise men, Hector wrote to say that after a lifetime of hesitation he had finally made his most important move. He had married Aunty Lillie. He explained that on the day they had met in Manila for Lester's funeral, their separate journeys had fallen into perspective. They had seen how their individual quests had been designed so that their paths would one day be brought to a point of true convergence. That point had finally been reached twelve years later in the propitious Year of the Rooster. The wedding had taken place at a small lodge in the misty Sri Lankan hill town of Haputale. They had both joined an eclectic but deeply rooted spiritual group. They were no longer permitted to travel, other than by land: never to touch the cruel sea was one of their precepts. Hector would have loved to bring Lillie to London, but could not now until Adam's bridge was built to link the island to India, and the Channel tunnel became a reality. It was not a joke. Their idea was to stay put, he wrote, and create an energy centre for world peace on an island of fractured dreams. Aunty Lillie had added a note on a page ripped out of a school exercise book. It turned out to be a prayer for national harmony through a fat-free diet. She'd remained faithful to her principles: ice cream was still a no-no.

Sunny sent them his congratulations. When he told Clara about the marriage, she laughed, as though they were the young ones, and she and Sunny knew better.

Clara was also undergoing a metamorphosis. After the summer holidays she had brought out all her old paint boxes that over the last decade had been shoved behind jigsaws, board games and puzzle books. She'd cut up her maternity dresses into smocks and started splashing colours about as if she was back in kindergarten.

'I've enrolled in an evening class. Art and Design.' Her hair was tied back tight. Her face gleamed as though she had been on a treadmill all afternoon. 'It will help me decide which way to go in the future.'

'What do you mean in the future?'

'I don't know whether fine arts or graphics is really my thing. I am not going to spend my whole life in Gumbo's office, you know.'

'Graphics?'

'Why not?'

'Photography as well?'

In the doldrums after the festive season, Sunny read Hector's card again and felt unsettled by it. Hector and Lillie had closed a gap, but in doing so had widened the cracks in him. The need to fix the past, to plug the holes, felt intolerable. At a loss, he suggested a family trip to Sri Lanka. 'You know, I think I would really like to go.'

Clara shut her London gallery guide and snorted. 'What? You think now that everyone has been bombed in that place, it'll all be hunky-dory?'

'The government has changed. The new President has come in on a peace ticket.' The reign of deaths squads and the dark days of the south and north, the dead and disappeared, were said to be over. 'There is a ceasefire. No hostilities. Peace talks.'

'Oh, right. What about malaria? Dengue?' Clara had no intention of going anywhere. She had signed up for the spring session at City and Guilds before she was halfway through her introductory graphics module. The class seemed to give her a real buzz. She wasn't going to be thwarted by a phoney peace. 'You don't want Mikey risking all that, do you?'

He didn't want to expose his son to any danger. 'Fine, I'll go on my own then.'

'If you must go, I guess it is better now than later.'

'I'll be back in two weeks. No one comes into the shop at this time anyway.'

'I wasn't thinking of the shop.'

Sunny knew that. But what was there to talk about? The gulf was growing in front of him as well as behind him. He didn't know how to cross it. He only knew he wanted to do something soon. If nothing else, to see the place of his birth, the country he had lost sight of for more than a quarter of a century, and make it his again. Possibly produce some pictures that would show something more than ruined monuments and moral debasement. He wanted to do it before he got old, before he started forgetting everything, or not caring; before Hector, and even Aunty Lillie, vanished from the world.

*

There was no question of staying with Aunty Lillie and Hector. That would have been going too far. Hector had understood and had arranged for Sunny to stay with a niece of his instead – Mrs Adel Fonseka – who ran a guest house in Havelock Town. The room he was given had doors that opened straight on to a sandy garden very much like his earliest stamping ground. It was a pleasant house in a time warp off the main road. Even the phone in the house was restricted and didn't have an international connection. He had to go to one of the tourist hotels to get a call through to London.

Adel had the appearance of someone who still lived in the 1950s: stretch-fabric slacks, blouses with big bold buttons, sharp collars, earrings like knuckledusters and hair bunched purposefully, as if she were ready for a morning at a riding school. The impression she gave was one of awkwardly concealed warmth and neurotic household efficiency. She was only a couple of years older than Sunny, but she made him feel like her long-lost son. She had a splendid meal prepared for him, and immediately plied him with beer and spirits.

'Anytime you want to eat just let me know. You can order whatever you like. Our cook Padma is very good. She can make anything. And if you want to have a drink, just help yourself. Beer, liquor, cream soda. The notebook is by the fridge. Just write it in and do a tick. Like a minibar, no?'

Adel didn't eat with him; she sat at the opposite end of the dark mournful table and watched. She said she'd already had her meal and claimed that she never touched alcohol at home. Suddenly she bawled out. '*Mey, koheda vatura*?' An alarmed elderly woman emerged from the kitchen clutching a bottle of chilled water. 'I'll take some water,' Adel explained with a bashful smile.

For the rest of the evening she interrogated him on his plans. She especially wanted to know when he was going to visit Lillie and Hector. She was very fond of Hector and evidently a little unhappy about the marriage.

'You haven't seen Aunty Lillie for a long time, no? Not since her joining this crazy group? Or what?'

Sunny said that he had last seen her at his father's funeral. Adel was shocked. Sunny tried to change the subject and complimented her on her cook's liver curry. 'Very tasty.'

'Not only rice and curry. She makes excellent Wiener schnitzel and chicken chasseur. Tomorrow you like to try schnitzel?'

'I'm out for the day.'

'If you go to Uncle and Aunty, you'll definitely need something. At least an omelette when you come back. You know they don't eat, those two. Ramazan all the time. And all the time she is in a really dowdy sari. I don't know why. *Tikak pissu*, no? A little mad. I think so.'

Adel seemed to want to take over his life. The paying-guest scheme was not an economic venture but a kind of kinship game. Her husband had died soon after their marriage; she had no children. Enticing guests into the house was a means of gaining and consuming the family she had longed for, amalgamating husband to son in one go. That first night, after he made his excuses and retired to his room, Sunny found it difficult to sleep. It was not only the heat; the place seemed haunted.

The next morning, after another huge meal, he set off

for Rajagiriya where Hector and Lillie communed with their inner spirits in land-locked sanctity.

The driver of the hired car was an excitable young man in his early twenties. An excess of curly hair was in constant danger of completely obscuring his vision and large, grey teeth dwarfed the rest of his eager face. When Sunny told him where he wanted to go, the man gave a squawk of delight. 'My sister there. In Wellampitiya right next door, sir.'

'OK.' Sunny had no idea of the geography, it was all new territory.

'Coming from England, sir?' He leant to one side to take the first hard bend as though his old jalopy was leading in the Grand Prix.

Sunny gripped the dashboard with one hand, his specs with the other. 'Yes.'

The driver stepped on the accelerator and the engine gurgled. In a high, nervous voice he asked what had happened to cricket in England, why the white people of the Queen could not play the great game any more. He said he'd heard they were in deep shit.

Sunny had to confess that he knew nothing of the troubles affecting the England team or any other team. As the car shuddered over a broken stretch of the road, the driver sang the praises of the new Sri Lankan cricket squad. 'One day,' he crowed triumphantly. 'One day to win, sir. Captain first-class. I have my small cousin, sir, he wants to be a champion.'

'How old?'

'Fourteen. Nothing in his head but cricket. I try to get him a job in a Matara garage. Mechanic, but all he wants is to play cricket by the sea. Now, I think, maybe that is his future. What do you think, sir? Better anyhow than becoming a murderer, no, sir? Everybody knows killing people is bad, but that is all they teach these days.'

'Doesn't he have to make a living?'

'Professional sportsman. Matara Malli, that's what they'll call him.'

'And you?'

'Name is Piyasena, sir.'

They got to Rajagiriya after what seemed like a catalogue of reversals, wrong turns and detours but which Sunny was assured were clever shortcuts to beat a number of leftover security checkpoints from the Pope's recent visit. 'Anti-LTT.' Piyasena cheerily dropped the last E and made the Liberation Tigers of Tamil Eelam sound like London Transport rather than a paramilitary organization. At the high-level road he turned to Sunny without slowing down. 'Now where, sir?'

Sunny repeated the address and told him he didn't know exactly where it was.

'That's no good, sir. I also don't know.' They coasted down close to a small kiosk and he yelled out the address at a man dozing behind the counter. 'Hector, Hector *mahathaya?*' he added.

The man behind the counter picked up a newspaper and fanned himself.

Piyasena repeated his question and then opened his door to get out. The car began to roll. Sunny pulled the hand-brake and shouted. 'Brake!'

'Sorry, sir. Sorry.' He twisted around, one foot out, one in, and lunged for the lever, then saw Sunny's hand on it. 'OK, sir. No problem. That's the one.'

He left the door open and went over to some bystanders, then came back with his teeth flaring up into an enormous grin. 'OK, sir. All fine.'

Sunny knew they had found the right place the moment he saw the shrouded house with its wide veranda and large porch where a huge, cream American car lay stranded; surely the only American car of that opulent size for miles around, if not on the whole island?

'Here.'

The driver slammed on the brakes and Sunny just managed to protect himself with his hands.

'Sorry, sir.' He leapt out of the car. A moment later he ducked back in to pull up the handbrake. 'Full stop, sir. Flat ground. No problem.'

Sunny got out and rattled the gate. A dog howled somewhere in the back of the house. No one appeared. He made his way towards the veranda.

Aunty Lillie was meditating on a mat at the far end. Her face was lowered and only her grey hair tied in a bun was visible. She was thinner and smaller than Sunny remembered, but unmistakable. She was wearing a sari the colour of ash.

She looked up. 'Oh,' she said, as though Sunny was in the habit of popping in every other morning. 'Sanath, you are here already.' She didn't get up from her lotus position.

A chair scraped on the hard cement floor of the room behind her and a big figure loomed out of the shadows. 'Ah, so you have made it,' Hector boomed. 'Come, son . . . Sunny.' He ran the words together to cover up his embarrassment. 'You found us. Good.'

Sunny rummaged in his bag and pulled out a bottle of Scotch and a large packet of Walker's shortbread. He gave Hector the whisky, and Aunty Lillie the shortbread. She looked at the packet with some suspicion. 'Butter?'

'Yes.'

'Oh dear. We don't eat butter.'

Hector put a hand on her shoulder. 'For guests, my dear. With the whisky, for guests.'

'Guests? We don't encourage guests.'

'I thought chocolates would melt,' Sunny explained.

'Chocolates have butter.' Lillie's voice was brimming with severely tried patience. By now her nephew should at least have learnt the ingredients of confectionery.

'I also brought you a tablecloth.' Sunny quickly handed her a thin square parcel, gift-wrapped in the West End.

'What's that for?'

'We thought you might like it. Clara said it cleans very easily.'

'Isn't she with you?'

'She didn't come this time. Mikey is in school. I wanted to make this trip on my own.'

Hector made a humming noise.

Lillie opened the parcel and unfolded the white nylon cloth with its beaded patterns. She pulled it through her fingers, measuring it by the arm, like someone examining a fishing net. 'Very thin.'

'Yes. Easy care.'

She let it drop in a heap next to her and examined the inside of the wrapping paper. 'This Clara he says is a paper girl. English?'

Hector shuffled over to the wicker chairs arranged in a small circle in the open lounge. 'Come, why don't we sit down on the chairs. Lillie, enough meditating for the morning?'

Lillie sighed and uncrossed her legs. Putting one hand on the floor she pushed herself up and straightened out. 'Tea? You drink tea at least.'

'No sugar, just milk.'

'Good. They take a lot of sugar in England, no?'

'Liverpool.' Hector added with a twinkle in his eye. 'I remember the sugar money there. Slave trade. What a business.' He paused, recollecting his visit of all those years ago. 'And how's Tifus? You see him at all?'

'I saw him last summer when we went up to Clara's parents.'

'So, how's the fellow?'

'All right.' Then Sunny thought of how Tifus had looked. 'Actually he's been a little unhappy about things.'

'Those randy clients not kicking the bucket fast enough for him, eh? Surely he must be up for retirement by now?'

'He likes his work. I think it's more to do with his son, Ranil.' Delora had told him that Tifus wanted Ranil to settle down with a girl as Sunny had, instead of drifting like a cloud in the Himalayas.

'I remember the chap. Far-thinking fellow. Good aura.'

'He's gone a bit too far . . .' Sunny was about to say *spiritually*, but managed to stop himself in time.

'Far is not enough, you see. Far is like deep. Often mistaken as sufficient. But you need to also think *wide*. You understand?' He turned to Lillie. 'That is what we, in our twilight years, are learning. Isn't that so, old girl? Width. Breadth.'

She looked out at the broad, dark garden of tangled trees. 'Who is that fellow at the gate?'

'What fellow?' Hector started.

Sunny told them it must be his driver.

Lillie was outraged. 'What is wrong with the bus? All you have to do is change in Nawala, no? Hector?'

Sunny said he didn't know about the buses, or the whereabouts of Nawala. He needed a car.

'We don't need a car here, you know.' She was back in the business of unfair reprimands. 'Your mother spoiled you. I told her, you'll become a very lazy boy. Now look what has happened.'

'You have a big American car out there, I saw.' He wasn't going to take it. Not at nearly forty, for God's sake. Boy?

'Ah,' sighed Hector, happily ignoring the mounting tension. His big face settled into an easy, relaxed smile. 'You saw it? Beauty, no? I brought it back from Manila. I couldn't leave it after all those years but, you see, we don't use it. Petrol is too expensive now, and the tyres went flat. You can't get those American tyres very easily here. There's a chap down the High Level road starting a business in spares, but he says it will cost me a fortune. He has to steal them from the damn American Embassy.'

'You better go and find out what he wants.' Lillie's beady eyes were still fastened on the figure lounging by the gate. 'He probably wants to eat. There's a *kadé* up the road he can go to. We have no food. We are fasting today.'

Sunny went and gave Piyasena some money for a bite. He told him he could go see his sister as well as long as he returned by four o'clock.

Back on the veranda Sunny asked Hector about the fasting. 'Is it like the business with the Señora? The one in Quezon City?'

Lillie's head jerked up. Her gaunt face hardened. 'Philippines?'

'Señora? No, no, we have moved beyond old Zaramazov. Here, Sunny, we are preparing for the twenty-first century. It will be a very important period, you know. They talk about it being the age of China and all that, but that is a misreading. China has lost its way, you see. I was there, after all, at Tiananmen.'

'You were at Tiananmen?' Sunny wondered if Hector, like Aunty Lillie, had gone completely loopy.

He smiled. 'Yes. The bank's annual meeting. I was retired, but I got the invitation and went. You see, a lifetime of work makes you pumped up with air. You get a little fat, but feel good. Then when you stop working and retire, old as a prune, it all passes out of your backside like so much useless gas. You end up wrinkled up and feeling exceedingly stupid. You should stop working early, you see, or never stop. Your father was very clever, Sunny. He didn't stop. Anyway, I went to the meeting to get a second wind, as it were. Old Navaratnam came too. You remember our cricket coach, Rudy? Rudolf? I knew he wouldn't be able to resist a trip to Beijing. It was quite fantastic. Zhao himself came to the ADB meeting and said how they were listening to the young people demonstrating outside, how everything was part of the remaking of China for the new era.' Hector's breath was heavy. He gazed up at a couple of sparrows that flew, chirping, into the eaves. His eyes had stopped twinkling. 'Poor fellow. Poor young people.'

'Were you there when the shooting started?'

'Oh, no. The meeting was over by then. The authorities wouldn't let anyone stay on. Rudolf tried, I remember, but no chance. There was enough commotion for them with Gorby coming from Moscow and all that. But we saw the initial demonstration. That in itself was traumatic enough for Rudolf. You see, he too was an internationalist. While we were waiting for the coach to pick us up from their Friendship Store, he told me, "The ideals of the LTTE are now so corrupted, my only hope is China." His only hope. And you see what happened. Even there you see how, in the end, the old want to kill the young. Just like in 1971 here. And now those fellows in the jungle. It is the material world that corrupts . . .'

Lillie who had been listening intently to Hector's reminiscences, suddenly broke in. 'Politics. Everywhere this politics spoils everything. Evil, these people are evil.'

Hector tried to pacify her. 'Not evil, my dear. People are not evil, they are misguided.'

'Don't be a chump, Hector. Misguided? These gunrunners, these warmongers, these rapists, arsonists, killers, running around with knives and guns and dead people's bones? They are all spiteful, hateful, evil little monsters. Misbegotten, not misguided. All they want to do is kill.'

Sunny told them he'd thought a truce had been declared. The Pope himself had come, from Manila of all places, carrying doves, pigeons and what-have-you. Peace *was* possible. Joseph Vaz was canonized. The year 1995, people claimed, was the first window of opportunity in a wall of oblivion.

'Ha!' She looked at Sunny in disbelief. 'Peace? The only peace anybody here wants is a piece of somebody else's fat cake. Bread and butter, eggs and flour, have made them all go nuts.'

'On Tuesdays and Thursdays we eat nothing,' Hector added.

'I see. Thursdays, too.'

Lillie glared at both husband and nephew and then picked up the tablecloth and knotted it around her fist. They waited for the air to clear, taking in the sounds of cars on the high road, crows by the garbage, the dog in the garden.

After a little while Hector continued. 'You will be amazed at the number of new bakeries in Colombo.'

'Is there one nearby? With *mas-pan*?' Sunny had a sudden hankering for a sweet bun baked with a meat curry filling.

'You are hungry? Does your son also eat and eat?' Aunty Lillie looked appalled at the realization that her brother and his wife had unleashed such avarice into the world.

'Only cake,' Sunny retorted with a kind of infantile zeal.

Hector laughed, relieving them from confrontation. 'A son. My goodness, I cannot believe that you have a boy. How old now?'

'He'll be nine this month.'

Hector whistled. 'I'm trying to remember how old you were when I used to see you in those Makati days.'

'A little older.'

'Come, let me show you something.' He eased himself up and led the way into the darker recesses of the room. There was a small bookcase filled with volumes on the world's lesser-known religions. On top stood a framed photograph of Mikey that Sunny had sent one Christmas. 'It is very good,' he nodded. 'Very good to see this boy. Does he play cricket?'

Sunny sighed, feeling another twinge of regret. 'No, we haven't tried to.'

'Ah, but you should, you know. Remember how you got us all playing, back in Manila? The Makati XI. Dear me, that was something else. I have been thinking about those days a great deal. So much so that I have become a bit of a cricket bore.'

'You joined a club?'

'Oh, no. But I have been following the sport. A very good team is coming up, you know. You watch those fellows. They are getting somewhere. That Ranatunga is not bad. Cunning fellow, despite his size.' He made the shape of a pot belly with his hand. 'For me it has also become something quite . . . spiritual. Shall I show you?'

'Please.' He was desperate to move away from Aunty Lillie's critical gaze.

'Come, we will go through to the other side.'

Sunny followed him.

'Look.' Hector pointed at the squashed tyres of his car. The rubber had oozed out from under the rims like fat. The paint had dulled and the glaze was lost in a rash of rust, dust and grime, but there was still something majestic about the car.

'Yes, it is a Buick. Getting on now, like all of us. This was the last one I had before I left Manila. Even bigger than old Lester's. You never saw it.'

'How weird.' For a moment he thought he could smell the burning peanut oil Beatriz used to use to fry her *lumpia*, a pungent sweet aroma that would waft into his Urdaneta practice arena, in the garage, outside the kitchen.

'Even the electrics – the windows are electric, you know – are gone.' Hector looked disappointed at the car's failure to maintain itself. He brushed a curled dry yellow leaf off the bonnet. 'Trouble is the roads in this place are not worth driving on. You've seen the state of them?'

'Potholes?' There were some terrific ones, worthy of an Indiana Jones film, but Sunny had seen some good new roads too. 'Not on every road.'

'That one going to parliament is very good,' Hector agreed. 'They certainly fixed that. But everywhere else, if the potholes don't get you, the roadblocks will.'

He shuffled out of the porch into the back garden. 'Come, you will like this.'

He headed for a big, brooding tree in the corner. It had a rope hanging from one of the horizontal branches. At the end of it, the old trick with the cricket ball, this time in an orange plastic net.

'I learnt this from you, remember? You had it in a sock, but I wanted to hear the leather and see the ball. What do you think?'

'Fantastic.' Sunny lost twenty-five years at a stroke.

'You see, I have discovered it is not from the old that you learn, but from the young. Isn't that so?'

'I am not so sure.' There seemed so much that he needed to teach Mikey. If only he knew how, and time was a little kinder.

'I remembered watching you with that ball, practising in your father's house in Urdaneta. I thought it was blissful. You would be completely lost in a world of your own, hitting that ball in its white sock and waiting for it to come back and be knocked again. That was the state we were all looking for, you know. It is what meditation is all about. You know what I mean?'

'Zaramazov?'

'Almost. Except that you must not try too hard. It is not an easy business. Even he, the Grand Master, did not quite know . . .'

'Zen cricket?'

'Well, I come and knock it about for a bit and some days I am lucky. I find it. Other days it is just a bloody cricket ball. You want a go?'

'Later, maybe.'

'So, tell me, what will you do now that you are here?' He stooped a little and searched his pockets.

'I wanted to see what was here. Lay some ghosts to rest.'

'Ah, yes. That is certainly important in this country.'

'I'd like to take some pictures.'

'From where?'

'Photographs. I want to take some photographs of the place. The country. You gave me my first proper camera. I became a photographer.' Sunny pulled the small leather-cased Voigtländer out of his bag. 'You must have known.'

Hector shrugged. Sunny wasn't sure whether he even remembered the camera.

'Good. Yes, that is good. My old friend Brendan is a photographer too, you know. A lot of people like to take pictures now. He guides them all over the place on photo-shoots, or something like that. Shooting is the big thing, as you can imagine. War zone and all that. Anyway you should meet him.'

'It's OK. I want to find my own angle.'

'Lionel Wendt was another fellow. And Alphonso. We used to go to their shows. Brendan knew the whole crowd. Lillie and your mother and, of course, Lester knew them too. The same sort of business, no? So, you are going into it as well?'

'Not exactly. I don't do journalism. I take more personal pictures.'

'Alphonso was an athlete, not a journalist. Aesthete, I mean. And what about Lionel Wendt? Very artistic. Naked bodies, coconuts, everything.'

'I know.'

'Let me get you Brendan's number.' He called out to Lillie. 'Where is that Brendan's number?'

'Why do you want to talk to that lunatic?'

'Sunny is going to take photographs. He should meet Brendan. When did we last see Lionel's pictures?'

'Who?

'Lionel Wendt.'

'Where?'

Hector rummaged around a side table in the lounge and discovered the household address book: an old metal case with a spring-loaded lid. Lester had given it to him as a birthday present. Sunny remembered going with his father to Greenhills to get it. Was it Alemar's, where they had all those bleached American paperbacks and tons of stationery? Lester had been so pleased with the purchase. Sunny could remember him tapping it and saying, 'Hector really needs something to keep track of people. For an administrator he is an amazingly disorganized fellow. Head in the clouds, all the time.'

Hector chuckled, as if recalling the same days. He slid a

small tarnished tab to the top of the faded gold alphabet and flipped it open. 'Pity old Alpho's gone. Passed away . . .' He clicked his tongue. 'Ah, here we are.' He picked up the pencil attached to the case and scribbled a number on an envelope that lay on the table. He handed the envelope to Sunny. 'There. Call the chap. He'll be only too glad to talk about nudes with you.'

'Don't you need this letter?'

'Why? What is it?'

'I don't know. It hasn't been opened. Looks official.'

Hector retrieved the envelope and ripped it open. 'Damn fool bank manager. Doesn't know what he is doing. This is the second letter on a deposit account that I closed six months ago.' He handed the empty envelope back.

Lillie tilted her chair back. 'Keep away from that idiot. He has spent too much of his life in a dark room to know anything about anything.'

Sunny wasn't sure whether she was talking about him, or Brendan.

On the way back to Adel's, Sunny stopped at a bakery and got a collection of savouries in lieu of his lunch.

Later, in the evening, when he came out to return the plate and glass to the kitchen, Adel waylaid him. 'You were eating, no?'

'Just some pastries?'

'From the Taj? Or Galadari?'

He said it was not from a five-star hotel, just a small bakery.

'Fab? On Galle Road?'

'No. Just a small place we passed on the way back from Rajagiriya.'

'You should be careful, really. Some of these places have things that are weeks old. Especially those savouries. Sweets at least have sugar to keep them.'

'It was fine.'

She made a scornful face and warned that patties and *mas-pan* were the worst. 'Biological time bombs. You must never buy from those roadside dives. If you want patties, just tell me. I can make them myself, very quickly.' She cupped her hands and wiggled them, patting this side and that.

Sunny promised he'd ask her next time.

'What about dinner?'

'I might take a stroll and try the Chinese restaurant at the top of the road.'

'Chinese? That one is not very good. You should go up to the roundabout. Anyway, listen, instead of wandering around alone like a madcap, why not come with me? I'm going to a demo-dinner at eight o'clock.'

'Demo-dinner?' She hardly looked a rebel.

Adel smiled, turning coy. 'We are all members of this din-din group, and we meet whenever Angie or Arnie come back from one of their trips; they are forever going to Singapore or Bangkok. They have a lovely dinner and demonstrate the latest gadgets they have brought.'

'Like what?'

'Oh, anything. Last time it was this special non-stick frying pan they had found which was amazing. They get all sorts of things. You never know what to expect.'

'So what? They just show off their latest kitchen toys?'

'No, no, silly. It is a business. They have a demo and then they sell the thing. You have to buy a ticket for the dinner.

Very reasonable and there is a paying bar for the serious drinkers. Tonight it's at The Tamarind Club.'

'Could we stop on the way for me to make a phone call?'

'To London?'

'If I could.'

'Oh, you can do that at the club. They are all set up for that.'

The Tamarind Club was based in what had been an early post-colonial residence about ten minutes' drive away.

Upstairs in a private function room about fifty chairs had been placed in a semicircle, most already filled by *habitués* in their middle years. Everyone, even the thin ones, looked quite buoyed up, as though the air-conditioning was pumped straight in under the skin. Sunny collected the complimentary drinks: rum punch for Adel, beer for him.

A woman in a green sari came up. 'Adel, where have you been, darling?'

Adel took a quick gulp of punch and giggled.

Sunny excused himself and went to find the telephone. The timing was just right to catch Clara in London. She was at home preparing prints for her next evening class. Mikey had gone to one of his innumerable parties at the Finsbury Park bowling alley.

'How is it?' Clara asked. 'Have you met them?'

He gave a simplified account of the visit to Rajagiriya.

'Where are you now?'

He tried to explain the business at the club. 'And what about you?'

She said she had found another course to go on at Easter. The application had to be in within three days.

'Good luck.'

'I want to get a portfolio together. Alex says I'd have no problem getting on to a degree course. He's been great. So supportive.'

'Alex?'

'You know? My teacher. The artist.'

'Supportive?'

'We had a long chat and he says I could do it. He's very encouraging.'

'I see. You want to go to art college?'

'Yes. I really want to do it.'

Back at the house, Adel leant against the door. 'That hair-brush and massager is the thing for me. Who needs hair curlers in *this* country, but that de-tention business with the electric massage is just the ticket. I get this ache, you know, some-times right across my shoulder.' She turned her shoulder to show where her tender flesh might once have been too taut.

'You should have bought one,' Sunny said.

She looked at him dreamily. '*Ah-ney*, Sunny, you gave your wife a son, no?'

'It is not like a gift . . .'

'My husband was going to,' she interrupted and then started shaking her head from side to side, 'I was young and ready but then he died.' She swayed forward.

'Oh, shame.'

'Impossible to believe it. He was young enough, but heart went kaput . . .' She was beginning to fall towards him. Sunny steadied her against the door. Her shoulder was soft and round. She gripped his arm.

'You better go to sleep.' He prised her fingers off one by one.

'You think so?' She looked at him, confused. Her hand trembled in his. 'Right, then. I suppose I had better . . . Goodnight.' She drew back and turned towards the stairs.

Sunny went to his room and closed the door. He sat on the edge of the bed and thought of the deceased. His father. His mother. Unrequited love. Hector. Lillie. Clara. Desire.

The next day Adel was as bright and cheerful as ever. She'd had her breakfast early and was busy with shopping lists and phone calls. 'Put your laundry out to be done,' she hollered as she left the house.

Outside a coucal was calling; birdsong that Sunny recognized and wondered how he could ever have forgotten. The bird was somewhere high up in the trees next door and its notes bounced from branch to branch. The echoes seemed to bring the world close in to Sunny. He noticed other sounds, high and low: smaller birds, insects. He tried to remember what it had been like to grow up in a place like this. A place full of contrast, light and shadow. The sun's rays seemed to slice through a hundred shades of green. This was light he understood, intuitively. Would Mikey, growing up with the softer grain of northern light, find it too vivid? Was it a question of latitude? The position of the sun? In Makati, the light had been as bright, but seemed flatter. Perhaps it was to do with the trees. Clara had done her autumn project on Van Gogh's move to Arles, highlighting the fervour of his description of southern light. Was that what was magnified here?

By mid-morning, he decided it was time to go to the house where he had lived with his mother and Lester. The road was not far from Adel's. He took the Voigtländer and set off on foot. The shade trees disappeared. The heat was stultifying. He found the road, but nothing looked quite the same. He reached number 23, the site of his first home. A small block of flats had taken its place. There was no sign of a garden. Grey concrete had covered what had once been a lawn; breeze-block walls had replaced hedges and fences. He kicked a small stone towards the gate. None of the things that had made up his early world, imprinted as images on his brain, existed any more. Everything had been violated. There was no past – no place, no people – except what he remembered. It frightened him.

When Sunny went back to see Hector and Lillie again, he found them eating plantains on the veranda.

'Our leading light says we must alternate the fast with the feast.' Hector held out an offering, which Sunny declined. He asked for a glass of water instead.

Lillie pointed to a jug perspiring on a side table. It had a saucer placed on top. There were two glasses on a tea-stained doily next to it.

'I got hold of Brendan. He is very keen to meet you, Sunny. Fellow was so happy when I told him about your hobby.' Hector peeled another small plantain and took a bite. 'Excellent plantain. You are sure you don't want one? These are not like those yellow plastic thingamies you get in England.'

Lillie sighed. 'Does this Adel give you fruit? If you are going to eat you should have fruit.'

'I had pineapple for breakfast.'

'Pineapple is much better in the afternoon. Morning time you must have plantains.'

Hector interrupted her. 'If you have your car and that driver fellow, we can go and see Brendan today. We can drop in for a spot of lunch.'

Lillie looked horrified. 'Lunch in that house?'

'He has a cook woman who makes him lunch.'

'She'll just give you some burnt *jahdi* and tinpot *pol-sambol*.'

Hector smiled. 'You stay, my dear. I'll take Sunny.'

'Where is his house?' Sunny asked.

'Not far.'

Back in his London shop, Sunny had no trouble dealing with photographers and would-be photographers, but the prospect of visiting a semi-professional of his father's generation made him nervous.

Lillie picked up a prayer book and turned a few pages. 'Why you want to look through a little hole in a box to see what you can see if you just open your eyes, I don't understand.'

They sat in silence for a little while. Then Hector yawned and got to his feet. 'I'll go and get my wallet. On the way back, we can pick up some fresh bread. If you don't mind, Sunny?'

Lillie harrumphed and continued to read.

Brendan's studio was enormous. A display cabinet bigger than Sunny's whole shop held vintage Hasselblads Sunny had only ever seen in catalogues that were themselves antiquarian. He also had a receptionist, a young girl with long wavy hair who was replicated in a couple of the portraits on the wall. Behind her a fridge with a glass door exhibited three small piles of film; on either side hung heavy crumpled black curtains.

'Is the boss in the shooting gallery?' Hector inquired with a polite nod.

'Mr Amarasinghe? He is here, sir, but can you wait a minute?'

'Of course.' He turned to Sunny and gave a conspiratorial smirk.

'He is in the darkroom.' She paused, clearly struggling to add to this information. Then her face lit up. 'Doing the training of our new staff.'

'New staff?'

'Yes, sir. Srimantha was here before, you remember him sir? He has gone. So now we have to start right from scratch with new staff. Priya came yesterday.'

She pressed a button on the telephone console in front of her. 'One moment, sir. I will go and tell . . .'

'Pretty girl,' Hector mused when she had disappeared. Sunny went over and examined the cameras in the glass case.

'Hallo, Hector.' The loud greeting was followed by a thunderclap. Sunny turned and found a man about half Hector's height and at least twice his girth standing with his hands clasped together in front of him. He had an angular mouth that stretched from ear to ear in a sharp grin.

'I thought I'd bring Sunny to meet you, otherwise he'd never make it . . .'

'Very good. Pleased to meet you, Sunny. I knew your father.'

'Hallo.' Sunny extended a hand. It was not going to be met. Brendan was not a hand shaker. Sunny diverted his hand. 'Fine old cameras,' he added, pointing at them.

'Fakes. I get a chap in Maradana to copy them – just the shell. Good, no?'

Sunny laughed. 'Great.'

He was pleased. 'You appreciate the joke. Tell you what, I'll get him to make you one, if you like.'

Hector didn't follow. 'What are you chaps so pleased about?'

'The illusion, Hector, the illusion. Welcome to the house of illusions. You want to see the studio?'

The large room was professionally kitted out with light stands, reflective umbrellas, black backdrops and white tents. 'We can create anything here,' he declared. 'But come, let's go in the house and I'll get some lunch sorted. You'll stay for lunch?'

'Oh, yes.' Hector answered for them both.

Brendan barked out a string of orders to an invisible retainer as they passed through to the main house. He took them into an air-conditioned room with frosted windows and proceeded to cross-examine Sunny about his photographic intentions. 'You want to do some jungle shooting? I can arrange it. Can't do Wilpattu, even with the bloody truce, but Yala is possible. You like to try? Leopard? Or how about the Habarana herd in the north? Elephants?'

'I'd prefer to find something different.'

'Oh, yes, I understand. We already have enough animal lovers. No need for another one to go wild. You want human drama? What about Trinco? I took a bunch of journos up there the other day.'

'Tiger country?' Hector asked.

'Good one, Hector. Very good. But these days, you know, the bloody elephants are far more dangerous. Ten fellows were killed up in Dambulla. Villagers, I mean, not elephants.'

'I wish I could capture what has gone. Disappeared,' Sunny mumbled.

Brendan fixed a bruised yellowy eye on him. 'Like old Lester? You know, a lot of the buggers who've been writing in the papers these days have been an insult to your father's profession. Now finally the media is getting its teeth back, but those thugs recently assaulting Jayantha is very worrying.'

Sunny was aware that murder and the intimidation of the press had taken place with grim regularity, especially since the late 1980s, but he didn't feel it involved him.

'I am not into journalism. My father wasn't either, in the end.' Sunny told Brendan how he had tried to find the house he'd been brought up in. What he wanted was to take a picture of that house now. Not find an old picture of the house, or to take a picture of what had replaced it, but somehow to recreate it with the camera. He wanted photographs that did more than say 'I am here' or 'that is there'. 'Maybe something that brings out what is in our minds, even if it is no longer in the world. Or never was . . .'

'Fantasy? Like Guinevere and Lancelot? The Pre-Raphaelites? No more fake truths, only true fakes.'

The comparison had not occurred to Sunny and came as a shock, especially since he would not have suspected Brendan of harbouring such an interest. He imagined Brendan in his studio with his receptionist draped in silk, her Pre-Raphaelite hair flowing into a garden of sandalwood and cinnamon. A leopard-skin garter.

Lunch was brought in. It was much as Lillie had warned: coconut *sambol*, charred segments of dried fish, a curry of unidentifiable bones and a mound of pebbly cold rice.

They moved over to the glass-top table and sat down.

Brendan reached over and helped himself to the rice and then urged Hector and Sunny to do the same. 'You know, I am glad Hector brought you over. You are welcome to make full use of the studio any time you like, Sunny. We have all the props. Models too are no problem. They are willing to do anything these days. All it takes is money. Open sesame. Anything goes . . .'

'What about you? What if your life had taken another turn? I'd like to take that picture.'

'You mean, what I would like to have been? King Arthur? Or Parakramabahu the Great?'

Sunny suggested that with Hector, a portrait in front of the Central Bank building, where he might have spent his whole career if he had not gone to Manila, would be interesting. 'I'd like to construct the picture as if that had been the life.'

Hector's face clouded. 'Yes, indeed. I wonder what it would have been like.'

'In that case,' Brendan said, 'do me as a captain.' He grinned. 'Captain of a cricket team.'

Brendan found his old regalia and got changed in the downstairs bathroom, hissing and cursing at the smell of mothballs. Although neither the trousers nor the shirt fitted, Sunny set him up in the studio in a way that hid the gaps. The receptionist, impressed by the sight of her boss bursting out of his cricket whites, wanted to know what it was all about. When Sunny explained, she said she had always wanted to be a singer. 'Deep down, that is my really true desire.'

'OK. Let's pretend you are a pop star.' Sunny took a very melancholy picture of her that he knew would fulfil Brendan's

Pre-Raphaelite fantasies. All throat, bust and big, moist eyes.

Hector offered to have a word with a friend to see if they could do him later, in the office of the governor of the Central Bank. 'That would be a coup.' The thought brought a smile to his face.

Brendan wanted to develop the pictures straightaway, but Sunny said, 'I still have ten shots left.' He had learned to be careful with money.

'Such patience,' Brendan said to Hector. 'Just like the father, no?'

Adel had placed Sunny's laundry, neatly ironed, on the bed. The shirts baked paper crisp, the socks carefully coupled, and even the underwear – cotton mesh briefs for the heat, and boxers striped and butterflied – pressed like they'd never been pressed before.

Adel knocked on the door. 'Would you like some tea?'

Sunny said he had been given tea, and thanked her for the laundry. Trying to be discreet, he added. 'You didn't need to iron everything.'

'Oh, but you must have your clothes ironed. I would hate to think of you in those, all crumpled up.'

'I could iron . . .'

'I didn't know they had buttons now. Is that how it is in London?'

'These are made here.'

'Really?' She picked up a pair of boxers and gently opened it up. She squinted at the label on the waistband. 'Made in Sri Lanka. Imagine that. Does everybody in England wear them now?' she purred. 'Anyway, I'd better leave you to get on with your bath or whatever.' She placed the garment back on the bed and straightened the fly. 'There you are. Perfect, no?'

That evening he declined an invitation to accompany her to Mt Lavinia. He wanted to think about things. Should he make more of an effort with Hector and Lillie? They were the closest links he had to a country he wanted to reclaim.

He phoned Hector and proposed a trip out together. 'Good idea. With this damn car out of action, we never go anywhere. I don't like the buses very much, actually.' Hector suggested one of Brendan's safaris. 'You don't have to take photos if you don't want to, but I wouldn't mind seeing those elephants he goes on about.'

They settled on a couple of days up at Habarana. Brendan said he would organize everything. He was still chuffed with his stint on the other side of the lens.

Sunny managed to get one more call through to Clara from the Galle Face Hotel. The time difference and her busy schedule made it impossible to do more. He got her just as she was downing her muesli before the school run. 'It's crazy,' she moaned down the line. 'Gumbo's driving me insane.'

'What about this Alex? Your art class?'

'Thank God for that. Alex has this wonderful new project. We'll be doing all the galleries. I just need some time.'

That's what I need too, Sunny thought when he put down the phone. Time. The chance to start again. Real time. Mikey would be nine the week he got back. So many years that he had been too busy photographing other babies, other children, and then locking and unlocking a cubicle full of obsolete machines. He walked on to the veranda and looked out at the huge open park bordered by the sea on one side and the tall buildings of the city at the far end. The ground used to be green, he remembered. Not any more. It had turned sepia. The colour had evaporated like everything else in the past. The ocean looked fierce and dark. Some kids were playing with a bat and a ball, but there were no kites flying in the sky. It made him worry not only about his life but also Mikey's childhood. That too was passing. Soon the kid would be in double digits. Then nothing of those earlier days would remain, except what Mikey might remember, and the pictures Sunny took, or regretted having failed to take. The thoughts kept swarming around in his head, the mental images he possessed began to fade. There was nothing he could hold on to.

Panic filled him. His chest hurt. He suddenly wanted to shoot film without stopping. Maybe that really was the only way to keep things from slipping away. He wanted to be back in his house, in his street, in his London, taking picture after picture after picture – *Mikey, me, Mikey, me, Mikey, Clara, me*. Saving them. Now. Quickly. Before it was too late.

Catch it, he wanted to say to his son. *These years will become as difficult for you to remember as mine are for me*. He yearned to be something more to Mikey than his father had been for him.

'Tootle-hoo, Sunny.' Brendan was in a khaki safari suit, looking quite the successful thug. 'Dawn patrol, eh?' He had a brand new Landrover Discovery at the gate. 'Turbocharged, no?' Brendan smiled proudly and stroked the leather trim.

Brendan's driver had eyes like boiled gumdrops; he preferred sound to sight, the horn to the brakes, and relied on a clarion blast every five seconds to clear the road. Most creatures – human and animal – scattered out of the way and whatever didn't disappeared anyway with their passing. By the time they got to Hector's house, the waking life of outer Colombo had been decimated. Hector and Lillie got into the vehicle with no idea of what was in store.

'Lunch in Kurunegala,' Brendan announced.

'Lunch?' Lillie hesitated.

Hector reminded her that it was permitted while travelling, as long as they went by land.

'Essential, my dear,' Brendan added. 'You cannot go on an empty stomach.' Not that he was likely to have experienced such a phenomenon.

The small wayside inn they stopped at for lunch had been cleaned out of its rice and curry by a coach tour about half an hour earlier. All that was left were some limp Chinese rolls.

A long hungry hot afternoon drive later, they reached their destination: the Lake View Hotel. Its plain whitewashed walls, sloping gardens and perfectly symmetrical blue swimming pool would have made it the ultimate in modern holiday resorts of the early 1960s. But now even the blistering garden shrubs had a vintage look to them. There were boulders in the drive and the walls at the front had begun to crumble.

'Is this another ruin?' Hector muttered as he slowly climbed out.

'I thought you would like it, Hector. Old-world. Quiet. Very good for meditative types.' Brendan lit a cigarette and chucked the match into a gutter. 'Now, where's the reception?' He marched inside and rang a desk bell.

The main foyer was spacious, with a view of the pool

and then the lake in the distance beyond. It had excellent natural light.

'I think the staff might have died some time ago.' Hector sat down on a rickety wicker chair and contemplated a three-year-old calendar pinned to the wall.

Brendan rang the bell with extra vigour.

Eventually a slender young man in a mud-coloured shirt emerged from the manager's office. 'Major Amarasinghe? Sir, here already?'

With barely contained excitement the manager showed them to their rooms and then went to ensure that tea was ready.

Out by the pool, the wind was up. When Sunny came out he found the hotel manager and his waiter pouncing on wafting paper serviettes and sandwiches like a pair of cats. The teapot had half the tablecloth flapping over it, ready to sail.

The surface of the water in the pool broke in a whoosh. 'What's up, men?' Brendan bellowed through the spray. He bobbed over to the climbing rail.

'Wind, sir.' The manager grabbed another piece of green garnish as it flew past. 'At this time it blows hard.'

'Can't you do something about it?'

'It is not in my power, sir. We have no climate control . . .'

'Windbreaker, man. You know, use a screen.'

The waiter dived behind him and missed the catch: a scrap of lettuce flew over the boundary parapet.

'Sir, we have a good wall.' The manager swung around, arms flailing, propelled by the wind. 'Dining room, sir? Or I can put the tea in the hall inside. Very nice sitting area there. Our Swiss guests used to like it very much.'

Brendan hauled himself out of the water and picked up his towel. He wiped those parts of his abdomen his small arms could reach without too much effort, and then let the towel flutter over his shoulders. 'Right. Do that then. How can you eat anything in this hurricane?'

'Not a hurricane, sir. This is our cool breeze.'

Brendan turned to Sunny and Hector who were watching him. 'These buggers say we must have tea inside. I'll put my clothes on and join you.'

'This place has not changed in years,' Hector said to Sunny. 'Not a bit.'

'I like that.'

'Oh, yes. I do too. But a young fellow like you, surely, you desire change? That's the world now, isn't it? Quick, fast, adaptable. I see it in *Time* magazine. These innovators, change agents, they are all young characters. Always under the age of forty.'

Sunny shrugged. 'It feels to me like everything changes too fast.'

'How? What do you mean?' He was challenging Sunny, just as he used to in Urdaneta when Sunny was fourteen and he was in his forties.

'Like Manila. It has all gone. There is nothing for me there. And there is nothing for me here, it seems now. Maybe, one day, there will be nothing for me in London either.'

Hector shook his head. 'I am not so sure. Things are not quite so easily lost, Sunny, except for money. Bits of paper. Sometimes I wonder if I shouldn't have stayed in Manila, like your father did. He really was the smart one. You remember that sparkling little Rosa?'

Brendan came in from the terrace and called out to the manager hovering by the dining room. 'Those changing rooms are infested with bloody mosquitoes, you know.'

'Sir, it is too windy outside for them, so they have to go in there.'

Brendan rolled his eyes in exasperation and sat down. 'Where is Lillie? No bathing beauty? What, Hector?'

'She is not used to travelling. She needs to rest. Meditate, you know.'

'Ah, yes. Like I said, perfect place for it. So, what about tea?' Brendan looked around for someone to pour it. The waiter hobbled over to the table and lifted the tea cosy. 'I will pour, sir?'

'What happened to your foot?'

'Fell, sir. Outside. The tomato sandwich.' He waved the tea cosy at the windswept terrace. 'Went too fast by.'

'Never mind. Put the milk first. You have milk?'

The waiter replaced the tea cosy, picked up the milk jug, checked it, poured a few drops into each cup and then proceeded with the tea and tea strainer. It was riveting. They all watched in silence, waiting for the hand to shake, the tea to spill, the foundations to crack.

Brendan lit another cigarette and watched until the last drop was safely poured.

'Now, then. What is the programme here? Are those elephants still roaming about? Will they come down to the tank in the evening?'

'Oh yes, sir. If you go in by the Forestry Department access road, you can see them. They will all come.'

'Now?'

The manager checked his watch. 'Oh, now is very good, sir. Before dark and tigers, et cetera, et cetera.'

'And you will have a good dinner for us tonight. You have prepared?'

'Yes, sir. We are very prepared.' He spoke in a rush, anxious to please. 'We have chicken-in-basket, potato chips, and for the alternative – pride pish.'

Brendan banged his forehead with the heel of his palm. 'Good God, man, have you no proper pud?'

'Sir?'

'Food? Dammit . . . Proper food instead of your children's menu and fried bloody fish. What about some stringhoppers? Any *pol-kiri-badung*? Game?'

'Oh, oh, oh. Local food? Can do, sir. Very good, sir. We can do.'

Brendan turned to Hector. 'You and the wife are eating, I take it? Or you want *kankun*, or pea soup, or something like that.'

Hector smiled and said that this week they were prepared to eat anything.

'Good, good.' Brendan glanced at Sunny. 'You have any peculiarities of the diet? You want the tourist menu?'

Sunny said Brendan's choice was perfect.

'Excellent. So, we will look for these damn elephants and come back ravenous.'

Lillie didn't join the safari; she'd had enough physical transportation for one day.

'No problem,' Brendan said. 'Let us go forth, just the three of us.' He sent the driver off to find a tracker.

Despite all his earlier protestations, once they entered the jungle Sunny could feel an excitement that was not to do with the calculation of aperture and depth of field, not to do with light and colour, creativity and perspective, but entirely to do with being in the right place at the right time. He looked at Hector and wondered if he had the same feeling.

Sunny wished he had Mikey with him, that they were taking a step together into the unknown. Making this place their own. Instead it was Hector and him; Hector the older man, but Sunny the father. Both out of kilter.

'*Mehen, mehen*.' The tracker gestured to the left. The driver swung the wheel and the jeep bumped on to another track. Soon the hushed trees gave way and they were out in the open. The water in the huge tank had retreated, leaving a kind of alluvial plane around it. The evening sun was mellow; the sky enormous and forgiving, with the blue seeping up from the surface of the lake to soften it. The grass at the water's edge was young, as green as new rice. This was a place where the air itself moved with a sense of belonging.

The tracker grabbed the driver's shoulder and rose in his seat. '*Ali, ali.*'

The vehicle stopped. Two elephants at the edge of the jungle about three hundred yards ahead jostled each other and ambled out into the open. They were heading for the water.

'We have to get closer,' Brendan hissed. 'Close up.'

The driver looked at the tracker, then at Brendan; he edged the vehicle forward. The elephants took no notice.

'Come, Sunny.' Brendan opened the door.

'Sir . . .' The tracker protested.

'Pah, the wind is blowing our way. Come. You know what

they say? If it is no good, it is only because you were not close enough.'

'Wait.' Hector held Sunny's arm. 'What the hell is he on about?'

'Photographer's saying . . .'

'Damn foolish. Don't go.'

Brendan was already waddling towards the animals. Sunny followed him. He swapped cameras, keeping the Nikon with the telephoto nestling in his shoulder bag within easy reach and used the Voigtländer to take a few shots. Brendan's arms moved up to his face. Sunny heard a click. A moment later a shrill trumpeting erupted behind them. He turned around and saw a bull elephant with its trunk raised, baring a single white tusk. The elephant stamped and pawed the ground.

'Quick, back.' Brendan headed for the jeep

There was another shrill trumpeting; the elephant charged as if to cut him off from the vehicle. The jeep jerked into life and started moving.

The elephant veered off and trotted back into position. He stamped the ground again. The jeep revved up, climbing over some broken branches. Hector had the door open and Sunny jumped in. Brendan clambered in front and they shot off as the elephant made another charge.

'There's a whole herd,' Hector bellowed. 'Look behind the fellow.' About fifteen other animals had emerged from the trees. 'Brendan you are a madman.'

While waiting for dinner that evening, out on the terrace, Brendan opened a bottle of arrack. Hector declined at first;

then changed his mind. 'After that fright, maybe I could do with something.'

'Good man.' Brendan poured him a shot. 'You are on the road, anyway. Surely it is allowed?'

Lillie pulled her sari close around her and gave Sunny a look of contempt. 'You went to take their picture, and they chased you off?'

Brendan told a story of once bringing a group of Dutch photographers to the same hotel. 'Two days and not even a dung ball to show.'

'They stayed here?' Hector asked.

'I don't think they will ever come back. You see, two of the party had severe food poisoning. Cricket is more likely to tempt them back than wildlife.'

'They ate here?'

'Different management, old chap. Not to worry. This fellow was trained at the Oberoi.'

Dinner, when it came, was fine. By then Brendan had knocked back half the bottle of arrack and was holding forth on everything from hotel management to elephantiasis. Hector goaded him every now and again with a lightly barbed remark, while Lillie stayed on autopilot, feeding the body and freeing the soul. She finished her plate of stringhoppers and green pigeon curry and said she must catch up on her sleep. She didn't wait for the *crème caramel*, donating to Sunny her share as though it might make up for any lingering neglect from her earlier stint of unwelcome parenting.

'Are you really a major?' Sunny asked Brendan. 'The manager called you Major Amarasinghe.'

Brendan took another gulp of arrack and studied the horticultural patterns on his bush shirt for a while. 'The Service went badly downhill, you know. Vendettas. Politics. Bad business. So I resigned. But sometimes you need a bit of rank to get things done. Usually I keep the uniform out of sight. Been a bit of a liability lately.' He went on to lecture them on the merits and demerits of international hotel management versus military incompetence and then, halfway through his dessert, came to an abrupt halt. 'Time for bed,' he announced. 'Crack of dawn, on the trail?'

The next morning they did another run around the tank, but saw only water buffalo and a couple of painted storks.

In the remaining few days in Colombo, Sunny went into manic overdrive. He rushed about collecting brass plates, oil lamps, batik prints, wooden toys, curry powder, books, postcards, anything that might help him recreate the richness of the place for Mikey, and also for Clara; to give them an idea of what he had seen. He hired Piyasena to run him around and took loads of pictures – snapshots, pure and simple. Pictures of buildings, cars, birds. Kids playing cricket in alleyways and wastelands, between tin cans and clothes lines, on streets and on the beach.

Overcoming his earlier reservations, he went to the Colombo cemetery too. Piyasena collared a doddery old watchman to help locate Sunny's mother's grave. It took about half an hour in the blazing heat to find it: an ordinary gravestone with an ordinary name, Irene Margaret Fernando, and a set of dates that surprised Sunny. He had never considered how much of a life she'd had before he had begun his own. He realized then how little he knew of her. Her true life, that incredible arc from birth to death, was lost to him. He had had only a glimpse of her. Then she had gone. Standing before her grave, Sunny felt oddly distant. He was hot and thirsty. His feet ached. Piyasena was the one who murmured, '*Amma*,' and crouched down to clear the weeds. Before they left, Sunny took a picture, but his heart was not in it. The light was all wrong.

On his last night he went back to Hector and Lillie. He wanted to talk to Hector. 'I didn't really find my world,' he said. 'I even went to *Amma*'s grave.'

'Maybe you are looking in the wrong place. Like I said to you before, Sunny, you have to choose the right time and the right place.'

At the airport, Piyasena asked him for his address in London. 'For my cousin, sir.' He was looking ahead to the day when the boy would come with the Sri Lankan team to play England. 'Next century,' he added. He knew how to build on hope.

'Two weeks in hell, while you were up yourself in paradise.' Clara slammed the door.

It was an exaggeration, of course. Sunny knew her hell was simply a mad boss. She'd had to work overtime the last week and had missed her evening class and a gallery outing with Alex. Her plan to get on to an Easter course had been scuppered. Mikey had had to stay with friends on three occasions. Not that he seemed too displeased about that. Mikey was still at an age when he could look pleased without loss of face. Sunny could still hold him, lift him, hug him – just.

'I saw elephants,' he told the boy. 'An elephant charged me.' He gave his rendition of an elephant's flourish and an abbreviated account of the safari.

Mikey's face glowed. 'Cool.'

But somehow he never got around to looking at the pictures Sunny had taken of wild elephants or kids playing cricket; growing up was all-consuming. The next birthday was only days ahead. Time was short.

Although he was still in primary school, Mikey was speeding towards a world that would soon eclipse his father's. Acceleration was everywhere, except in the realm of words, as he grew into a state of teenage inarticulacy. There seemed nothing Sunny could do about the ever-widening gap. Was that perhaps what his mother had seen, and his father? A gulf from which they believed they could only retreat?

'Gumbo is finished,' Clara announced one day. 'He put all his money in that dud bank that's crashed. He's done for.' She got a job at the Rondell Foundation. The hours were longer and it was full-time, but she got better perks, including proper study leave.

'You'll do the art course?'

'No, that's on the back burner. Alex's thing is fine for now. I want to do a professional qualification instead. Management accounting, maybe?'

The pay was good, but not enough to make up for Sunny's shortcomings. The Footsie tumbled, his money shrank and the cubby-hole shop began to sink. He did nothing about it. After the trip to Sri Lanka, a kind of paralysis grew over him that was in direct proportion to the increasing need for action. Perhaps it was visiting the cemetery in Colombo that had done it.

Whisky began to offer some consolation, a semblance of control; he could be sure he knew what was going on between sips, even if at no other time. The familiarity of repetitive worries and a shrinking boundary lightened the load. Clara became barely visible in the semi-darkness. Mikey blossomed but Sunny missed everything except his daily tipple. He even missed the first news of the big explosion in Colombo.

It was the week that Clara had gone on Alex's four-day art tour of Italy. Sunny had his hands full with Mikey and a deteriorating business plan. It was only a remark made when he collected Mikey after a music lesson that alerted him. A parent of another budding musician said, 'Terrible news, isn't it?' She mentioned suicide bombers in Sri Lanka. The pictures of the devastation were on TV, briefly, and in the newspapers the next day: short reports of a small city shrouded in smoke. Scores of office workers, insurance clerks, peons, street vendors had been killed and injured in the huge blast; the Central Bank, Ceylinco and several other buildings leading up to the old clock tower destroyed. But soon news had moved on, quick to forget small tropical islands in trouble.

He called Hector in Colombo; Lillie answered. 'Thank God, he is alive. He was due to go to the bank in the afternoon . . . But Brendan was not so lucky. He was just passing by, walked right into it . . .' The carnage, the destruction, the instant reconfiguration of the city and their world was too much for Hector. Lillie said he was in a deep depression.

'He sits in his chair and mumbles that the landmarks have disappeared. He isn't himself. Colombo is not the same.' Brendan had been his friend; the Central Bank, a kind of home. Life before 31 January 1996 was for him a ruptured dream.

Six weeks later Sri Lanka won the World Cup in cricket for the first time. The country was jubilant and the cricketers became national heroes. But did that make a real difference? Sunny didn't think so. He knew things did not balance quite so easily, no matter how drunk you got.

The crunch came for Sunny two years later, after Mikey had settled into his local secondary school. The music department offered options in the history of the Hammond organ and psychedelic guitar lessons. Jimi Hendrix had been transcribed. Mikey got into keyboards and practised variations of chromatic scales which Sunny remembered his mother's pupils playing. 'You should be proud of him carrying on the tradition.' Clara tried to soothe him but she had no idea what it did to his head. She had already completed Part 1 of her management accounting exams and was being encouraged by the persistent Alex to think again of art school.

The shop seemed to have become almost invisible. Sometimes days would go by without a single customer; the only person to come in would be the postman, or someone looking for a spare camcorder battery. Photography had taken a dive. After Princess Di's death, Sunny reckoned no one really wanted to be seen with a camera. Taking pictures was no longer done; *paparazzi* was a swear word even among news editors.

On the way back home one evening, Sunny stopped at the supermarket for a special-offer whisky deal and some pretzels that lately had regained a hold on him. The woman in front of him at the checkout dropped her lottery ticket and Sunny picked it up for her.

'Oh, thank you.' She looked at him with pale wide eyes, enlarged by soft contacts and curled lashes clotted with mascara. 'Aren't you Mikey's father?' She spoke as though she was on camera, barely moving her thin, glossed-up lips.

'Yes. Mikey.' Sunny was struck by how his identity had shifted from son to father.

'My daughter is in his class.' She smiled as though this made them conspirators. 'I saw you with him at parents' evening.'

'Right, yes. Homework.'

'My daughter says he is very good in the band.'

'Band?' It was news to him.

'It's perhaps because you play. Or his mother?'

'My mother's dead.'

'I'm so sorry.' She lowered her eyes as though there might be some comfort she could offer.

Sunny wished her luck with the lottery. Then realized he had confused Clara with his mother. His head hurt. He needed a jackpot too. He didn't know what to do about the lease. The shop was doomed. To continue was impossible. To think was impossible, with or without a drink.

In the end, he gave up the business. He brought the last few old cameras back into the house and stored them up in the loft along with his mother's portrait, the old cardboard suitcases from Manila and a fleet of Pampers boxes stuffed with baby toys and useless clothes. A gleeful gay couple from Margate who had acquired the adjoining premises took over the lease and swiftly turned the whole thing into yet another hairdressers' salon. They called it *Snip-Snap* and gave Sunny and Clara vouchers for free cuts for a year. 'We can do matching highlights.'

Clara was not amused. 'What are you going to do with yourself now?'

'Take some time out.'

'Isn't that what this has been?'

'What do you mean?'

'The last couple of years. You haven't exactly been rushed off your feet have you, except between that Victoria Wine and the bottle bank.'

'Wines?'

'Whatever . . .'

'You think I should have tried harder with the shop? Is that it?'

The brown pleats in her eyes were set solid, like glass. Distant. Hard. 'I think you could just try, Sunny. You give up so easily. Like you have nothing in you any more.'

'Nothing in me any more?'

'Maybe you never did.'

That was unfair. Uncalled for. She'd spent too many evenings with a brush in her hand. He had plenty inside him. She knew it. Plenty of fluid, at least, of one sort or another. But the world was spinning too fast. There were things that he simply could not handle. It wasn't that he was pushing his luck, or her. No. The world was pushing in on him. There were empty jam jars and whisky bottles by the tumble dryer waiting to be taken out, old newspapers overflowing from wastepaper baskets all over the house. The jasmine, the geranium and the *ficus benjamina* were all brown. Maybe it was his fault, but then he thought, couldn't it also be hers?

Mikey soon slid from the 'A Train' to something he called 'da real mutherfuckin' world' and exchanged the piano stool for the couch. His preferred instrument became the CD, to which Sunny's usual response was, 'Can't you play something that doesn't thump so much?' It was not that he wanted a different beat or rhythm; he didn't know what he wanted, other than a double-fingered Scotch.

'I can't go back to taking pictures,' he grumbled to Clara. 'Nobody wants photos any more.'

'I'm not sure you are right about that. People are really into it these days. Alex says everyone is doing it. We all need to make something, you know, and with the cameras you get now, anyone can take pictures.'

'Precisely.' Sunny slumped a little lower in his chair. 'I want a job where I get a wage. Something simple and straightforward like yours.'

'Then why don't you get one?'

A couple of weeks later Clara came home with the news that a photo-lab was opening next to the local newsagent. 'They need staff.'

'You want me to be humiliated?'

She stared at the fish cakes smouldering under the grill. 'I think they would appreciate your . . . experience.'

The owner turned out to be one of Sunny's first buyers – Freddy Ismail. A man of many investments. A collector.

They'd chatted about vintage cameras and he'd enjoyed Sunny's stories about the pieces he had in the shop.

'I saw you closed the shop, Mr Fernando. No good?' He was very direct.

'Early retirement. I liked the cameras too much, you know, to let anyone buy them.'

'I remember,' he smiled. 'That huge Hasselblad, you wouldn't part with that for anything, would you? No one could even touch it.'

Sunny smiled politely. The fake camera that Brendan had given him in Colombo was one of his true treasures. He said he was looking for something to occupy his time.

'It's all Adobe Photoshop and electronics now. Not like in the old darkroom.' Freddy added that he wanted to develop a studio. 'Portraits. You like to be the pro? The photographer, Mr Fernando? A small sideline, not a full-time thing. But I need an older hand, some real expertise to give us an edge in the market. Chips is fine, but you need the human eye, right? Would new technology interest you?'

'Sounds perfect,' Sunny perked up. 'I started with portraits, you know?' It would be a chance to catch up on all those new imaging techniques Clara drooled over, and to gape at something other than the bottom of a glass. They came to an amicable agreement: Sunny would run the studio for him and oversee picture quality three afternoons a week and all day Saturday; Freddy would pay him a regular wage.

Clara laughed happily, like she used to, when Sunny told her he had a job. Her generous lips bloomed again. They needed no gloss. He knew that. He had always known that. 'See, they do want you.'

He remembered everything that he used to feel.

Things began to look up. Tony Blair was in his first term flush, and seemed an honest enough man to lead the country into a new and beatified age. Sunny had no problem with his earnestness; he hoped some of it might even rub off on the younger generation sloping around the house. Even the London light appeared fuller and freer. And Freddy Ismail's new digital machines were quite impressive in their own way. At first Sunny didn't do much more than the occasional passport photograph, which he tried to make a little more Julia Cameronish than the usual booth affair. His efforts were appreciated and soon many of the aspiring actors and party people in the area began to drop in, keen for something quirky to send to an agency or a constituency committee. Some days Sunny felt better even without a drink.

Clara had been right. Image was back in business. The look. The eye. Software. Art classes for all ages. Mikey's hair got spiky, his sockets darkened under the lower rims. He walked as though he was being watched; sometimes like the out-of-work actors in front of Sunny's lens, other times incognito, hooded. Sunny couldn't believe he was already a real teenager.

'What's up?' he asked his son one day.

Mikey was sitting on a stool in the kitchen staring at the fridge magnets they'd bought in Welshpool one year. 'Have you ever smoked?' he asked, dissolving back into the little boy he had so recently been.

'I was never much of a smoker.'

'What? Never?'

'Well, I tried a bit. Now and then.'

'Why? Didn't you know about cancer?'

He tried to think of something to say about the nature of the tobacco industry, the mistakes of youth, America, vested interests, the economics of development. 'It wasn't like now. People did. They just did.'

'You tried to smoke because everyone else did?'

'I suppose so.' Robby was the real smoker, and Herbie, who would've inhaled burning beetroot if he'd thought it would make him high.

'That's so dumb.' Mikey opened the fridge and took out some milk and poured himself a glass. 'You know what your lungs look like?' Sunny watched him drink the milk in one long draught that seemed to last longer than his whole young sweet life. He could see his son's teeth through the glass, magnified, and a kind of hunger for the unknown that Sunny no longer had. Sunny wanted nothing to do with the unknown. He wanted only the known. The familiar. His chair, his light, his book, his bottle, his glass, his world. Everything in its place, unmoving. Solid. Tremors were for the young.

'So, your friends are smoking?'

Mikey gave his father a withering look. 'They were smoking in primary school. It's just a dumb thing dumb people do.'

'What else?'

Mikey put his empty glass on the table. 'What else what?'

Sunny wanted him to talk some more, but didn't know where to begin. The boy had opened a window and then closed it again. Sunny remembered how he used to do the same. Open, slowly open, and then in a rush, a panic, close everything down. What are the thoughts you keep to yourself? Which ones do you share? He didn't know.

'How's the band?' But he was too late. Mikey was out of

the kitchen, heading for the TV. The dark room of flickering images, one-way talk, electronic signals that one can safely take in from pre-puberty to post-dotage.

Maybe it was the impending millennium, the closing-down of the twentieth century, or maybe it was simply his age, the point when the big hurdles of thirty, even forty, begin to look rosy in retrospect, something that belonged to youth. Maybe it was the fact that Mikey had entered his teens and Sunny was just beginning to realize what crossing that threshold had meant for him thirty-odd years ago; how there would be no transition quite like that again. Maybe it was the accumulation of disappointments, the dismay at the realization that after all this time he may still not have reached the inner core of another – not just Mikey, but Clara too. That he had learnt nothing from the failures of those who had been this way before. Whatever it was, he withdrew further into himself.

Freddy Ismail, with his aura of effortless accomplishment and prosperity, was a source of some comfort. He was in his early thirties, and right from his muted gold sunglasses to his soft pigskin shoes he was a picture of easy success and cultural compromise. He was always smiling; his teeth more than perfect. 'Mr Fernando,' he would say, 'you are a real A1 artist, sir.' He'd put Sunny's portraits up in the shop window. 'The council should pay us for having these fucking masterpieces adorning the street.'

Sunny did take some good ones in that first year. As good as any portrait Clara painted. Terry, the actor, for example, in stunning profile. A Caesar staring at a beam of light that would splinter and break, destroying a dream and stabbing him from behind. One beam of light – it was perfect.

Olympus. Then Fiona. 'A little too keen on punt and cleavage,' according to Freddy, but as mesmerizing as a mermaid when seen from across the street. And Cordelia, in a composition where Sunny had exchanged black for white and discovered a luminosity that rivalled even the great Alphonso's. Sunny hoped that Mikey might be inspired and go hunting for Shakespeare in the library, or get involved in something really artistic. But the boy seemed completely impervious.

When he came to choose his GCSE subjects, Mikey shunned all the arts options. 'What do you want to do when you grow up?' Sunny asked.

He looked at his father in a way that left Sunny in no doubt of what he thought of the question. He was already catching up. He had a long neck and feet too big for his father's shoes.

'OK, sorry. Stupid question.'

'I want to be an engineer.'

Sunny wasn't sure whether this was the time to mention his own disastrous foray. 'I didn't think anyone was interested in engineering these days.'

'Isn't that what Grandpa did?'

'Yes. Absolutely. Are you into tunnels?'

'Maybe . . . umm, rockets?'

'I see.'

'Or, like, bridges. Roads.'

'You want to go places. Be on the move.'

Mikey looked blank, perhaps having already left the room, with that adolescent habit of slipping from one world to another as if through a sliding door. 'Huh?'

'Never mind. Technology can be . . . good. You need to be able to make things work.' Sunny thought he'd plant a seed. Mikey and most of his friends, as far as Sunny could tell, fixed nothing. If anything broke, they moved on. If a cassette got stuck, it was chucked; if a CD skipped, they skipped the track. If a button fell off, whatever it was would stay unbuttoned. A philosophy of ease, true, but it didn't promise great leaps for civilization. They were nomads, going from one room to another in search of the momentarily cool. No one ever spliced a tape the way he had done to save a Feliciano strum, or an Otis Redding chord. But then cassettes had no screws now, to undo and repair. No little fix-it bits. Widgets were nowhere to be found, except in cans of Guinness. Sunny shook his head sadly. What would happen to the world, when it got damaged? Would they just throw it away? Use and throw. As Kodak did with their 24-exposure egg boxes. He had a sudden yearning for things he could properly handle. Cogs, levers, thumbscrews. Metal cameras.

'Yeah. Right. Or I might just do gigs with a band.'

'I'm not worried,' Clara told Sunny. 'He won't turn out like you. He knows what he wants.' Sunny was not so sure. Kids didn't seem to know much in this age of disinformation. They seemed mostly to be asleep.

Mikey's new friend Benjy was the exception. He was smaller than Mikey, but full of energy. He'd bound up and talk to Sunny, even on the street where the passing world might see him. He didn't have that shame the young sometimes had of the old. He had become Mikey's friend in the second year at the big school. He had small eyes and high buoyant cheekbones. One of the first things he said to Sunny was, 'Hey *kumusta*, Pops?'

'Where'd you learn *kumusta*?'

It turned out that his mother was from the Visayas, in the Philippines. His father, a priest from Connemara, had been on a mission. At the market in Cebu their bicycles had collided and they'd fallen in love. Before the first child was born they'd left both the church and the Philippines; they'd come to live in London and now sold kitchen units in Wood Green.

'Mikey says you have a *barong*?' Benjy said. 'My Dad has one too.'

'Does he wear it?'

'My birthday is the same day as his number one fiesta. For that he gets really spruced, like *barong*, black trousers, shiny shoes. He's got cool *capice* cufflinks.'

Benjy was not only quick and talkative, he was also good with his hands. In his fingers even a chocolate bar looked like a tool. When Mikey's Nokia fizzled, Benjy was the one who knew how to fix it.

Clara was less impressed by the lad. She thought Benjy was a little wayward. 'He's got too much free time.' She, of course, had none: exams, maths, art, correspondence courses . . . Quite apart from her hyper-life as a flexitime mother.

'That's because he's quicker than the rest.'

'No. He just knows how to cut corners. Mikey should be careful.'

As a result, they never met Benjy's parents, who seemed to Sunny to exist on edge of the Mindanao Sea along with his fantasies of Legaspi, Palawan and Zamboanga, rather than in the slipstream of the North Circular road.

Every year Freddy Ismail expanded his shop, and 2001 was the third successive year of improvement.

Sunny had a week off while the shop was being refitted. He was going to use the time to paint the front of the house. Not exactly fine art, he said to Clara, but necessary. The window sills were pitted and cracked; the front door showed more grime than paint. He should have done it in the summer, but he was waiting for his hands to grow steady again. Now there was not much time left; soon the cold weather and damp would make the task impossible.

'Black OK?' he had asked Clara.

'You have some malaise?'

'Malaise?' The word had turned in his head like a loose petal blown in from the garden. 'Malaise? What is this malaise?' He put down his bottle and grabbed at a passing shadow. *Mal* might mean bad in most of the EU but it sounded like flower in Sinhala. Where did that leave *mal*-aise? He was in a whirlwind. 'Malaysia?'

'What is it with you these days?'

In the end they compromised: white window sills, but a dark bottle green for the door.

The sun shone all morning and it was hot on the front steps. A rose was out, peachy with scarlet wry smiles, a little shaky at coming out so late in the front garden where he'd dumped the summer's debris of broken trellises and busted pots, but in flower nevertheless. He undid the screws of the brass door handle, and removed the house number and letter-box flap. He spread newspapers underneath. The sports pages had multiplied recently and were good for the main panels. For the nooks and crannies he used the freebie Sri Lankan advertiser he'd picked up from the Tamil shop a few days earlier. The news was not hopeful. The spate of elections on the island had created confusion. Prospects were poor. The official death toll in the long war with the LTTE was over 60,000 men, women and children. Sunny scraped the door with a metal stripper until the small flakes of old paint, crumbs and powder smothered the headlines. The sound of steel on wood was hypnotic.

By midday he'd taken the worst of it off. Close to the bare wood of the door, nurturing the soot and sun of long-dead decades – the sixties or maybe even the twenties – he discovered an early coat of green paint. He made a mental note to keep a small bit of the door cut to it to show Clara when she got back from work: heritage was instinct with him. The next job was to smooth the surface. Rough paper first and then the fine grade. He'd never paid quite so much attention to preparation before. He wanted to keep it going; the moment, the peace of having just one problem to solve. It took him right back to his younger days when he could spend hours in front of a picture, or follow a thought – a ball on a string – for days. Hector would have said, 'Ah, Zen, no?'

It was not comfort he wanted now, not even reassurance. Simply a quietness. Peace in his mind. Clara seemed more content recently, all her interests feeding each other. Mikey had settled something in his own mind too. Sunny had figured out how many glasses he needed to keep things in focus. 'We each have our own lives, borrowed as they may be,' he said out loud.

Before breaking for lunch he applied a grey primer on the door. There'd be time for it to dry then, before he started again in the afternoon with the dark, deep everlasting green.

It was only when he'd made his toasted sandwich and sat

in front of the TV with a beer that he discovered what was happening. He was just in time to see the first tower fall in New York. He stayed, transfixed by the cameras that had taken over from the commentators. Everyone was bewildered.

Hours later – two? three? – he heard the front door open. He stepped away from the TV which was stuck in a perpetual loop of showing and re-showing the same unbelievable images of a plane flying straight into a skyscraper. In the hall, Mikey was staring at the grey door. 'What happened?' He dropped his school bag.

'The next world war . . .' Sunny started to say, but then noticed the tears in his son's eyes; he was struggling to hold them back. 'You've seen what's been happening?'

'It was a fight,' Mikey said. 'Massive fight.'

'You saw TV at school?'

Mikey's long neck tensed and he shook his head. He looked at his father as though he had gone crazy.

Sunny bundled him into the sitting room. 'Look.' There was that plane again. An arrow becoming a fireball. He watched what he'd seen too many times already. 'Look,' he said again to Mikey who was fiddling with his trainers. Mikey pulled out a tissue and started wiping one of them. His limbs had grown disjointed.

'What are you doing?' Sunny couldn't believe he was cleaning his shoes. Not watching. Not hooked. Not terrified.

Mikey got up and headed for the hall. 'I have to wash this . . .'

'Hey, do you know what is happening? That's a real building.'

Mikey came back, surprised at his father's tone. He stared unflinchingly. 'Benjy was in a fight.'

Sunny made a sound conveying sympathy, but the dust cloud on the screen seemed to spread into the room and cover everything.

It was only later that night that he learnt from Clara's few clipped words what had happened to Benjy. He'd been in a fight with a bunch of Turkish boys near the old shop. Mikey had been in detention and got there only when the ambulance had arrived. Benjy had been rushed to casualty. While Sunny was out at the off-licence, Clara and Mikey had called Benjy's house but there had been no answer.

'What about the hospital?'

'The switchboard kept putting us on hold.'

They didn't know who else to call.

By the time Sunny went upstairs to say something to Mikey, he was fast asleep. When he came back down, Clara had gone to her computer. On TV the newscasters were beginning to manage the news once more; they had their pictures back under control. When Sunny lay down to sleep that night he couldn't sort the images of New York from those of Colombo five years earlier. As for little Benjy . . . he didn't know what to think. Nothing would be quite the same again in their separate worlds: Mikey's, Benjy's and his. But then, he wondered, was it ever?

CHOWKIDAR

2002

SUNNY LOOKED at Hector's letter again: *2002 might be a year to remember.*

He showed Mikey the enclosed cheque and told him what Hector had suggested, *a good bat*. Mikey shrugged. An MP3 player was more his thing than cricket kit.

On the night of his birthday, Mikey went out with a gaggle of odd hoods while Sunny and Clara watched what Sunny called the Bush, Blair and Bin Laden show on TV. The remains of a chocolate cake subsided on the coffee table next to the birthday Cava and Sunny's nearly depleted Bell's. Sunny collected the bits of wrapping paper from the birthday presents – CDs, a video, a jumper, a new pay-as-you-go mobile – and stuffed them into a recycled carrier bag.

'Is that it then? No longer a kid?' He poured himself another stiff drink.

'Don't be silly. There's summer after summer of exam stress to come. He needs to build himself up to it. I guess you wouldn't know about that.'

Sunny gagged. She of course had plenty of experience,

with her graphics and oil paint and diplomas part 1 to infinity. 'Mikey? Stress? Maybe over garage and grunge.'

After the news was over, Clara switched off the TV. Sunny handed her Hector's letter. He would like it to be a year to remember. He began tentatively by saying that he thought it was pretty unlikely that Mikey would want another holiday with them, however sunny the green valleys of Wales might be. Not unless they were going by black Maserati, or the Harlech Festival was headlining So Solid Crew and Barry White reloaded in a striped djellaba. The newly peaceful Sri Lanka of Hector, with its requirement of major capital outlay, was more likely to catch his interest. 'What do you think? Shall we all go to Sri Lanka this time?'

She read the letter slowly and then sighed. 'Weren't there supposed to be peace talks when you went last time? And then, didn't they just go and launch a full-scale war?'

There had been Operation Riviresa, followed by Operation Jayasikuru and then Rivibala and on and on . . . Yes, he knew that, but things can change. Wasn't that the lesson he was meant to learn?

'Second innings, second chance. It's all up for grabs.' For him too, perhaps.

'Yes, and where do we suddenly get the money from? Has Hector sent a cheque for that too?'

Earlier in the day, at the library, he had noticed a flyer for a national photography competition. The first prize was five thousand pounds. Enough to make a real difference for him, for Clara, for Mikey. He had fantasized about it while waiting for another drunk to finish with the newspaper. Now it formed into a holiday in Sri Lanka. A wide screen

TV. *Bahala na*, Robby's favourite Tagalog expression came back to him. *Que sera, sera*. Whatever will be, will be. Luck. Fate. Or was it *bahala na kayo?* It's up to you?

The first day of the first Test match at Lord's between Sri Lanka and England – Thursday, 16 May 2002 – was glorious. The sun had come out for the Sri Lankan tourists. The temperature soared for the first time all year. The visitors abandoned their thermals and played like they were on the beach at home. Roasting England, as the delighted pundits said, the ones who – countering the loyalty test – favoured the team with the longest names in the game. Perhaps they'd invested too much time practising the pronunciation of Jayawardene, Jayasurya, Muralitharan, to let nationality form a boundary, or maybe they just liked good cricket, sunshine and memories of palm trees.

Sunny was in the studio most of the afternoon setting up some new equipment Freddy had splashed out on with more of his unstoppable wealth. When he came out Freddy chuckled. 'Hey, you guys are doing all right, eh?' He'd heard on the radio that somebody had already got his first century – Mahela Jayawardene?

Sunny caught the highlights on Channel 4 and was hooked. He realized then that Hector was right. He *had* to go to Lord's and rediscover the passions of his youth. Suddenly the most important thing in the world was to see Sri Lanka play England in a full Test match in London. He had to make his life turn the way he wanted it to, like a true spinner's ball. It was up to him. *Bahala na kayo*. His head was throbbing with an excitement he hadn't felt for years. He got out his vintage

Leica and a cleaning kit. He was sure that he would take the perfect picture at the match, a sporting photo which would bag him the photography prize and allow him to breathe easy at last. It all fitted together. He could hardly wait.

'What's wrong?' Clara asked when he went into the kitchen. 'You want a camomile tea?' She had an Oxford Street *lungi* wrapped around her and knotted high on her front. Her hair was up, in a tangle, her shoulders bare and moist after her bath.

Sunny started to dismantle the camera. He wanted it in perfect working order. The viewfinder and the lens absolutely clear. He told her that the match had been on TV. The words tumbled out but didn't rouse much interest in her. She made her night drink in a mug – a Tate Modern souvenir she liked to hug. His head was pounding. His hands trembled. He put down the camera. The spice rack behind her, crammed with cardamoms, cinnamon and garam masala, was half off the wall. The screws were not right, the wall plugs loose. She pursed her lips for another sip and he remembered everything that had happened in his life. Everything. He saw her again as he had the first time, in Mrs Veeraswamy's kitchen.

'You know, sometimes I feel I want to burst open this head of mine and show you what's inside.' Sunny leant forward, his elbows on the kitchen table, his fingers stretched out around his skull as though he was about to prise it open. His nails dug into the skin of his forehead. 'I want it to be yours.' He looked up and caught her eyes; it hurt him to hold the gaze. 'Do you know what I mean?'

He wasn't used to talking like this. From the inside. He

hadn't done it for years. Perhaps he never had. He didn't like to be the one to break a silence, but at that moment he wanted to say everything. He was too full of words. They were churning, making him unsteady. Drunk. 'Do you?' Sunny asked again. His fingers drummed at his head.

Her dark eyes wavered. 'Mine?'

He glanced down at the camera in pieces on the table, the lens brush and cotton bud, the cheap cut-glass tumbler of whisky next to it. 'Do you want to come with me tomorrow?' It felt as though he hadn't asked her anything so direct in a long time.

She took a sip of her herbal tea. 'I don't think so. This is the last weekend to get Mikey revising. And there's the school concert in the afternoon.' She put down her mug and picked up a pencil. Her thumb pressed against the middle of it. 'I want to get a load of paints too, you know, for my new class. I'll need the car.'

His breath was warm. Too warm. Something was burning up inside him. He wasn't sure whether there should be more to this moment, or less. Life seemed to have become too fraught. The glass of whisky moved out of focus. She had her life; he had his, even if sometimes it seemed he'd lost his grip. He wanted to ask about her new class. Was it Alex again? Something snagged on the side of his leg – an involuntary contraction of a muscle that pinched the notorious sciatic nerve his father had complained about. Or, maybe, just a premonition of another clumsy step he was about to take. Ever since Hector's letter arrived he had been tense, as though his body knew that time was running out. He felt he'd fluffed everything; now he just wanted that second chance.

'OK, take the car. The clutch is slipping, but if you keep a steady speed you'll be all right.' He had thought he might be able to make some adjustment, tighten a cable, and save himself the three hundred pounds he would be charged by the local garage. He just hadn't got around to it. 'I should have had it fixed. I'm sorry.'

She bit her lower lip. 'I'll manage.'

The pencil snapped.

He saw her in the car: that lip drawn in, eyes sharp, sitting high. A determined, exacting driver who, quite rightly, expected things to work as they should. For her, the engine must start at the first turn of the key, the car move smoothly at the press of the accelerator, stop at the touch of the brake pedal. Traffic lights will switch from red to amber and then logically, inevitably, to green in correct accountable unfuckable steps. For Sunny, increasingly, nothing ever worked quite according to plan.

He hadn't been to Lord's before; never seen a Test match for real. He had no idea what he might be letting himself in for; his only experience of cricket in England came from country drives and those sleepy affairs behind the tennis courts, off Park Road, that he used to pass with Mikey when he was a toddler: sunlit oaks, a blue sky, a pavilion from the colonial era with picket teeth and gin rims. He packed a bottle of water, a little hip flask, the old Leica with the cleaned Super-Angulon 1:4/21 Leitz lens and a small palm TV in case he couldn't get into the grounds. He wasn't going to be alone. If this was the most fun batting team in the world, then the place may be already full – a hundred thousand London Sri Lankans might be there, celebrating the end of the war and the rebirth of Test cricket. It was about time.

He bought a newspaper and took the W7 to Finsbury Park. There was no one on board who looked ready for cricket. Off the bus, he headed straight down the tube like a devout saboteur. He knew he had the look, these days, clean-shaven or not. The dark hue, the loaded eye, the prescription sunglasses. A fruit vendor stared at him with suspicion, as if he could tell they were on different sides.

'You fail the Norman Wisdom cricket test, right?' Freddy had chuckled as Sunny was putting away the tripods the previous evening.

'What's that?'

'That bald fella who told us to "get on your bike". He said vagrants like you and me never support England. We confuse the home team.'

'Immigrants,' Sunny corrected him. 'It all depends who they play.' He remembered the complexities of loyalty even in the Philippines. 'Anyway, it wasn't Norman Wisdom. He was a joker.'

At King's Cross he made the mistake of assuming the shorter route was the quicker one and got fouled up by the Circle Line; then, at Baker Street, he began to sense something. There were definitely *aficionados* in his Jubilee line carriage. Solitary types in khaki shorts, carrying small canvas sacks packed with newspapers. Sunny picked out half a dozen of them, each one trying in vain to look inconspicuous. As the train pulled into St John's Wood they rose from their seats at the same time. Sunny followed them down the platform at a discreet distance. Despite the prospect of sunshine, they did not look like happy people.

As he reached the escalator, festive laughter tumbled down towards him. More fans materialized, donning sun hats, carrying umbrellas, picnic baskets, carrier bags of plonk and beer.

As soon as he got through at the top, he was accosted by ticket touts.

'Best seats, forty quid.'

'Today's last seats.'

Sunny avoided them all and followed the crowd down Wellington Terrace. He noticed that everybody else was ignoring them too. He had no idea of the official price of a ticket; he didn't even know what one looked like.

He headed down to what had to be the grounds, although it was difficult to imagine where among the villas and luxury blocks it could be hidden. He spoke to no one and no one spoke to him, but there was a sense of solidarity. Sides, at that particular moment, seemed not to matter. He was at last that arrow he had always wanted to be: just released, in motion, heading for his proper place. Pure Zen. Clara had her thing; he had his. Perhaps the fact that their lives had slowly separated didn't matter. He reached the grounds. A queue at least 300 yards long snaked round a bend in the road. Towering above them was a media pod that looked like a spaceship. He joined the queue and heard a roar inside, where something wonderful in cricket had happened.

A Sri Lankan gang in a new Mercedes rolled past, the driver peering out looking for a familiar face to cajole, glancing up at the sky from time to time, ready to take evasive action if a ball came at him out of nowhere, as they are known to do in gardens and stadiums all over the world. Another ticket tout approached the queue. The price had dropped to thirty pounds. Someone in the line called him over. The rest watched as two men examined what the tout had to offer. They exchanged notes and headed for the turnstiles. The man in front of Sunny nudged his companion, 'Let's see if they get in.' They did. The tout disappeared. The queue moved and there was another roar from inside, then a huge collective sigh.

Picture reception was terrible and Sunny's vintage palm TV couldn't quite cope with the glare of the sun, but he managed to catch the score and passed it around: 343 for 3. He felt he was joining a religion, or something akin to one. The man next to him explained that Atapattu, a name he pronounced without hesitation, had achieved a milestone. 'You heard the cheer?' he explained. The Sri Lankan stalwart had hit a boundary to cross the century-and-a-half mark. Sunny smiled, beginning to understand. The day was looking even better.

When he reached the ticket booth he was told the Compton stand was good. Thirty pounds to be up on top. 'You can see the scoreboard and the replay screen.'

'What if it rains?' The weather report claimed rain was on the way.

'They won't play if it rains. You take shelter underneath.'

He collected the ticket and went in. The security guard rummaged around in his bag and pointed out that the water bottle was leaking. The *Guardian* had saved the camera. The other bottle was safe. Sunny thanked the woman and she wished him luck as though she knew how much he needed it.

Inside the gates he entered a fairground. There were nets to the left, toilets to the right, and people milling about looking at everything but the match taking place in the centre. He found his way to the Compton stand; a metal spiral staircase led to the upper tier. He climbed up into the open and stood amazed before a green lung holding its breath every minute or so, as a ball flew down and a perfect straight bat blocked it. The scoreboard gave the names of the batsmen, the bowler and any fielder who touched the ball. It was a world away from those games Sunny had passed in the middle-distant countryside, where the beer was warm and the mayflies snored and matchstick figures played an indistinct game. The replay screen on the other side ensured that nothing was missed: that boundary thwacked as you bend for your beer, or the wicket that falls as you sink into your paper. The art of the near miss, the spectator's true sport, was almost impossible. Anxiety – the very heart of art – now had to focus on not missing the actual moment because the camera was always there, never blinking, recording everything for a posterity limited only by technology. It was no longer the case that you might miss it, only that you may not see it *as it happened*. Sunny found himself intent on every ball. The here and the now. No Clara, no Mikey. No father, no mother. No other thought.

In front of him, two men in white sun hats were drinking champagne out of plastic flutes. They had been there for a while – the bottle was nearly empty. Their faces were florid, but they kept their ties and blazers on. Beyond them, out at the crease, the famous Sri Lankan batsman Aravinda de Silva was hopping like a bird, patting the earth with his bat, casting quick furtive glances around the field, getting ready to fly. *Watch out*, Sunny wanted to yell. The bowler, England's Caddick, was already on his run-up. Only when the ball was released, after a forlorn grunt, did de Silva seem to notice what was happening. Startled, he let fly – another boundary. The two men in front giggled and touched plastic. 'Cheers.' When de Silva got to 48 there was an announcement that he had reached a career record of six thousand Test runs. 'Bloody good show,' the Englishman on the left said, and poured out the last of the champagne. The stadium wasn't full, there weren't many brown faces in the crowd – not the thousands Sunny had expected – but the cheer was loud. Then Atapattu fell for a smart trap and played the hook he'd resisted all morning. Suddenly the knocking back and forth of the ball, the minutes ticking by for no reason, stopped. Everything stopped except the ball, falling. On the field all the players tensed up as one. The trap had been sprung. Trescothick made the catch. The man was given out. The wind changed. Sunny stood with the rest of the stadium to give the batsman his standing ovation as he took off his gloves and shuffled into the pavilion and a page in sporting history.

When lunch was called, the pair in front opened a bottle of red wine and started to munch corned beef sandwiches. Sunny took a quick nip of old gold and went down to see if he could find a Sri Lankan snack. He came across fish and chips, crêpes, burgers and a tikka masala stall. No *vadai*, no *bola cutlis*, no *lampries*.

Then he saw her.

He would not have recognized her if she hadn't turned. She wore a long brick-coloured tunic that hid her figure and she was chattering. She stopped and looked down her long quivering, gorgeous nose at a white polystyrene dish of golden chips. The oval face was unmistakable, even with the glittering nose stud. She picked up a large square-cut potato, the size of a finger, and put it daintily in her mouth.

He adjusted his sunglasses. 'Tina?'

She must have been ten yards away. She couldn't have heard him, but she looked up. Her face broadened as she laboured to quickly swallow her chip. 'Sunny?' She dabbed off the excess ketchup. 'Sunny?'

'Yes.' He went up to her. Full on, for a moment she seemed a caricature of the young girl in Makati who had tormented his youth. She was still a knockout.

'Sunny? You haven't changed a tick.'

Could he say the same to her? What could he say? 'Tina.'

'I can't believe it.'

Sunny shrugged. 'Neither can I. What are you doing here?'

'After yesterday, we just had to come back to watch more.'

Only then did he notice her red-haired companion. Steve Thompson grunted a greeting, as apish as he'd been three decades earlier.

'You remember Steve?' Tina clutched his arm as though he might slip away to deep square leg.

'Of course, Steve. How are you?'

'Good. I'm good. You? Good?'

'I live here.'

'Yeah, we heard,' Tina teased. 'Goodness, in London?'

Steve leant forward. 'You like a beer?'

'Oh, Steve darling, you were going to get the beer, weren't you? So go. I am so thirsty. Sunny, come, let's sit. Get him a beer, Steve. Yes?'

Sunny had never heard her say so much. Her voice was full of disbelief at the luck of a charmed life. 'Sure. A beer would be great.'

'Foster's?'

'Sure. Whatever.'

'Good. That's . . . good.'

While Steve donned his anorak and headed for the good beer counter, Tina settled herself into a plastic chair. 'So, Sunny, how have you been? Tell me.'

'OK. I've been living here.'

'Married, right?'

'Not exactly.' The glare off the white plastic table was almost too much.

'You have a son?'

'How did you know that?'

Tina simpered over another chip. 'I heard. Here, have some of these. They are just so delicious.'

Sunny tried one. They were greasy and seemed to be still frying in the heat of the sun. 'You don't live in London, do you?'

'Oh, no. Just here on a hop about. Steve and I live in Sydney. Tomorrow morning we are off to Paris. We are doing Europe. All the concert halls. I've always been mad about orchestras, you know. But we'll nip back from Berlin for the India-Sri Lanka ODI, next month and then it will be all over.'

'Yeah?'

'The One-day International? That's the real thing. Adrenalin, no? Steve goes crazy with cricket. And now, guess what? Sri Lanka. We've just been in Colombo, on the way. Short stop, you know. He loves it. He wants us to move there. We did a quick beach and culture trip. Now all he wants is to play in a sarong and eat coconut. I don't know what Daddy would say if he heard. I am hoping that when we go to Rome, he'll see the light. All those saints can surely do something, don't you think?'

'How is your Dad? Your mother?'

'Fine. They are fine. They live in Washington. Very happy. Well as can be expected in these days of the great American siege, and Daddy's tummy problems. They are both staunch Republicans.'

'Republicans? What about China?'

She nibbled some more, thinking. 'That was a long time ago. After we moved to America, things changed. He was diagnosed as having a food allergy.'

'Soya?'

'No, seriously. First we thought it was just MSG – monosodium glutamate. Then curry was ruled out too. Cumin, coriander. Onions. Asian cuisine was causing him major problems. You see, he tried to cook for himself. Thank God, he's stopped that nonsense now. Mom is so happy. And Daddy does smile a lot more. He says he feels healthier. And he was a fan of Nixon, you know. So it all sort of makes sense.'

Steve arrived with the beer. He placed the bottles on the table and sat down slightly apart from the other two, looking sombre.

'I was saying,' Tina explained, 'you'd love to live in some beach house in Sri Lanka, isn't that right, Stevie? But Daddy doesn't trust anyone there, not even the place – beach, jungle or sea. He thinks the peace won't last. War is now everywhere, how can it disappear from that one little place?'

'They are reopening the Jaffna library.'

'Yes, Steve darling, but you know what's going on. With those assholes everywhere, excuse me but warmongers are the pits . . .'

Sunny couldn't work out what Tina was doing. Why was she talking in this way? It was as though she was hungry for a life that had escaped her. How could she – who'd been such a free spirit, in whom the future had glowed – be so entangled, so stuck, in the world she had started out in? And with Steve? What about women's cricket?

'Sunny, you'd never believe where I met him again?'

'Steve? At the zoo?'

She paused. 'Why do you say zoo? No, not the zoo. At the library. The State library in Sydney. I was doing research for my thesis – on resins, you know – and there he was. Steve.'

'Also doing research?'

'Temporary job. Cleaning . . . Good job.'

'It was fantastic.' Tina dug into her dwindling collection of potato chips.

'Really?'

'Now we both are into sticky drugs.'

That might have explained something, but then she mentioned the pharmaceutical industry. They both worked for a multinational. 'Steve reckons he can open a lab in Sri Lanka. Get in on the ayurvedic front before all the patents go. Anyway, what about you, Sunny? What's been happening with you?'

'I've been here. London. I do a bit of photography . . .'

'Fantastic. We love taking pictures. Steve, show him the camera we got in Singapore. Show him. He'd love it.' While Steve fumbled with a leather pouch, she continued. 'Digital. It does video. Everything. Oh, darling,' she squeezed Steve's arm. 'Do we have those Colombo pictures in there still?'

Steve dipped his head a little lower. 'That lot was downloaded.'

Tina gave a sexy little whinny. 'I thought we could keep hundreds, no? What were all those megabytes for?' Her face quivered, disappointed. 'You'd never believe who we met there. Never.' Her eyes brightened. 'Guess?'

'Prabhakaran?' The LTTE supremo had given his first press conference the previous month. Sunny had seen his picture on the net. He could have been a junior game warden in his neat safari suit rather than the leader of the most famous guerrilla army in the world.

'No, silly. Someone you know. From Makati?'

'Hector?'

'Robby! We met Robby, there in Colombo. Can you believe it? He was staying at a friend of my cousin's. Adel's. You know her. She said you stayed with her once.'

'In Havelock Town?'

'Yes. She talked a lot about you. She really liked having you there. She *lurved* your clothes.'

Sunny didn't want to talk about Adel. 'What's Robby doing there?'

'Garment factory. Much to Adel's delight. But of course you know all about that, no? He said he met you while doing the same thing here.'

Sunny blushed. 'No, no. I wasn't in his line of business. We just met, like this. You know how it is. London.'

'I know. I know. We've done Trafalgar Square and the South Bank.'

'Festival Hall,' Steve added knowingly. 'Very good.'

Tina said they had arrived a week earlier and had spent the whole of Sunday on a double-decker tour bus seeing the city at treetop height. 'I know it like a pigeon,' she squealed, fluttering her hand.

Steve laughed too, as though they were on honeymoon, or one of Herbie's illicit substances.

For a moment, Sunny felt a twinge of envy. Not so much for Steve, but for what they seemed to have together. Gladstone's famous London bus ride, a stroll on the South Bank, an urge to laugh at the same time. A shared sense of a mad spinning world.

'Yesterday, in my opinion, was the best.' Steve's fulsome sentence gave Sunny hope. Perhaps there was some divergence in their lives.

He was wrong.

'Oh, God, yes.'

It sounded like sex. Sunny didn't want to know.

Steve held Tina's hand in one fist and lifted his beer with

the other. He sipped and smiled at the same time. 'It could have gone on all night.'

'But Daddy always said that in England the balls tend to wobble after . . .' Tina hesitated.

Sunny didn't know what to say.

'He would have loved to have been here with us,' Steve added.

'Your dad?' Rudy? Sunny remembered his penchant for group activity.

'Uh-huh. He is almost all-American. He has completely given up curry and sesame oil, but he'll never swap cricket for baseball. He would have loved to see Mahela Jayawardene pulling his hundred yesterday.'

'Cover drive.' Steve raised his eyes.

'I understand.' Sunny finally caught the true drift of their pillow talk. 'It was a good start.'

'But this wicket falling before lunch, that is not good news.' Steve looked into his tumbler, downcast. 'Not good at all.'

'The President can give them a pep talk,' Tina laughed.

'Which President? MCC?'

'Sri Lanka's President, dummy. Chandrika. She's here. We saw her going into the pavilion.' She screwed up her mouth and twisted it from side to side as if to suppress her amusement.

Sunny reckoned Tina was joking. 'What, while the Tigers come out to play in Kilinochchi, she's here to watch cricket? What about the peace talks?'

'That's not her thing, no? That's Ranil's business.'

'Ranil's?' Then he remembered Ranil was the name of

the Prime Minister in Sri Lanka. He rubbed his temples. The world seemed very crowded.

'Anyway, whatever the reason, she is here. And the boys need a cheerleader.'

Steve sniggered.

It was announced that the match was about to continue. Tina stood up. 'Toilets. Then we better get to our seats. Shall we meet here at the break? Sunny?'

'Sure, teatime.' He watched them go, hand in hand, both a little wider than before but happy.

Back on the upper tier the two sozzled enthusiasts in the front row were exchanging reminiscences. Sunny listened to their talk, letting the sound of other voices fill the void in him.

'You ready for a beer now?' one of them said, as the crowd cheered another boundary.

'I'll wait for the next wicket.'

His companion gave a muffled laugh. 'Another Sri *Langkin* wicket? That's their Arnold? Isn't it? Poor England. They could do with a bloody crate of beer. Look at Hussain. Looks like a bleeding ghost with all that white sun slop.'

The new batsman looked set to be there for a while. A bored England fielder near the boundary started to practise his golf swing. Beyond the media pod hanging over the edge of the grounds rain clouds were gathering. Somewhere Tina and Steve were watching the same game; the President of Sri Lanka was watching it. Hector might be in a house in Colombo with satellite TV, and maybe Piyasena with his cousin Matara Malli in a *vadai kadé* off Galle Road. Perhaps even the Tigers' leader in his camouflaged bunker was biting his nails . . . All watching the same game. Slowly the world, Sunny's world, was rearranging itself. Those watching would remember this peculiar event for ever; those who missed it would never know its thrill. Sunny saw how Clara and Mikey would be on one side; the others, from the supreme commander to Matara Malli, on the other.

Clouds rolled closer. England's bowlers – Caddick and Flintoff – seemed revitalized by the smell of rain; aggressive, even from the Nursery End. The crowd started to egg them on, thirsting for a wicket. The batting was simply not exciting enough to hold them, the fans had had enough. By three o'clock the whole atmosphere had changed. Arnold reached his half-century and got his cheer, but something was held back. The deal was off. The crowd wanted blood. The desire was palpable. A supermarket carrier bag wafted over the playing field like a clown's balloon, misshapen, mocking. With the very next ball Arnold was out – bowled by Hoggard, also caught by Trescothick. Then, within eight balls, Aravinda de Silva was out. 'By George, they've got it,' the man in the front row yelled. 'England.' He switched to beer and passed a can to his companion. By the mid-afternoon interval, they had entered a different world.

Sunny went back to the food court to meet Tina and Steve. They were eating ice creams and looking miserable.

'Tea?'

'No bloody Ceylon tea,' Steve whined. 'These bloody people don't serve any good bloody tea.'

'Yeah. They don't have any Sri Lankan food either.'

'No chicken curry, no *vadai*, no tea. No wonder our boys are so glum.' Tina licked the vanilla drips off her fingers.

Sunny nodded. 'They might have had a *baila* band, at least, and some bottles.'

The carnival atmosphere that had been all pervasive earlier had evaporated. They were at a much darker event now: more like a public execution. The expectation was for wickets to fall, rather than for runs to stack up.

'You staying until the bitter end?'

'Oh, yes. Shall we go for a drink after the game? Or a meal? We heard there are some Filipino restaurants in Earls Court.'

Steve endorsed the proposal. 'Good.'

'I have to get back, but maybe a quick drink round here.'

'Sure, sure. A quickie then. We'll be having an early night anyway. We have to be at Waterloo before seven tomorrow.'

'Eurostar?'

'Yes, under the sea we are going.'

Eric would be pleased, Sunny thought. Clara's father longed for more people to experience the Chunnel.

He noticed raindrops soon after he got back to his seat. The batting had turned to blocking. There was booing. Then, some time before Zoysa hit the only two sixes of the whole match, Sunny got a call on his mobile. It was Clara. The car wouldn't start; it was stuck at the car park of John Jones's art shop.

'The AA card is out of date.' She sounded incredulous that he had neglected to pay up for roadside rescue.

'Yes. I was thinking about that.'

The crowd chanted as the bowler pawed the ground. Then he charged . . . 'Whoooooo-aagh!'

'What's happening?' Clara asked.

'The mob. They want action.'

'What shall I do? The gates close at six.'

'If it won't start it is the carburettor, not the clutch. You go on to Mikey's concert. I'll fix the car and bring it home. I have my keys.'

He asked her to video the end of the match. The team would have to battle on their own. There was nothing he could do about Tina and Steve. He didn't know where they were sitting. He hadn't given them his phone number. They had no way of contacting each other. Did it matter? He decided to trust in luck. Fate and destiny. If they were to meet again, they would. At the Oval for the ODI.

When Clara got home, she looked as though she was still upset.

Sunny shrugged. 'I am sorry about the AA. I'll sort it out tomorrow. But even they might have missed it. It's a tiny tube that comes loose sometimes. It only took a minute . . .'

'Mikey wasn't there,' she blurted out. 'He didn't come to the concert.'

'Why?'

'I don't know. He didn't turn up. It's not like him to let down his band.'

'Did you try his phone?'

'It just goes to voicemail.'

'Have you tried calling any of his friends?'

'Not yet.'

Sunny wondered whether it was to do with his French oral, but that was not until Monday. Mikey wasn't the type to lose sleep over exams. He sent him a text message. 'Let's wait and see for a couple of hours.' Mikey was sixteen. He could do what he wanted.

Sunny poured himself a whisky and settled down to watch the last of the day's play, rewound on tape. Fingertip control had its attractions after all. He could stop the action, pause the ball, go back a frame, forward a frame. See the fielder's howl, the captain's frown. It may not have been real, but it was almost his game now. The technology was utterly seductive, even if the Zen went, as Hector would say, when you began to identify the player by his face rather than his stroke.

When Sri Lanka got to 555, after some laborious batting, the captain declared the innings.

The bowling, the experts warned, was going to be the problem. There was no Murali – possibly the greatest spin bowler in the world. He was not fit to play. Sri Lanka had never won an overseas Test without him. Vaas, the fast bowler, came out and crossed himself. Involuntarily Sunny did too. Not for them, but for everything else that seemed to be gathering around the edges. Mostly for Mikey. He hadn't replied to the text. Sunny keyed in another, but resisted sending it. He would wait. Patience. Anxiety must be swallowed. Transformed. The brand of cigarettes Lester had smoked in Colombo was 555. He'd blow smoke rings, one through the other, like ripples of magic breath. The small through the big until another shot right through and dispersed the earlier ones.

At about eight o'clock Mikey finally replied. His message was typically brief. *sori* about the concert and a *c u l8r.*

'He's OK,' Sunny told Clara.

They had dinner, each preoccupied with their own thoughts. Halfway through the lasagne Clara asked about the match. 'Was it any good?'

'Depends what you mean by good.'

'Worth going?'

'It isn't easy to describe. Bit like a religious experience.'

'Dad used to play, you know. Every Sunday. Drove Mum nuts.'

'Was that the problem?'

'The rows? I don't know. They expected too much, I guess.'

'Is that why you expect so little?'

She shrugged. 'Maybe.'

'Anyway, I'm not about to start playing.'

Sunny went back to the TV to watch the highlights. He drew the curtains and switched on the small lamp on the piano. He got his chair in position and put a cushion for his back and another on a stool for his feet. He poured himself another drink and turned on the telly.

She pushed open the door and peered in. 'Haven't you seen it all?'

'I want to get the full picture.' To get it into the blood. Somehow it was important. Something had to be important.

'Sounds like an addiction.'

He settled down to watch the replay of the two sixes that had come, one after the other. Was that when he was on the tube, or in the car park, under the hood, twiddling with rubber hoses? He would have liked to have seen the sixes, two in a row, in real life. He might have taken a seriously good picture. A second chance like that doesn't come very often.

Only then did Sunny realize he hadn't taken a single picture. Not even of Tina, or Steve in his gooseberry anorak. The day had been too surreal; he had been in a trance. He'd completely forgotten the photography competition.

At midnight he sent another text to Mikey. A reminder. He didn't expect a reply. Clara had gone to bed. Everywhere small fissures, fault lines, new cracks were widening. Mikey in a world Sunny would never see, Clara in retreat, and then Tina, who had appeared and disappeared – now tucked into some Bloomsbury hotel with her man, watching the replay on a minuscule TV and wondering why he hadn't turned up at the end of the day. It was not his fault, but Sunny felt he'd made a bad move; been forced to make a bad move by the way things were. He stayed in the sitting room with the TV on, thinking, until the bottle of Scotch was empty. Perhaps it was not so strange for Tina, people appearing and disappearing. Her life still revolved around the people she'd known in her teens: her mother, her father, Steve. She'd moved from country to country but the people in her life remained the same. Clara's life was surprisingly similar. He'd first met her when she was sixteen; the rest of her circle from that time, and earlier, were still around her. She remained attached, despite her reservations about her parents. She'd discarded no one, except for Gumbo, and easily added new ones like Alex and her painting group.

Sunny wished he had taken Mikey to the game. But it was too late. Mikey was off on his own already. And tomorrow Sunny had to go to Freddy's studio. There were appointments to keep. A job to do. There was no guarantee that Mikey would be back before midday, and in any case there were exams on Monday.

Sunny felt unsettled when he found that Clara was still awake. She was in bed, with a magazine next to her. He put the phone on the bedside table.

She had the duvet up over her breasts, held in place by her arms. The wall behind the bedhead needed repainting. There was a sheen where his head had touched it for sixteen fugitive years. They had gone for muted tones, all those years ago, when they had been happy to pore over colour charts and furniture catalogues. They had liked the idea of a cosy room; now it seemed dark and unbearably confining. White might have been the better option, even if it had turned grey by now. The whole interior of the house needed redoing.

'I met a couple from Manila.' He tried to engage her.

'Where?'

'Today. At the match.'

'Do they play cricket in the Philippines?'

'They are not Filipino. They are like me. We happened to be there, in Manila, at the same time.' He remembered how Robby had broken through first, then Hector. Linking the past and the present, a needle flashing in and out with a thread made of memory.

'Will you meet up again?'

He said he had forgotten to exchange numbers and that in any case they'd be off touring Europe. 'They just came and went. It was . . . weird.'

A police car with its siren wailing raced down the escape lane by the park.

'I wonder why Mikey missed the concert.'

'Maybe he got tired of playing the same three chords.' He checked the phone to make sure it was on signal. The transmitter icon blinked.

'Better get some sleep.' He turned off the light.

Another siren sounded in the distance. It might have been better, he thought, if he had gone a little easier on the whisky.

At about 5 a.m. he heard the front door open and close. The jangle of keys being tossed into a drawer. When he woke again, it was nearly nine.

He had three appointments and then some enlargements to oversee. There was no TV in the shop, and the lad who worked the machines in the back hadn't brought his radio. Sunny heard nothing about the match until teatime when he went to the newsagent's. 'England in deep shit.' The shopkeeper's words created an echo in his head that bounced from Colombo to London. 'Hussain out, caught by that Sangakkara.'

When Sunny got home at the end of the day he found that the England team were on their second innings in a humiliating follow on. There were complaints made – unfair wily bowling, a crisis in confidence – and a hint of rain in the air.

Sunny watched the repeat on TV as though it were live.

Clara peeped in during a drinks break. 'Have you talked to Mikey?'

'I haven't seen him.'

'When is the match over?'

'At this rate, pretty soon.' England had made only 275 in the first innings. They might be all done for less than that in the morning. 'But there are two more matches in the series.'

Clara watched Ruchira Perera release a ball on screen.

'He's met a girl.'

'Who?'

'Mikey.'

She was smiling.

'It's not the first time, is it?'

'He looks pretty pleased with himself.'

'Doesn't he have a French exam on Monday?'

Clara smiled again. 'I think he'll be all right. I don't know who she is. He wouldn't say anything, but he did have a big grin on his face.'

Sunny didn't see him that evening either. Exam or no exam, it was Saturday night. He hadn't seen Mikey on a Saturday night for quite some time. He indulged in non-stop televised cricket and even left it on while Clara dished up her latest culinary experiment.

'Will you talk to him tomorrow?' She released a slice of salmon into a stream of pad thai sauce. 'Show some interest?'

'Sure, *oui*.' The game would be over by the time Mikey woke up, he had no doubt about that.

Sunday turned out to be not quite so straightforward. The Sri Lankan skipper dropped all his catches. His team-mates looked flabbergasted. The wickets refused to fall. England began to build up runs that no one had thought possible. By the time Mikey stumbled down the stairs, rubbing his eyes, Sunny was ready to turn off the TV and rub his own.

'So, who is this girl?' He had no wish to waste time.
'What?'
'Some new girl?' Sunny added, unsure what else to say.
'What are you on about, Dad?'
'Hope she can speak French. You got an exam tomorrow, right?'
'I know *that*. You don't need to tell me that.' He went over to the piano and started on an unexpected Gershwin tune.
'Good. That's fine, then.' He retreated back to the gloom of the TV. He would have liked to have said, just tell me what's going on, son. But he couldn't. It was too late.
The telephone rang. Sunny waited to see if Mikey would answer it. He did. A moment later, he called out. 'It's for you, Dad.'
Sunny took the phone.
'You don't recognize me, Sunny, do you?'
'Recognize you? Why, of course . . .' All he needed was another second. One, two, three. The voice was strained, but familiar. 'Ranil?'
'I've only just come back. My father is in hospital. He's . . . very ill.'
Sunny sat down. 'What happened?'
'I got here in time to bless him.'
Sunny wanted to stop him. Stop the voice. Stop everything. He never cared for telephones. No good ever came out of the wretched machines. 'What do you mean?'
'He hasn't got much longer, they say.'
Sunny couldn't imagine Tifus propped up in a hospital bed. Tifus should always be in a room full of people, bounding

from group to group offering peanuts and olives, cracking ghoulish jokes about the route from this world to the next. Delora would be devastated. 'Your mother?'

'She's being brave.'

'I am so sorry. Clara will be very upset.'

There was a pause. 'Is she there? Can I speak to her?'

'Sure. Of course. Let me get her.'

He went and found her at her computer searching the internet for more vivid fish dishes. He told her what had happened and gave her the phone. He knew she'd know what to say, even though Sunny was the one who had a father and a mother dead.

The final Test match was going to be at Old Trafford in a month. As the first one looked like it might be heading for a draw – England were batting solidly through the day and aiming for one – the last might be worth watching. Sunny wondered if he could get to it and see Tifus at the same time.

When Clara came downstairs, he asked her what she thought they should do.

'I don't think there is anything we can do, except pray.'

'Ranil can do that for all of us. He is the expert.' It was unnecessary, but he couldn't stop himself.

'What's your problem?'

'The match is going to be a draw.'

'So?'

'They should have won. The first two days were all theirs. It's so . . . disappointing.' Was that the right word?

'It's only a game. How do you think Ranil feels?'

★

Monday's TV showed a practically empty Lord's. Tickets were on sale for a tenner. There'd be no touts, no queues. But Sunny didn't want to go. It would be unbearable. Then, as he watched the TV, Sunny began to see the game in a different light. When he had gone to Lord's, he had got too excited. Drummed up expectations that could not be met. That was not the nature of the sport. It was not meant to be about expectations. The experience ought to be meditative. Let the captains and the cheerleaders shoot adrenalin and shout and swagger, but not the spectators. Bawling and baying for blood was not the right way to approach this game. The way to do it, he reckoned, was to do it pissed. The pair in front of him had got it right. The game, like life, was at best a slow slide from cold champagne to tepid beer, with plenty of nodding off in the sun when the going got rough. Let us have spin bowlers and googlies. Ignore the bouncers. Get rid of the batsmen's helmets and stick to crotch boxes. An occasional boundary, a rare six, and for the rest of time boggle and twaddle and take the chance to catch up on news made untroubling by print. Leave off the photographs, the yahoo, the boo, the *baila* and the witches' brew. Scratch a ball, stroke a bat, dream the dream. As the master Po-chang might have said: first there was cricket, then there was enlightenment. Then there was cricket again. No change. No big deal. Plain Zen and soda.

When Mikey came back home from his French exam in the afternoon, he looked like he'd had a better time than the cricket fans had had falling asleep on the stands in St John's Wood. England had inched to an unglamorous and dispiriting draw that satisfied no one.

He grunted in a very Gallic way when Sunny asked him about the exam. And that, it seemed, was that.

Tifus died three weeks later, crushed by cancer of the gut. He'd had a week out of hospital, at home. Ranil was there all the way through. The funeral was set for Tuesday, 18 June, the day after the last Test. Clara and Sunny drove up on the Sunday.

Sunny didn't have much hope for Sri Lanka at Old Trafford. There was little point in watching. England had won against Denmark in the football and was into the quarter-final, which in a displaced kind of way he was happy to applaud; nobody talked about the cricket match in which England had reached the 'comfort zone' with 512 in the pocket.

They met Ranil at his house. His hair had turned entirely grey. Not only his hair, but also his skin. His mother was upstairs, resting. Clara gave him a hug and Sunny shook his hand, mumbling vaguely about how sorry he was.

'It's no great shock,' Ranil said. 'In this family we know death.' He uttered the word with greater relish than Tifus would have used. Ranil looked much bigger. He was broader, thicker. Perhaps taller than he had been before. More comfortable, despite the bereavement. His face was heavier, graver, like that of a man who had seen a lot and learned a lot.

'Can we do anything to help?' Clara asked.

Ranil raised his hands, like a priest. 'Everything has been taken care of. The procedure was all set out and the firm runs like clockwork. I find it fits me, you know. It is like a vocation. I just didn't know it, until he stepped aside.'

'You'll go into the business?' Sunny asked.

He shrugged. 'I am the business. I've already got a website under way.'

He offered coffee and Garibaldi biscuits in the sitting room. 'Dad's favourites, you know, these squashed fly biscuits. We thought he'd like it if we served them to visitors. It's the kind of special touch he would have added.'

Clara murmured praise and approval while Sunny took a bite out of the wafer-thin, gummy biscuit that Tifus had offered him on his first visit. They sat in silence as the intervening years receded in each of their heads.

'So, no more roaming about, then? All that travelling . . .'

Ranil breathed in slowly as though he needed to fill his lungs before he began. 'We are all searching, are we not? You remember, I went to the Himalayas. I went to Lhasa. I went to Angkor Wat. I went all the way to Japan – there were no football crowds like there are now, you know, just Shinto. Sunny, I wanted to go to the Philippines too – there was a chap performing miracles in San Fernando, as it happened. I thought of you. But then I met up with a group who convinced me we had to get to Bangor immediately . . .'

'There is always a miracle maker . . .'

'That's what I reckoned. You will find your miracle when you need it. And now, coming home from a good long stint in Bangor, I find that in this place, in Dad's business, there is the fit. It is the glove. You understand? My home.'

Sunny saw that in some miraculous way, Tifus was resurrected in Ranil. When he moved his hands, when he spoke, Tifus was there, the smaller father ensconced within the larger son. Sunny thought of how Mikey was already bigger than him. Am I in him? Is my father inside me, observing? Is he the one in my mind turning the world from pictures to words?

While Clara rummaged around her parents' house, Sunny slipped away to Manchester to witness a few overs of the last day of the last sad match at Old Trafford. In the end, he couldn't help himself. He'd read that it was possibly Aravinda de Silva's closing innings before retiring from Test cricket. The finality of it all appealed to him. And this time, he reckoned, he might find the photograph he needed for the competition. Something had to happen soon.

The sun was out as he pulled into the field opposite the grounds. He found his way expertly to his seat in a practically empty row, donned his hat and sunglasses and defiantly opened a bottle of Tiger beer. 'Play it again, Aravinda.' He allowed himself a cheer as the batsman hooked and pulled and let fly as though rejuvenated and right back at the beginning of his glittering game rather than the end of a very special career. The batting was better than anyone had expected, and the score crept up. Arnold, with equal finesse, clocked up a good century. By the time the side was out, England had 50 to make from six overs and it didn't look likely. The match, as Tifus might have said, was a dead cert draw. But then the crowd urged their team and the slow game turned England's way: the ball flew, runs multiplied. Sunny stayed too long, too late and saw too much. Cruising back down the M62 motorway he went over and over the game. This match, in which he'd told himself nothing mattered, not even the passing of time, had become one where every minute, every ball counted as though the future of the world depended on it. He had taken a few pictures but he knew they wouldn't come close to capturing the apocalyptic spirit.

He drove back through Liverpool, wanting an excuse to go through the Mersey tunnel, go under water. Think. Not think. Take a picture. A pure picture. The picture. Or sink.

Opposite the Adelphi he saw that the Army & Navy Stores, where he had gone with Ranil nearly thirty years earlier, had turned into the Kumar Brothers. Would he find hawkers by Bold Street? Betel-chewers by the Cavern?

Birkenhead tunnel was cordoned off by traffic cones and he had to use the one into Wallasey. When he came out he decided to drive over to New Brighton to see the waterfront. Across the Mersey a string of modern spindly windmills waved their lazy arms. He watched for a while. Then from there he followed his nose towards Birkenhead and Clara's parents' house. There were some new housing developments starting up in the richer areas: security fences, road barriers and sentry boxes. It looked as though the world was dividing between the villages of the Domesday book and those of the fast and rich. Veera had been right, all those years ago. Exclusivity had taken root again. An abandoned school was being turned into a site for executive homes trading on small deceits, short memories and mythical heritage: Old School Lane, Tuck Shop Corner. Assorted deadly confectionery.

He got to the house later than he had planned. Clara asked, 'What happened?'

'I got lost.'

Her father, Eric, laughed. 'Can't blame you. I heard the score.'

Sunny explained that he'd driven back through Liverpool and had taken a couple of wrong turnings.

'Not hard to do, the way these town planners keep messing with everything. Except the tunnel, of course. At least that is safe.'

'The Birkenhead one was closed.'

'Oh, really?' Eric looked concerned.

Beryl said that she'd kept some dinner warm. 'A little bit of *cassoulet*. You know it, of course? Although I must say I much prefer Delia's recipe to this new one.'

'I'm sorry I'm so late.'

'Don't worry. Eric was never back from a cricket match in time for his hotpot, were you, dear?' She turned to her husband. 'Ever?' She added a little testily.

He raised his shoulders helplessly. 'It's a game where time plays tricks . . .'

Sunny wore a fat, black polyester tie for the funeral. Clara wore a black hat. So did Delora and Beryl. They could hardly recognize each other. Everyone was boiling; their faces streaming with perspiration. Tears were superfluous. It was a typical Tifus joke. 'Now you people know what it is like. I did this almost every day – togged up for the pegged-out.'

At the crematorium, despite the heat, Ranil was calm and commanding. Big and handsome. He guided his mother, accepted condolences, thanked the flock and generally impressed the crowd. 'He is amazing,' Sunny said to Clara.

She smiled. 'Yes.'

After the service, everyone was invited back to the house. Ranil had the place decked out in white chrysanthemums and there was a garlanded picture of Tifus in the sitting room. If Ranil had intended a sales pitch, he couldn't have done better. Some of the older guests nodded as they passed by, as if to make a mental note to put his name down in a codicil on their own exit procedure.

Several people came up to Sunny. 'Too bad about the match,' said one. 'What happened? I expected more sparkle from your Sri Lankan boys,' said another.

Closer friends of Tifus tried to present the bigger picture. 'Lost the cricket, but won the peace, eh? At least no war and terror any more.'

Sunny didn't think the two – cricket and war – were on the same scale, but he accepted the need to look for compensation wherever one could. Delora came and sat on a nearby chair. 'I am so glad he came back in time.'

'Ranil?'

Her face tightened as she forced herself to look into a future she could not imagine. 'And your Mikey is now sixteen. I can't believe it.'

'Yes, GCSEs now. Wants to be an engineer, but music is probably more his thing than serious studies.'

'Funerals are not necessary for . . .' she stopped. Her eyes trembled as she looked around the room, searching for someone. 'It is not easy, this dealing with the dead. Neither of us are from here, you know, Sunny, but we made it our home. Poor Ranil has always been looking for something else. He needs that. To be looking. What a barney he had with Tifus the last time. But I understand, you know. After all, I left Wrexham for Liverpool when I was nineteen. Perhaps my mother's Portuguese blood required a port. Sea air.'

'Would you like some water?'

She nodded, grateful for anything.

Sunny brought her a glass of water. Someone else was by her side, speaking about the tribulations of shopping at the new hypermarket. 'It is not aimed at the single person at all. We become invisible, my dear . . .'

'Here you are. Sorry.'

'Thank you.' Delora collected the glass in a thin hand knotted with blue veins. She took a slow tiny sip. The water seemed to fill her eyes. 'That's good. He always said funerals made for thirsty work.'

'I know.'

'I had a letter from Hector,' Delora continued. 'He must have posted it straightaway. A sweet letter.' She asked the other woman whether she remembered Hector, the gentleman from Manila who came all those years ago. 'A lovely man.'

Sunny drifted into the garden. He wondered how Hector had known about Tifus. Maybe he was on email. He always knew more than Sunny gave him credit for; he should have been the reporter. Hector was close to Lester's age; then there was Tifus and then Irene. But she went first, then Lester, now Tifus. There wasn't a pattern to the way we fall. Or was there? Sunny thought of Ranil, Robby, Tina and Clara. The false steps they might each take; the true ones. The batting order. *Our lives had been too tentative*. Whose phrase was that in his head?

He saw his mother in her Colombo home, detaching herself from all that had grown around her. Retreating into a still photograph where nothing could touch her; where nothing would change. Where there was no past, no future. A place with music that only she could hear. Why had his father not understood what she was going through? Hector would have understood her artistic temperament. Her need for space. Composure. Peace. Love. To give and to receive. Her fingers were long and beautiful . . . Sunny heard a crashing of chords, the slamming of the piano lid, wood cracking. He is in his childhood garden. He has a bat in his hand. He can't sing. He can't play . . . He sees his mother come out on to the balcony in an ivory satin gown, tearing newspapers and casting old scores into the bushes. She is hissing at Lester. 'What's this? What's this? What's this shit you write for these toady rags?' Sunny's ears hurt. He sees a chest, a trunk. Someone has thrown away the key. Why? *I don't understand. I don't understand why she is doing this*. His father says something about money and there is another angry outburst. 'Don't you fucking touch me.' A cloud of ripped newsprint floats in the hot, humid air. Sunny hears another word. Child. Then there is silence. Stillness. He doesn't hear anything else. Did his father have no better words with which to reach her? *Child?* Who said it? Did she? What did his father say to her before they were married? Before she died? Sunny realizes there is no one who can tell him what was really said. What should have been said. The right words. Everything had moved out of reach.

The right words were what he always lacked, despite the syllables sloshing round inside his head. He hadn't the right words for Clara, for Mikey. For himself. Not for his mother, nor his father. He didn't know what to tell Delora about her husband, he had nothing to offer Ranil. He watched Ranil speaking to some of Tifus's colleagues – his now. Clara appeared with a glass of wine for Ranil. They were both in the same picture for a moment, framed by the window. Sunny remembered how he'd first seen them together, the Crisp 'n Dry. It didn't seem so long ago. She looked like she was closer to where she belonged now, standing next to Ranil. Sunny felt frightened at the way things had turned out, as though someone might have been playing with them. Another game he had not learned or understood in time.

The first ten days after their return to London were eerily quiet. The sun was warm and summery. The back garden turned to weed. Mikey – exams over – was either asleep or out; Clara was busier than ever between her work, her oils and the internet. When she found Robby's new online store, she'd frowned. 'This is really OTT.' Sunny didn't look. He didn't want to hear any more voices from the past. He'd had enough of the dead and departed. He wanted to latch on to something ahead. At the library he saw again the looming deadline for the photo competition; he still had nothing to send.

He took to walking everywhere with a camera in his hand, in case an angel might fall out of the sky. He had to trust to luck – *bahala na* – fate. On the days he went to the lab, he would watch with envy as customers trooped in carrying their rolls of 35 mm film, APS cartridges and digital media. He tried to spot competitors, the more sallow, serious types – no holiday snaps there, no baby pics. He even took a photograph of one. A subtle shot of what seemed like hope fluttering at the counter, a shaky hand with loose change, a whispered name. Freddy saw him do it and asked what he was up to. 'You think we need CCTV in here?' Sunny told him that he was just trying out a lens. Creative experimentation. That pleased Freddy. 'Fantastic,' he said, thrilled at the idea that his shop might be the fount of such spontaneous inspiration.

Sunny wanted to photograph hope embedded in love. Or love embedded in hope. Something promising despite the true nature of the world. Against the odds. Something more all-encompassing than that Parisian kiss imprinted in a million heads. Something that could be found, just as it was lost, like life itself. Unexpectedly. Undeservedly. He remembered the conversation with Hector in the tea room in West Kirby, his words on love, unrequited and requited. He wished he had captured the hope, love and care in Hector's face then. His mortality. Could he find it in another face? In another image? Before the end of the month? Ever? *Bahala* bloody *na*.

One evening, on the way back from the library, he took a photograph of the darkening empty road. When he got home, Clara was on the phone. She was laughing. 'OK, love.'

Sunny stored his camera away in the cupboard under the stairs.

'That was Mikey.' She put down the phone. 'He's coming back with some friends in about an hour. They want to watch a video.'

'Might that not be too energetic?'

'I think he might bring the girl.'

'He said that?'

She shrugged. 'No. It's a mother's hunch.'

'I see. Some mothers do have them, I guess.'

Mikey appeared with four others. Sunny recognized only Benjy, lankier but as bright as ever. Mikey didn't bother with introductions, but Benjy did.

'This is my cousin, Vicky. She's come to stay with us.' He turned to her. 'Mikey's dad knows the Philippines.'

Sunny asked her where her home was, once more unsure where his own was.

'Cebu.' She smiled dazzlingly.

'I'm sorry not to have ever visited it.'

'*Ai*, you must see Cebu. You maa . . . st.' She stretched her eyes wide and the crucial words. 'Ree-ally, you have to go to Cebu city.'

The other two slouched into the sitting room. 'That one is Daniella and that's Joe,' Benjy added. The girl raised a hand in a sort of lame greeting, the boy twitched a shoulder weak from the weight of permanent hip-hop.

'We are going to the match on Sunday,' Mikey said suddenly, speaking to Sunny after what seemed like years.

'Which match?'

'Vicky wants to see a cricket match. We're going to the Sri Lanka-India game.'

'At the Oval?' Sunny had been so dismayed about the looming competition that he'd forgotten the one-day match. 'You have tickets?'

'A friend of Benjy's got us tickets. I used Hector's money.'

'Come with us, Mr Fernando. Plee-ease come. Mikey says you know all about it.' Vicky peered at him, searching for the words she needed. 'Benjy's buddy tol' us it'll be reelly, reelly exciting. One-day match. I wanna learn cricket. Back home no one can play.' She was standing very close to Mikey, slender and sweet. He looked happier than Sunny had seen him since he was about nine. His face had lifted, his shoulders broadened. There was solid flesh where before there had only been space for him to grow into. He was born with Sunny's face in baby shape; now adolescence seemed to have brought more of his mother to the surface. He stood there, sixteen years old, his hair in highlights, his skin alloyed and his hands remarkably steady.

'Bring missus. She likes the matches, no?' Vicky added.

'I might see you kids somewhere in the crowd, if I can get a ticket.'

The next day he managed to get one on the other side of the stadium from Mikey and his friends.

The day before the match Clara mentioned that Ranil was coming to London. 'He's invited us for lunch on Sunday. A special place off the Edgware Road, near where he is staying.'

'I'm going to the match.'

'Another one? You know Ranil does need some support.' Her voice was sharp.

'I thought he had God at his side.'

'You are one of his oldest friends.' Clara's face was losing the summer colour she'd gained recently, as though her blood was gathering somewhere else. Something was not quite right.

'You go. You were the sweetheart.'

'Don't be ridiculous. That was twenty years ago. Thirty. He is just trying to get us all together again. He wants his old friends around him.'

'That's the way you see it, so that's the way it is, huh? Everything according to the gospel of Clara.'

'What exactly are you trying to say?'

Sunny said he had to go to the match. He had older friends than Ranil to see. And Mikey was going to the match. They'd be there together even if not next to each other. 'You don't understand what it means. It's a roots thing.' He wanted to say, we could all learn from our sixteen-year-old selves. We should go back for a day. The youngsters in real time; Clara and Ranil, Sunny, Tina and Steve on rewind.

Clara picked up a biro and drew a rough triangle on the pad that served as her shopping jotter, then started to make bobbles on each corner. She spoke again only after she finished the third one. 'Maybe we should get married after all.'

Sunny hadn't touched a drink all morning. Sometimes he heard voices in his head. He tried not to open his mouth when he was confused, but he had to ask. 'Why? Why do you say that? Why now? What would be the point of it?'

'Mikey's growing up. He might beat us to it. Kids these days seem keen on old conventions. Maybe they know something we don't. Sometimes I wonder if I have been too . . . prejudiced. Maybe it is the right time now for us to renew things.' She put the pen down. 'We could even have another baby.'

'At our age?'

'Cherie had one. Or we can adopt. What do you say? It is never too late.'

Sunny needed a drink. A bloody great eye-opener, he said to himself. And then, aloud, 'I need to think.'

'Think about what?'

'Thoughts. Us. Everything. What about art school? Your Alex?'

She blinked. 'I've decided mandalas are enough. I know what I want. I know what is important to me. Do you?'

The atmosphere at the Oval was extraordinary, the noise level astounding. The stadium throbbed, ready to burst. Even before the toss, the crowd – predominantly South Asian this time – was in a frenzy.

Sri Lanka batted first. It wasn't a good start, wickets fell fast, but the play was for runs, runs, runs. Anything cautious was booed. There was no sign of Mikey and his friends, or Tina and Steve. Sunny was in a stand mostly full of Indian supporters, with a handful of neutrals and a small contingent of Sri Lankans two rows back. There were trumpets and drum rolls, klaxons and whistles and rattles and chants and screams. This was cricket at full decibel. A game where every ball was a missile and the field an arena of gladiators. Sunny realized he had known nothing about real One-day cricket. Nothing. These fans had not come to watch but to participate: the players were not kings but servants of the crowd. They existed only to please the crowd. Do their bidding or be hauled off. Earn respect only with every ball; glory from the past was not enough, except perhaps for the legendary Sachin Tendulkar, who raised a cheeer every time he moved, even if it was only to snap a bit of elastic.

Someone in the row behind issued a stern reminder, 'This is not a Test match, you silly buggers.' He was one of a Sri Lankan party: two young boys with flags, a girl of about ten, mother, father and several other adults who looked like they might be related. The speaker cradled a box of Banrock shiraz. A large red thermal container in the centre of the row held the rest of the day's provisions. When the captain finally carved a six over third man with a stunning leap, the whole family jumped to their feet and cheered. The Indian fans around were amazed. 'OK.' There was a blast of music to celebrate the boundary; a snatch of 'That's the Way I Like It'.

By 11.30 a.m. the Sri Lankan captain was out – caught by Dravid to a huge roar. 'Ooh, ah, Indi-ah,' was chanted again and again until fifteen minutes later, when another wicket fell – lbw. Then a new and more menacing chant: 'Are you watching, Pakistan?' India had come from a win over England the day before. Their fans were on a roll. They had Pakistan in their sights. The commentator among the Sri Lankan family clicked his tongue and poured himself some wine. 'What has happened?' he moaned. 'In 1996 we were the champions of the world. What the hell has gone wrong?'

'What goes up, must come down, no *machang*? Even when you hit a six?' His companion was a philosopher.

'So what, *men*? Then you hit another six. What is this looking down business all the bloody time? How will they ever do anything? Everybody in our bloody country blames every bloody body else. No wonder we always end up fighting each other like stupid buggers.'

The youngest boy in the family, further down the row, took refuge in his gameboy.

The stand's Indian cheerleader strutted to the front. He looked like one of the lads Sunny had worked with in the accounts department all those years ago. This man had probably only just turned thirty. He was small, tubby, prematurely balding. He had a fat beak and a big voice. He gave full vent to a stream of racy chants: anti-colonial, anti-white and anti-Pakistani. The old codgers with the only bottle of fizz in the stand simply raised their beakers at the relatively mild 'white boys' taunts, as if recognizing this abuse as juvenilia from the previous century. Everyone was letting go. The cheerleader embarked on a public interview. 'Hey man, you people ever been to India?'

The oldest of the bubbly party replied that he had not only been there, but lived in India for thirty-five years. He had been in the railways.

The cheerleader said that he himself had never been to India. 'What's your name, man? Who do you support then? India?' He doubled up with a loud guffaw.

'Of course. My name is Hutton.'

The cheerleader turned to the crowd astonished. 'Hey, Hutton is an Indian, Hutton is an Indian.' Then twisted it. 'Mutton, man.'

The chant was taken up by everybody. 'Mutton is an Indian.' Then someone else ratcheted up the tempo. 'Beckham is an Indian, Beckham is an Indian.' Then, 'Becker was an Indian. Becker was an Indian.' A moment later, 'Henman will be an Indian. *Yarr.*' It was the new badge of honour. All heroes had to be Indian.

Another wicket fell.

'Look out, Pakistan.'

The food container in the Sri Lankan row was opened and some *vadai* and patties were passed around. The man with the box of wine gobbled a snack and stood up in disgust. He was tall and wore a blue, white and gold Sri Lankan cricket shirt. 'Give us a four, you lazy fellows,' he bellowed. The cheerleader looked at him in surprise as if 'lazy fellows' was the worst curse he had ever heard in his life. He wiped his brow with his sleeve. 'Whoa.' Then he took up the chant himself. 'A four here, a four there, here, there, everywhere . . .' Suddenly the whole stand was cheering for a Sri Lankan boundary. 'Come on, you lazy fellows . . .' Everyone was now Sri Lankan. Another boundary, and a big hurrah erupted. For a moment everything was topsy-turvy. Samosas were passed around from the Indian fans down to the Sri Lankan row with congratulations and a cascade of laughter. The man in the Sri Lankan cricket shirt leant back with a box of patties and offered them around. 'Hey, you eat meat? *Meat*?'

A jovial Indian supporter took a patty and offered a crispy vegetable pakora in return. 'Very good,' he chuckled. 'We want you guys to play well, you know, before we turn you into mincemeat. We have to show Pakistan what we can do.'

'*Yarr*, but we have some scores to settle with you Lankan wankers too,' one of his friends butted in.

A beer carrier and a curry bucket arrived. The cheerleader leapt to his feet again and tried to wind up the crowd with more insults at Pakistan, England and Sri Lanka. He started on anal dreams and ghee fingers and tried a couple of lewd openly racist taunts. He got a laugh but not enough support. He changed tack and reassured the women in the family near him. 'We are all good Asian boys, really, Mummy. Don't you worry, we just need to juice up, no?'

The runs had slowed. The sky was overcast. The Sri Lankan batsmen on the pitch were hunched, looking cold, while the Indian team strutted about in warm, fluffy blue. Sunny needed to calm his nerves. He wanted to find Tina. He couldn't quite focus on what Clara had been trying to say. What did she really mean? Why get married now, after all these years? Haven't we been through it all? He wanted to see Mikey and Vicky. Young love. Timing was everything. And there had to be a picture for him here. This was the final day before the deadline. His last chance. He had to be ready for an image to enter the mirror chamber like a ball to the perfectly angled plane of a bat. He took the cap off the lens, ready to roll, and went down behind the stands.

Crowds paraded carrying drums, flags, trumpets and hooters, but there was no sign of Mikey or his friends. He looked for Tina. On several occasions Sunny thought he'd spotted her distinctive face before it dissolved into the shape of some other elongated profile, closer perhaps to that of his mother's. Age and memory were playing tricks. Fortunately he managed to stop himself, each time, from greeting the wrong person. He took pictures instead. With a camera he could do anything. Held correctly, it made the professional photographer practically invisible. He could go right up to anyone and press the shutter, catching a sari, a flag, a bare midriff or a swaying beer gut. He took pictures of silver belly buttons, cool chakras, hennaed hands. The New Cricket. He didn't know what he would say to Tina if he found her. He had never told her that he'd gone to Baguio that Valentine's weekend in Ricardo's car, only to find she wasn't there – but that wasn't it, surely? What could he say now? Maybe he could take her picture instead, pretend she was about to hit a Bollywood six and do a belly roll with Steve.

Overhead, the crowds stomping on the upper tiers went berserk. The Sri Lankan batting had come to an end. The score was 202 for 8. It was not heady stuff but enough, with luck, to make for a tight finish.

Sunny thought of Ranil in his spiritual cul-de-sac on the other side of town. Clara was the one he wanted there anyway. What was it she really wanted? He thought of the moments she'd been happiest. Their lives seemed to be slipping by so fast, he could barely tell which year they were in any more. How could she think they could start again, as if everything would simply get better, as if nothing would age, go sour, decline, erode and slip away? Was it the prospect of menopause? Had there been anything with Alex? Did he care if there had?

He wished he had brought his mobile, then he could have found Mikey at least. He'd never been to a match like this with Lester. Now he and his son were at least in the grounds together. Perhaps it was possible to get what you really wanted. Clara had said once, 'Much as I love you, I don't want Mikey to be just another you.' But he could learn from Mikey, couldn't he? Or had she said, 'Much as I loved you . . .'?

Someone on the other side of the ground started a Mexican wave. Block after block of people stood and swayed together, leaning into the next, creating a tidal wave of rising and falling bodies that rippled across the stands. When Sunny stood and swayed and clamoured with the bunch of meat-eating Mummy's boys led by the young hooligan, it seemed as though they had all become one. The ripple effect went around the stadium six, seven, eight times, stirring it. Stirring up the game. He photographed the movement. A long exposure to catch the human ripple in the low reddish light that had descended. A double exposure to follow. A wave. And then, another wave. A vortex.

Two Indian wickets had fallen; there was some faint hope among the Sri Lankans. Then Tendulkar stepped forward and smashed a long hard drive. The ball, a round, white bullet, shot across the grass towards a few fat pigeons congregated on an empty patch of the ground. The birds were pecking at the earth and waddling about, ignoring the mad momentous game around them, unaware of the tribal needs, the chameleon identities, the laws of science and the art of hitting ducks. The ball sped into their midst and caused a flurry. The bird in the middle didn't stand a chance. The ball hit it. The pigeon keeled over. Play stopped. The whole of the Oval was hushed. The nearest fielder walked over and picked the bird up as though it were the dove of peace. He carried it slowly towards the boundary. Sunny knew then that this was the picture for him. He ran down to the rope faster than a long leg might streak to stop a boundary ball. He kept the lens aperture small, knowing that in his photograph the sky would be a bowl where newspaper confetti floated like circling buzzards, while in the centre a pair of clasped hands prayed to a dying bird. Its feathers trembled just enough to blur, in and out of perfect focus, like life itself. He clicked the shutter before the groundsman's bucket swung into view to collect the corpse. He didn't even need a light meter. There was something significant happening here, he knew, no matter what the outcome of the game would be. Perhaps it was the power to silence that comes with death, however small the life, and our need to overcome it. To find some brief moment of care. Hope. The tender possibility of renewal. This man, this game, this bird was salvation. The timing was perfect. Anything seemed possible: peace, love, joy, life everlasting . . . It was all in the frame. Sunny saw it all. And in that moment he understood something about himself. The life he had and how far it could take him.

More wickets fell. 'Vindaloo, vindaloo' became the new cry. 'Pigeon vindaloo' the new taunt. A win for India seemed inevitable; the drumbeats and the honking grew louder. Everyone was waiting for the final stroke to mark the end of the day. The sky was turning redder.

The cheerleader lost his grip. He was no longer necessary. His anguished appeal: 'We want a fuckin' riot, we want a riot . . . guys. Per-lease . . .' was completely ignored. When the game ended with a final undisputed boundary for India, he gave a last drowned-out hurrah. A little boy climbed the stairs and the cheerleader hugged him in relief. 'Hey, little fellow, come to Uncle. How'd you like your first match?' His answer was lost in the din.

Then, down by the hastily erected podium, Sunny saw

Tina. She was in a denim outfit that belonged to the early seventies. Next to her Steve was dancing. He wore a Sri Lankan flag like a sarong around his jeans and carried a beer. They both lurched towards the TV crew gathering around the players. Sunny could have gone down and joined the throng. He could have reached them and made contact, but he didn't want to any more. He wanted to go home instead. If it had been Clara there . . . Something in his head finally was clearing. He saw how each frame in his life was stitched to another. How he couldn't be what he was, and where he was, without what had been. Without Tina, Steve, Junior and Herbie in Manila, without Robby and Ranil, without Hector and Aunty Lillie, even Major Brendan, Rudy and Anjuli. Without Bradman, Weekes, Walcott and Worrel, troubadours and cricketers. And his mother and his father. Without Mikey running ahead. Without Clara appearing out of nowhere. Each in their place for ever, and settling him in his. He checked his watch. He put the camera in his bag and took the back stairs to the exit, afraid that somehow once again he would be too late.

The walk to Vauxhall tube was like the aftermath of a rock concert. Fans on both sides swaggered and cheered each other. Drums were beating, horns blaring. Kids roamed everywhere. Sunny caught a glimpse of Mikey and Vicky by the traffic cones before the crowd surged and swallowed them. Our side might have collapsed, he thought, but we shared the day. It felt good. He knew what it was like to be in the same place at the same time as his own. Next to him a bunch of teenagers sporting Sri Lankan cricket shirts were chatting excitedly in Tamil. Further on another group were singing in Sinhala.

Both supporting the same team. Despite the sad defeat, the poor showing all summer, the madness infecting the rest of the world, it seemed that on this June evening some divisions, at least, were close to healing. One suicidal war possibly over. The warmongers tamed. The bloodlust and the hate dissipated. He saw the dead bird become a phoenix. Its image rise from the strip of film and gain a new life. Things could be renewed. He clutched his camera bag tight, fearing his foolishness, fearing the future. Perhaps there is too much greed in the old world to let things become better, for there to be winners without losers. Some new calamity would open other wounds now this one was healing. He thought of his father and his mother and how their world had spun so unpredictably. He thought of Mikey. He wanted him to be able to look back on some happiness. And he thought of Clara . . . how she must know what he wanted to say.

When he got home he found the front door locked. No light was visible through the frosted glass. Clara evidently had not come back. He had paid up for all the rescue services: home-start, roadside assistance, relay, the works. She should have made it home by now no matter what had happened to the car.

He undid the locks and pushed open the door. He had missed the bottom of the frame when he'd painted the woodwork. It needed to be done. He turned and shut the door. The glow in the summer sky above the fretted rooftops of Hornsey filtered through the top window. He could see small birds wheeling high above. The swallows from their nests in Wales.

The answerphone blinked on the hall table. Sunny pressed

the button. Static, white noise and then a garbled voice that could have been Clara's. He tried 1471. The operator informed him that the last number could not be traced.

He wondered how he could reach her. He couldn't remember where she said Ranil was staying. The words in his head turned, a lateness in his blood.

He collected the empties from around the house and put them away. He got some milk from the fridge and drank it. He didn't want anything else. Nothing harder. Not now. Maybe not any more. At least, not yet. He went and sat in the room that had been his son's nursery and then, once Mikey had moved into a teenage loft, a picture gallery and then a music room. Sunny unloaded his camera. There would be time enough tomorrow to develop the film and take it in to the Soho office before the competition closed. Plenty of time for pictures. For images that hold breath. He knew he had the right photograph. It was a good camera. Now he could do nothing but wait for the phone to ring and hope there was still time for words. Time to erase his mistakes and make amends. Time to speak. Time to say yes. *Yes, let's do it. Let's go now to the Registry Office. Sign the papers, say what we have to say. Renew ourselves*. After that, maybe he could begin to formulate the words of the rest of his life. Words that would bring peace to his own mind if not to the world. And possibly, with luck, if the light and the timing were right, create a picture in someone else's and make his life a little more worthwhile. Words that might make room for hope. Perhaps something more than his father had managed. If only there was a place to start. A halfway house. Too much, it seemed, was too easy to squander.

Then he heard a key turn in the front door.. He came out into the hall as the door opened and saw her at the threshold. She had his light meter like a garland around her neck.

She lifted the cord over her head and held it out. 'I went to the match to find you. I thought you might need this.'

Sunny reached out. Her fingers were cold and, like his, needed warming. He could do it. At that moment anything seemed possible. He remembered seeing fresh fettucine in the fridge. 'I got the picture.'

'I know,' Clara said. 'I can see.' Her face opened and caught the last of the warm light spilling from the sky.

A Declaration of Thanks

I would like to thank the players mentioned, on all sides, whom I've had the pleasure to watch over the years. Also 'Anyone for Cricket' organiser, M. Kentake, for a timely invitation, and the other participants, Mike Phillips and Chris England, for their unexpected leg-spins on the day; the Gunawardenas for a welcome pitch in Colombo to stay in; the Aluvihares ditto for a second innings; my agent Bill Hamilton, and his team at A.M. Heath; Alexandra Pringle, Victoria Millar, Margaret Stead and everyone at Bloomsbury.

My very special thanks, long overdue, for everything from stories to stringhoppers, to my father and mother, Douglas and Miriam Gunesekera; also to Michele, Andy, Liz, Paul, Darin, Chandrika; John and Gwenda Pick. In addition, Jamie, Nissanka, stalwarts both, new fielder Bobby and new runner Charu.

And finally thank you Shanthi and Tanisa, who light up the day, and Helen for more than just the match.

A NOTE ON THE AUTHOR

Romesh Gunesekera was born in Sri Lanka and lives in London. He is the author of four books: *Reef* (shortlisted for both the Booker Prize and the *Guardian* Fiction Prize in 1994), *Monkfish Moon*, a collection of short stories, *The Sandglass* (BBC Asia Award) and *Heaven's Edge* (shortlisted for the best book award in the Eurasia region for the Commonwealth Writers Prize 2003, and named as a *New York Times* Notable Book of the Year).